I0547667

ACCOUNTS OF HUMANITY

"The greatness of humanity is not in being human, but in being humane." – Mahatma Gandhi

This book is a collection of six unusual short stories. While each tale stands on its own, there is a deeper connection between them, but I will leave it to the reader to uncover what it is.

(C. Traven, First Edition ©2021)

CONTENTS

1. THE MASSACRE

Gary Hastings wasn't married and had never been married. Sure, he had his share of girlfriends, but no relationship ever evolved to the level or the depth of matrimony. Currently, he was single again but in no hurry to find a new companion. Gary always thought that solitude was a rare gift in an overcrowded and overstimulated society – the world was over-socialized by quantity but woefully under-socialized by quality! Gary valued being able to think clearly without a myriad of distractions. Quietly reading a good book satisfied him a lot more than any noisy, wild social gathering could ever hope to accomplish. He was alone but not lonely, which was just fine with Gary.

He has worked at branch office #37 for the last 15 years. The office had quite the employee turnover, and Gary was the only one left from the day when Corporate had opened this branch in the city. Gary was considered a good employee - punctual, competent, efficient, and low maintenance according to his performance evaluations. He was courteous and professional, but he always saw his job strictly as a paycheck. Gary didn't try to climb the company ladder, nor did he socialize with his coworkers beyond the necessary. They were coworkers, not friends, and he always maintained that distinction.

This morning was the annual office meeting. The branch manager would show a lengthy, boring presentation to the entire staff, and afterward, they would enjoy coffee and donuts in the lobby. It had been that way for as long as Gary could remember. The big conference room on the second floor seemed crowded, and the air was stale with all 30 employees cramped into it. The branch manager had problems with the projection system, and the guy from IT was trying to fix it. Gary took advantage of the unscheduled delay, excused himself, and went to the restroom.

The branch office was located in an old brick building, and the restrooms were situated in its basement. While the upper floors had been retrofitted to a modern office environment's needs, the old cellar was left nearly untouched: thick stone walls and floors, a labyrinth of dimly lit corridors, and small, primarily empty storage rooms. There were rattling water and sewer pipes, a loud furnace, and a million electrical wires crisscrossing on the ceiling. Gary speculated that the contractors who remodeled this building forgot about bathrooms upstairs and then added them to this dungeon at the last minute.

On his way there, he walked through the reception area. A man with a big duffle bag crossed the foyer, running towards the elevators. That was a little odd because nobody should be able to enter the building without a card key unless Melissa, the receptionist, buzzed them in. But of course, Melissa was in the conference room right now. Gary figured that she must have left the front door unlocked for the catering service, and this guy was probably just delivering the donuts. After Gary had relieved himself, he washed his hands. As he was toweling off, he thought he heard some banging noises, but it was hard to say with the roaring furnace in the boiler room next door. Gary threw the wet paper towel in the wastebasket and returned to the upstairs offices.

When he got back, he spotted bullet holes in the door to the conference room. On that hunch, he speculated that the meeting must not be going swell this year, which made his stomach churn. He turned around, stopped by his cubical, and sent a quick message to his supervisor about not feeling well. Of course, unbeknownst to Gary, his supervisor was currently bleeding out next door and would never read emails again. Gary logged out, grabbed his lunch bag from the desk, and swiftly exited the building. The van from the catering service was still parked at the front door, hazards flashing. As Gary was driving off the parking lot, a caravan of police cars and ambulances was speeding by him, sirens blaring. Gary figured that whatever had happened in that conference room must have been pretty big.

Self-preservation was only one reason Gary left so swiftly: he wasn't afraid of death, unlike most people. He would have preferred a quick bullet to prolonged suffering from debilitating disease until the body can only be sustained by a bunch of tubes and machinery or the hellish nightmare of losing one's identity to slow but inevitable mental degradation. But Gary wasn't in any hurry to get on with the dying just yet, and he had no idea if danger was still lurking at the office. He also didn't want to stick around to talk to the cops because he didn't feel like pretending. They would expect to find someone in shock or emotionally distraught, and Gary was neither - he was just numb! He simply didn't care what had happened here, he wasn't inquisitive to find out, and he certainly didn't want to get involved on any level. But such a socially unacceptable response would likely incriminate him as a suspect or accomplice, and Gary didn't want that trouble: he knew that *innocent until proven guilty* was just an idealist notion that had little factual basis in the American legal system. Gary assumed that the police would eventually come to him, but he should be better prepared for their questions by that time.

When he got home, he turned on the TV. Every news channel reported the mass shooting at his branch office. Twenty-eight people had died, and two were in critical condition. Nothing was known about the assailant or the motive yet. Gary let that sink in for a moment, unsure how he should feel about the fact that all his coworkers were dead or dying now. After a minute of reflection, Gary knew that he still didn't care and didn't want to care, but he recognized that it would be very hard on his coworkers' families, making him sad and depressed. Gary also realized that he should update his résumé promptly because with the branch office depopulated, Gary was effectively out of a job now, and soon, the bills would start piling up. Lastly, he gave a silent nod to his weak bladder, for it had truly saved his life today!

Gary left the TV on and listened to the reporters while making coffee. His two cats were delighted to have him at home at this unusual time. Misha just wanted love and attention, but Leila was eager to have a second breakfast. Gary filled up their bowls with kibbles, took his coffee cup, and returned to the TV. The latest update stated that the death toll now stood at 30. Both critically injured victims had died on the way to the hospital or shortly thereafter. The victims' names had yet to be released, but Gary could do the math and concluded that he must be the only surviving employee of Branch #37. Gary turned on his lap-top and checked the newsfeed for more details, but details were still scarce, except that the police had found several handguns, many rounds of ammunition, and a powerful automatic rifle. Gary turned off the computer, finished his coffee, and switched to beer.

With a brew in hand, he sat down on the couch. Misha immedi-ately jumped on his lap and curled up. Gary wondered who of his former coworkers would have been most likely to go postal. Most of them had some quirks, but most appeared to be harmless. Of course, it is hard to tell in a nation where nearly half the popula-tion had mental issues at one point or another during their lives, and those were just the ones on record. So, Gary's first guess was Leroy Washington. A couple of weeks ago, he was fired after Cor-porate had discovered that he was diverting money to fund his gambling habit. But last Gary had heard, Leroy was locked up on other charges, and the judge had denied bail. Perhaps it was Catherine Walker, or Crazy Cate, as she was known around the office? Her screaming meltdowns were legendary, and her desk looked like a pharmacy with all those prescription pill bottles stacked on it. She gave off some serious Lizzie Borden vibes, but Gary didn't think she was the type who would go on a shooting spree. Cate had problems finding the power switch on the coffeemaker, so it was unlikely that she would know how to operate an assault rifle. Maybe poison or blunt instruments, or perhaps a butcher knife, were more her style. It could have been portly Donald Tucker with the red political baseball cap that he never seemed to remove from his balding head. He was a doomsday prepper and conspiracy nut, eager to tell anyone who cared to listen about the upcoming race war. Then again, the excitement of a massacre would probably be way too much for his burger-clogged arteries. Maybe it was Ahmed from accounting then? A devout Muslim, praying daily in his office and complaining every summer about the immodest wardrobes of his female colleagues. But Ahmed was well into retirement age, and it was hard to picture him slaughtering infidels to get his 72 virgins this late in life. Gary doubted that Ahmed could even remember what to do with them. That left Gunnery Sergeant Miller, a true patriot and a war hero. His number of combat tours was only surpassed by the number of PTSD symptoms he exhibited. If a car misfired in the parking lot, the good sergeant would be lying flat under his desk. But he certainly had the skill, training and probably knew where to get the firepower, too. So, Gary's money was on the broken hero, but Misha on his lap woke up and seemed to disagree. She bet a few kibbles on the fat, closet supremacist, while Leila seemed bored with the whole affair and got high on her catnip toy instead. Smart cat thought Gary and finished his beer.

Gary didn't understand the American obsession with firearms, and he had never owned one himself. Some of his buddies took him to a shooting range for some manly fun when he was younger. Gary fired a few rounds from rifles and handguns. He didn't like the noise, he didn't like the acrid smell, and his wrist was sore from the recoil. On top of that, he discovered that he had a lousy aim. It wasn't fun at all, and it certainly didn't heighten his masculinity. Gary agreed that guns in private hands had their place in a country like Switzerland, where citizens were also army reservists. Or maybe in war-torn nations like Syria or Somalia, where the possibility of violent encounters was fairly high. But in the USA, a developed, democratic nation with a stable government, it made no sense to have more guns in the hands of the public than there were people in the country! He concluded that his fellow citizens were either unbelievably paranoid or thought that only possessing a deadly weapon could boost their abysmal self-esteem. In Gary's humble opinion, neither group was stable enough to be anywhere near a firearm!

With every new slaughter, the media ratings, left or right, sky-rocketed, and in turn, the advertisers paid a premium to run their commercials during the coverage, which was no different this time. The lady from the catering service who had found the bloody mess in the conference room was giving interviews to every news station, reveling in her 15 minutes of fame. The NRA blamed the shooting on video games and proclaimed that it could have been prevented if only all the employees had packed heat. Of course! The politicians and pundits to the left demanded more gun control, while the ones to the right vehemently opposed that and offered thoughts and prayers instead. But simultaneously, both sides reaped in more campaign funding from competing lobbyists. Meanwhile, the fearful public went out to buy a lot more guns and ammo, much to the delight of Smith & Wesson and their ilk. In a sense, it was almost biblical: violence begets fear, and fear begets more violence – the circle of death, one might call it. So yes, mass-shooting were good for the economy, and what was good for the economy was good for America. In a few days, this tragedy would be forgotten again until the next slaughter in the very near future would deliver more lucrative opportunities – rinse and repeat ad nausea.

Around noontime, Richard Turnbull, the CEO of Gary's company, released a moving, compassionate statement to the media. At great length, he sympathized with the victims and their families and announced that all offices would be closed for the rest of the day. He promised that the company would do all it could to ensure the safety and well-being of its valued workers in the future. In addition, Corporate would also offer free therapy sessions for all 12,000 employees worldwide to deal with this traumatic situation. Gary was impressed: the board must have hired a speechwriter for Turnbull! Last year, when Corporate laid off nearly half of the company in a cost-cutting move, Turnbull just blamed the lazy employees for his managerial failures. By the way, that move was well received by Wall Street, as the company stock went way up, and Turnbull's golden parachute became even more golden. Of course, there was an economic reason why Corporate issued this rather sensible public statement: inevitably, the victims' families would sue the company for damages, and the board certainly wanted to mitigate the cost of the financial settlement as much as possible. If they had left the wording to Turnbull's depravity, any future jury would probably add punitive damages that, unlike the settlement itself, might not qualify for a tax write-off.

Just after lunch, Gary decided to call his ex-girlfriend Becky. They had parted on good terms, and Becky had always loved Leila and Misha. But Becky didn't pick up, so Gary just left her a short message. She called him back only a few minutes later.

"Gary! I saw what happened at your work. Are you OK?" exclaimed Becky.

"Yes, I'm fine, Becky. But could you please take Leila and Misha for a while?" asked Gary.

"Sure, I can stop by on my way home, if that works for you?" wondered Becky.

"Great, thank you. I'm not sure how long the cats have to stay with you, but probably just for a few days, if that's not too much of a hassle?" wondered Gary and offered, "I will give you a big bag of cat food and some of their toys, too!"

"No hassle at all!" confirmed Becky and asked, "Gary, does that have to do with the shooting? Tell me, what's going on?"

"Becky, I'm not the shooter, if that's what you are asking?" remarked Gary.

"Of course, you are not the shooter!" replied Becky and observed, "but you are not telling me everything!"

"There is nothing to tell. I just have a hunch that I might not be able to take care of Leila and Misha for a few days, that's all," answered Gary vaguely.

"A hunch? What does that mean?" Becky pressed on.

"Becky, please just take my cats if you can?" begged Gary, unable to explain to her the bad feeling he had in his gut.

"Fine, if you don't want to tell me. I'll be there around 4:00 PM!" promised Becky.

"Thanks, I'll see you then!" confirmed Gary and hung up.

While he was scanning job ads and working on his résumé, Gary continued to listen to the TV, but no new information was coming in. Gary stopped looking at jobs listings and used a laser pointer to play with Leila for a while until the cat got bored and curled up on the couch. Gary turned off the TV and had an early dinner. Halfway through the chicken salad, Becky rang the doorbell. Gary let her in and offered her some of his food, but she was in a hurry and declined. After Gary corralled Leila and Misha and put them in their pet carriers, he helped Becky load them into her car. Becky said she would call him again tomorrow when she had more time. Gary felt a little better knowing that his cats were safe and sound when she drove off. Hopefully, he will be able to reunite with them very soon.

Gary was having another beer while checking his work emails. As expected, all employees had received Turnbull's earlier statement in their inbox. Next was an urgent message from Security that advised all employees to carry their magnetic identification cards with them at all times, and nobody without one would be permitted to enter any company facility. Gary expected that, but he was surprised by an email from HR: they were already busy scheduling therapy sessions for the employees. Usually, it took HR weeks just to process a simple vacation request, so he paid extra attention to that message:

Our company is thoroughly committed to the safety and well-being of its employees. In light of today's tragic circumstances, every employee should immediately contact their supervisor or branch manager to schedule a therapy appointment as soon as possible. Your supervisor or branch manager has a list of mental health professionals in your area. Only a professional on that list is acceptable, and all appointments must be scheduled outside of regular work hours, but the cost of your visit will be reimbursed if you provide valid documentation. Failure to schedule or complete a therapy session will have disciplinary consequences, up to and including termination.

Ah, this wasn't therapy, but a psychological evaluation, probably planned long beforehand, but today's massacre would undoubtedly make it easier for the workers to swallow. After a moment, Gary sent a brief email to HR, but he couldn't help being a little sarcastic:

Since my supervisor and branch manager are deceased, whom would I have to contact to schedule the mandatory psychological evaluation? Please advise, Gary Hastings, Employee number A4519, Branch Office #37.

Only a few minutes later, he received a response.

Mr. Hastings, we have scheduled your therapy appointment for 6:00 AM tomorrow at HQ building #2. Please complete all attached forms before your visit, and sign in at your arrival. The receptionist will give you further instructions. Lisa Lambert, HR assistant.

Gary laughed out loud and typed in his reply:

Unfortunately, I'm located about 2,000 miles away from HQ. There is simply no way to make that appointment on this short notice. Best regards, and, please advise, Gary Hastings.

Gary waited for a while, but there was no further correspondence. It was late in the workday, and Gary assumed he wouldn't hear from HR again until tomorrow morning.

Late that evening, the Chief of Police announced some preliminary results of the ongoing investigation: it turned out that neither Gary nor Misha were correct: the assailant wasn't one of Gary's unstable coworkers. No, the picture on TV showed the guy with the duffle bag whom Gary had spotted on his way to the restroom. His name was Alexander Fields, with previous convictions for sexual assault. Apparently, Alex hadn't come to deliver donuts as Gary had thought but to put a bullet into Mary Jenkins' head. Mary was working in marketing, and she was quite the looker. Alex had met her at a pub a few weeks ago, but Mary had repeatedly refused his sexual advances. Unbeknownst to poor Mary, Alex didn't take very kindly to rejections by pretty women. The police had searched his home and found an angry social media post on one of those Incel hangouts:

I'm entitled to sleep with beautiful women, and if Mary doesn't let me, I will end that cunt for good!

That was the plan when Alex entered Branch #37. Of course, like all other employees, Mary wasn't in her office but in the main conference room at that time. When Alex found her there, he did what he intended, but since Alex had brought enough guns and ammo to stop a small army, he continued to vent his not-so-righteous anger on the remaining 28 people in the room. When he was finished, perhaps in a lucid moment while standing ankle-deep in blood or just because it was part of his plan all along, Alex blew his own brains out to make it an even 30 fatalities.

Gary was surprised that the police hadn't shown up at his place yet, but with the circumstances so quickly resolving, there was probably no rush, and that was just fine with Gary since he didn't have much to add to this investigation anyway. But Gary still had the feeling that this wasn't over yet. The public wanted someone to be punished for this heinous act, but Mr. Fields had deprived them of that satisfaction with his suicide.

When Gary got up the following day, he missed his cats. Leila and Misha would sleep on his bed every night, and it felt odd not to have them there. But Gary knew that Becky would take good care of them, and that would have to do for now. He brewed some fresh coffee and turned on his laptop.

First, he checked the newsfeed. The mass shooting was still on the front pages. The Chief of Police said that the case would remain open until further notice, but the police department had released all the victims' names and notified their next of kin. In the coming days, relatives would be permitted to claim the victims' personal belongings at Branch #37. The Chief had to answer some uncomfortable questions from the reporters at the news conference: Why was a known sexual predator allowed to roam the streets? Why had the police ignored Mary Jenkins' complaints? Where did the assailant get the illegal firearms? Why did nobody monitor his extremist online activities? The Chief was hard-pressed, and all he could say was that there were still more leads to follow, and his Detectives would leave no stone unturned. Meanwhile, a sizeable vigil with flowers, candles, and pictures was created by the community in the parking lot of the branch office, and a small group of activists had gathered there to protest against dangerous misogynist groups.

Gary wondered if he should go there and collect his personal belongings as well. But he had always kept his office desk clean of personal items, except for a coffee mug and a picture of Leila and Misha as kittens. But the cup was old and generic, and he had lots of copies of that picture, so he decided that it wasn't worth the drive. Next, Gary logged into his work email again. He had received a new message from HR:

Mr. Hastings, you have failed to appear for your scheduled appointment. We request that you reschedule with your supervisor or branch manager immediately! Lisa Lambert, HR assistant.

Now, Gary was a bit irritated! Either this Lisa Lambert never read his previous messages, or she was willfully ignorant of the situation!

Ms. Lambert, I'm working at Branch #37, the place that got shot up; maybe you have heard of that? My supervisor and branch manager are dead, so is every one of my coworkers. I'm willing to attend your so-called therapy, but please make reasonable arrangements for that! Thank you, Gary Hastings.

Gary left his inbox open, but there was no immediate reply. Perhaps he should call HR and get someone competent on the line? Maybe later, he thought. Right now, Gary wasn't in the mood to talk to idiots. Still upset, Gary left the house to take a short walk to the grocery store by the corner. He needed some milk and figured the fresh air would do him good. When he returned, he had another cup of coffee and rechecked his work email. HR had finally responded:

Mr. Hasting, since you have refused the mandatory therapy, we regret to inform you that the company no longer requires your services. Please complete all attached forms and meet for an immediate exit interview with your supervisor or branch manager! You may collect your personal belongings, then wait at your desk for security to escort you off the premises. Dan Wellington, Director of Human Resources.

For a brief moment, Gary envisioned himself storming into HQ with an assault rifle and mowing down scores of HR workers, especially Lisa Lambert and Dan Wellington! But that was not Gary's way. Besides, he already knew when the shooting at Branch #37 happened that his days with the company were numbered. The best he could have hoped for was either a meager severance package or a transfer to some other branch, hundreds of miles away. But now, the company had decided it was more cost-efficient to remove him for a cause instead. Gary was not even surprised. He printed the forms out and closed his work email. When he exited the program, a notification popped up to inform him that IT had already revoked his user permissions.

It was 10:15 AM when the swat team busted through Gary's front door!

"Get down on the floor, get down on the floor!" shouted the heavily-geared officer, pointing an assault rifle straight at Gary's chest. Gary was nearly blinded because another officer shone a powerful flashlight in his face, which was odd since it was broad daylight, and Gary's place was well illuminated.

"Get down! I'm not going to say it again!" shouted the man. Gary laid down on the carpet, but slowly, as not to make sudden moves and get shot by mistake.

"Hands behind your back! Now!" yelled the officer, and Gary complied. The other officer turned off the flashlight and took out some handcuffs. He stepped over Gary's prone body, reached for his wrists, and slapped the restraints on too tightly. Then he patted Gary down very thoroughly. When he was satisfied that Gary was secured, the officer stepped back again but kicked Gary's ribs hard with his heavy, steel-toed boots. It was excruciatingly painful, and Gary immediately knew that it had been no accident. The swat team continued to sweep his apartment. After a few moments, one of them called the all-clear. A third man entered the room, but from his position on the floor, Gary couldn't see his face.

"Gary Hastings, you are under arrest!" he said but didn't bother reading Gary his rights, "Take him to the van and tell forensics that they are cleared to enter!"

Two swat team members lifted Gary off the ground. When he was standing, a third one jammed the butt of his rifle hard into Gary's back.

"Move!" he ordered, and Gary started walking. They herded him to a police van parked outside his residence. The doors in the back opened, and Gary was brutally pushed inside the vehicle. He hit his head on the door frame and suffered a nasty cut right above his left eye. Blood was streaming over his face as he was chained to the bench in the van. Two swat team members sat to either side of him, another just across with his rifle trained on Gary.

They didn't bother cleaning him up when Gary was processed at the precinct, not even for the mug shot. The eye was already swelling up, and blood was still dripping from his cheek. After a few minutes, two officers put Gary into an interrogation room, sat him down, chained him to the table, and left without a word. Gary couldn't feel his hands because the tight cuffs restricted blood flow, and his head and eye hurt pretty severely now. But it was the ribs that made every breath excruciating. Gary suspected that some of them must have cracked.

The interrogation room was a small, stuffy room with a recording device on the table and a camera in a corner just above the door. Bright lights shone from the ceiling. The door had a keypad lock and a small window. The table and the chair Gary was sitting on were bolted down to the floor. He sat in the room for at least an hour without anything happening. Gary had expected a visit from the police all along, perhaps even prolonged interrogation with uncomfortable questions, but he had been entirely unprepared for such a violent arrest.

Finally, two men and a woman entered without a word. The two men sat down across from Gary, but the woman remained standing behind them. For a moment, they just sat there and looked at some papers in a folder.

"I'm Detective Madden, and this is Detective Harris!" said one of the men finally, but they did not introduce the woman. Gary suspected that she must be an FBI agent, perhaps a profiler. He immediately recognized Detective Madden's voice from the arrest.

At first, the interrogation proceeded as Gary was expecting. The police had found out that Gary was at Branch #37 when the shooting had happened. He truthfully told them everything, except that he had seen the bullet holes in the conference room door and that Gary had left the building because he didn't want to get involved. Instead, Gary said he left because he felt ill, which wasn't a lie, and that he didn't learn of the mass shooting until he saw the news on TV, and strictly speaking, that wasn't a lie either.

Over the next hour or so, Gary had to repeat the same story at least a dozen times. As the interrogation dragged on, Gary's ribs hurt more and more. Detective Harris seemed to notice, and he was getting increasingly more uncomfortable. The FBI agent who had paid close attention to Gary's every word, gesture, and facial expression earlier now seemed almost bored, but Detective Madden continued to bombard Gary with question after question. Gary answered them all as best as possible, but it was exhausting.

Suddenly, someone was knocking loudly on the door. Gary saw a face in the small window. He recognized the man from the campaign ads that were all over town. It was the District Attorney who was running in the upcoming election. The Detectives stopped the interrogation, got up from their chairs, and left the room along with the FBI agent. When they opened the door, Gary saw that the Chief of Police was standing next to the District Attorney. Detective Harris was the last one to exit, and he failed to close the door completely. In fact, Gary noticed that he held it open with his hand while talking to the visitors. Gary wondered if this was an oversight or intentional. Either way, he was able to hear the conversation now.

"What have you found?" asked the District Attorney loudly.

"Not much, I'm afraid. I believe this guy just happened to be in the building, lucky to be alive," said Detective Harris and shrugged his shoulders.

"I concur with the Detective. As expected, the suspect is nervous and in considerable discomfort because of his injuries, but his story fits the evidence. He might have omitted something, but I doubt that it would be a game-changer!" summarized the FBI agent and added pointedly, "Someone needs to tend to his wounds!"

"Of course, we will see to that!" said the Chief of Police quickly, and Gary could see through the small crack that the Chief was guiding the agent away from the interrogation room. The District Attorney and the two Detectives remained at the door.

"This reflects poorly on me, on us! We have 29 dead people, and the public demands to know what we will do about it. They want to see someone – anyone - getting their just desserts, not pictures of some dead asshole! Gary Hastings is all we got, so we need to tie him to Alexander Fields and the Incels!" said the District Attorney in a more subdued voice.

"What about the catering service?" wondered Detective Madden.

"No, she is a woman. It would be difficult to link her to a misogynist. Besides, she played it well, and the public sympathizes with her now. It has to be Hastings!" insisted the District Attorney and added, "find something, anything – we'll charge him with a parking ticket if we must, and Judge McKenzie will rubberstamp it at the hearing. Then we can prepare for the trial, stack the deck against the suspect, and show that we are doing something to protect the public!" proposed the District Attorney. Just then, the Chief of Police returned without the FBI agent.

"But he might be innocent!" Detective Harris pointed out.

"In the eyes of the public, an arrest alone proves that he must be guilty of something!" interjected the Chief of Police.

"Right, and have you seen Hastings' mug shot, Detective? That's not what an innocent man looks like!" added the District Attorney and laughed at his own joke.

"Has he asked for a lawyer yet?" inquired the Chief of Police.

"No, I think he still believes he doesn't need it!" said Detective Harris.

"Good, good," mumbled the District Attorney, and then he observed, "Hastings isn't the kind of guy who would have a top-shelf lawyer on retainer, so when he asks for one, it will just be some public defender. We can live with that. Tomorrow, we will arraign him; McKenzie will deny bail and set a date for the hearing. I'll press for the earliest one!"

"Push him hard, fellas!" instructed the Chief of Police and patted Detective Madden on the back.

"OK, we'll work on the scumbag until he cracks!" agreed Detective Madden, turned around, and entered the interrogation room again. Detective Harris followed him and closed the door. They sat down, and the interrogation resumed.

"We know you conspired with Alexander Fields. Did you pay him to kill those people?" insinuated Detective Madden.

"I didn't know the guy, and I didn't conspire with anybody!" insisted Gary.

"We will find out eventually! The longer you refuse to tell us, the worse it will get for you!" warned Madden.

"There is nothing to find!" countered Gary and insisted, "everything I have told you was true!"

"Yeah, sure, next thing you'll deny that you had the hots for Mary Jenkins, too!" said Madden sarcastically.

"I was never interested in Mary. She was a colleague, nothing more!" countered Gary.

"You're lying; we saw the emails!" yelled the Detective.

"I never emailed her outside of work, and whatever I've sent her from work was related to company projects!" refuted Gary.

"How did you communicate with Alexander Fields?" asked Madden.

"I never talked to him!" answered Gary.

"Did you use social media for that?" inquired Madden, ignoring Gary's reply.

"I never talked to him!" responded Gary unhappily.

"What social media accounts did you use?" Madden demanded to know.

"I don't have any social media accounts!" insisted Gary.

"Did you buy the guns for Alexander Fields? Where did you get them?" questioned the Detective.

"May I have some water, please?" asked Gary. His throat felt like sandpaper.

"No, this isn't a restaurant!" replied Detective Madden, "You get nothing until you tell us how you know Alexander Fields!"

Gary noticed that only Detective Madden was asking questions. Detective Harris was quietly taking notes but didn't say a word. Suddenly, a police officer in uniform knocked on the door. Detective Madden got up and opened it.

"Detective, you asked us to tell you when we have located the women. I have left their contact information on your desk!" noted the officer.

"Oh yeah, I better call the broads and find out what they know!"

grumbled Madden and exited the interrogation room. A moment later, Detective Harris got up, turned the recording device off, and left the room as well. But very soon, he returned with a bottle of water, opened it, and placed it in front of Gary. Gary was very thirsty, but he wasn't sure if he should drink.

"Are you the good cop to Detective Madden's bad one?" inquired Gary sarcastically.

"No," replied Harris and asked, "Did you hear what the District Attorney said earlier?"

"You left the door open on purpose...," noted Gary and tried to pick up the water bottle, but his hands were so numb, he couldn't hold it. Detective Harris noticed and loosened the restraints. Blood rushed back into Gary's hands with a painful, burning sensation. With some difficulty, Gary brought the bottle to his mouth and emptied it with a few big gulps.

"You are being railroaded!" said Detective Harris quietly after Gary had finished the water.

"I've noticed. Any idea what I should do, Detective?" wondered Gary.

"Ask for a lawyer, but get a good one, not a public defender – they are useless!" advised Harris and put a business card in Gary's shirt pocket, "call that number, say it's urgent, and that Jack Harris referred you!"

"Thank you, Detective!" replied Gary and nodded. Detective Harris took the empty plastic bottle and left the room again. Gary figured that he didn't want his colleague to see it. Gary moved his fingers, and slowly the feeling returned to them, but his ribs hurt more and more. Gary started to worry that it might be something more severe than just cracks and bruises. About half an hour later, both Detectives returned to the interrogation room.

"I would like to call my attorney now!" announced Gary.

"Ah, an admission of guilt!" stated Detective Madden and added, "you can do that later; we still have things to discuss!"

"No, I want my attorney right now!" insisted Gary.

"Later!" countered Madden dismissively, but Detective Harris took him aside.

"Frank, he has the right to counsel. We can't cross that line!" warned Harris.

"Are you going soft on me, Jack? You heard the District Attorney; we need to produce results!" insisted Madden, but after a moment, he relented and said to Gary: "Fine, you can make your phone call!"

Gary was led to a phone, and he dialed the number on the business card. After a moment, a woman picked up. Gary repeated what Detective Harris told him to say. The woman, who appeared to be the attorney's secretary, replied that Mr. Huntsman was not in the office at the moment, but she promised that she would relay the message immediately. After that, Gary asked if he could use the restroom, but Detective Madden took him right back to the interrogation room instead. After he was chained to the table again, Detective Madden resumed his barrage of questions.

"Do you know Amy Leong and Janice Alvarado?" he asked.

"Yes, I do," responded Gary truthfully.

"They say that you've beaten them and threatened to kill them!" remarked the Detective nonchalantly.

"That's not true!" gasped Gary. His relationships with Amy and Janice didn't end well, but he couldn't believe that they would have lied so blatantly about him.

"I talked to them myself, and we have their depositions! They swear that you hate women!" insisted Madden.

"Whatever they have told you is not true!" countered Gary. If not for his talk with Detective Harris earlier, Gary would have seriously wondered if Amy or Janice had been so spiteful as to claim that he had abused them. But now, he knew that these questions were just meant to throw him off.

"Give it up already! You are one of those Incels, like your buddy, Alex!" proclaimed Detective Madden loudly.

"Vexing," remarked Gary.

"What's do damn vexing?" grumbled Madden.

"Are they lying about me, or are you lying about their deposition?" wondered Gary pointedly.

"Don't get smart with me!" yelled Madden, and it looked as if he was about to hit Gary, but Detective Harris pulled his arm back just in time. Madden glared at his colleague, but then he calmed down it again.

"I need the restroom!" stated Gary.

"No, you need to give us access to your social media accounts!" screamed Madden.

"I don't have any!" insisted Gary and added urgently, "but I urgently need the restroom now!"

"No! How do you know Alexander Fields? How did you let him in the building? What did you say to him in the foyer?" the Detective pressed on.

"I don't know him!" replied Gary.

"What did you wipe from your computer? What was your relationship with Mary Jenkins?" Madden demanded to know. Gary couldn't control his bladder any longer, and to his shame, he had to relieve himself on his chair!

"Oh, fuck's sake!" yelled Detective Madden, "the swine pissed his pants!"

As embarrassing as it was, Gary's mishap ended the questioning for the day. He was removed from the interrogation room and handed over to a uniformed officer.

"Put him in holding, but hose him down first. I don't want to smell piss when we arraign him in the morning!" instructed Detective Madden with a big grin on his face, and the officer nodded his acknowledgment.

While in the holding cell, Gary tried to clean himself up as best he could. The dried blood on his cheeks washed off, but his face still looked awful. The orange county jail jumpsuit was a little too big for him and very rough to the touch but not uncomfortable. He stretched out on the narrow cot, careful not to aggravate his sore ribs. Only a moment later, Gary fell asleep from exhaustion.

The arraignment in the morning only took a few minutes. Judge McKenzie read the charges, Gary pleaded not guilty, but in light of the severity of the alleged crimes, the Judge denied bail. Surprisingly, he set the preliminary hearing for the very next day! That was quite unusual because the legal system was chronically overwhelmed and rarely moved that fast, but the prosecutor seemed delighted. Initially, Gary was supposed to be transferred to the county jail after the arraignment, but because the hearing was set early the following day, the police ferried him back to the precinct. While loaded into the police van, he overheard the prosecutor talking to one of his campaign aides.

"It's better that way! We don't want our sacrificial lamb to end up with a shiv in his back while he is in county jail!" the man said with a chuckle, and Gary knew for sure that all odds were stacked against him.

When Gary was back in the holding cell, his health took a turn for the worse. His left eye was shut entirely now, and his face was grotesquely swollen, but the head wasn't hurting that much anymore. However, the pain in his side was nearly unbearable now. More and more often, he had to cough and spit out wads of mucus. He tried to lay very still on his cot because every movement seemed to worsen the pain. It was about 10:00 AM when his cell door was unlocked, and a sharply dressed, older man with glasses entered.

"Hello, Mr. Hasting, I'm Malcolm Huntsman!" said the man and extended his hand. Gary got up very slowly because of the pain, and Mr. Huntsman noticed that.

"Oh, please remain seated, Mr. Hastings. Jack told me that you had a rough couple of days, and I must say, you really look awful!" remarked the attorney.

"Thanks, I guess!" replied Gary with a bit of a smile.

"So, I got most the information already. But I wanted to ask you a few questions before the hearing tomorrow if that's alright?" asked the attorney.

"Of course!" agreed Gary readily.

"Is there anything that you had omitted when the police questioned you, or anything you want to change or retract? You can speak freely, Mr. Hastings; this is all protected by attorney-client privilege!" assured the attorney.

"No, I told the police everything I knew, and it was all true!" answered Gary. He wasn't going to tell this man that he saw the bullet holes in the conference room door.

"I wonder, how did you know that the front door of the building was unlocked?" asked the attorney while he was leafing through Gary's file.

"I didn't really know that, but it's been like that for the last few years: Melissa would leave it open during the annual meeting for the caterer! I honestly thought that shooter was just delivering donuts!" explained Gary and shrugged his shoulders.

"Yes, that makes sense!" concurred Huntsman and inquired, "clients often don't want to reveal their personal relationships, but I have to ask about this one: is there anything that ties you to Mary Jenkins, other than your work?"

"No, Mr. Huntsman. Mary was a good-looking woman, but there was nothing between us, and it never even crossed my mind!" replied Gary truthfully.

"Understood!" acknowledged the attorney and asked, "the last question: do you have any social media accounts? Something that you might have forgotten about?"

"No, I don't, and I never signed up for anything. I use email and sometimes text messages, but the social media craze isn't me. I'm a pretty private person, and honestly, I'm appalled by how exhibitionist it all is!" elaborated Gary.

"I see!" said Mr. Huntsman and concluded, "Mr. Hastings, the charges filed against you are frivolous, and normally, we both should laugh at all of this. But after talking to Jack, I know this situation isn't normal, and no laughing matters. Our biggest obstacle is Judge McKenzie. If he is in the pocket of the prosecution, facts won't matter tomorrow."

"I can see that. What is the best course of action?" wondered Gary.

"If the Judge doesn't dismiss the charges, we will ask for a new hearing with a new Judge. Any reasonable Judge will throw this nonsense out!" advised the attorney, but then he warned, "however, bail was denied, so you will have to spend some time in jail while we wait for that!"

"Thanks for being so forward, Mr. Huntsman!" replied Gary and nodded.

"We'll take it one step at a time. I will see you tomorrow at the hearing!" said Mr. Huntsman and added, "get some rest, Mr. Hastings; you don't seem well!"

"I will; thank you for coming here, Mr. Huntsman!" said Gary and shook his attorney's hand.

When Gary arrived at the hearing the next day, his new attorney was already waiting for him. The prosecutor was also present and surprised to see Mr. Huntsman speaking with Gary. He quickly walked over to them with a big smile on his face. Gary wasn't sure if it was genuine and faked.

"Malcolm, it's been a long time!" he exclaimed with excitement in his voice.

"Hello, Bill! How's the campaign going?" replied Malcolm Huntsman courteously.

"Splendid, remind me to send you an invite for the next fundraiser. It will be at a plush resort!" promised the prosecutor.

"Oh, thank you, but you know that I try to stay out of politics!" answered Huntsman and smiled.

"You shouldn't, and you are one us! Law and order, Malcolm, law and order!" remarked the prosecutor loudly.

Gary thought that if his new attorney and the prosecutor were friends, his chances just took a severe nosedive. Perhaps it would be better to defend himself? Mr. Huntsman sensed Gary's apprehension and took him aside.

"Don't worry, I'm supporting his opponent!" he said quietly and grinned.

The proceedings were about to start, and unbeknownst to Gary, today was his lucky day. Judge McKenzie had an emergency appendectomy last night, and a new Judge was presiding over the preliminary hearing. Judge Nakamura had a reputation for being no-nonsense on the bench and tough as nails with defendants, witnesses, and Counsel alike.

"All rise for the Honorable Judge Nakamura!" announced the bailiff. Gary noticed that the prosecutor looked very displeased, but his own attorney wasn't too happy either.

"Tough one, but fair! Be on your best behavior, Mr. Hastings!" whispered his attorney.

This can't be good, thought Gary, and he wasn't sure what to expect from this new Judge. But when the diminutive lady, who looked too young to be a Judge, strode into the courtroom, Gary was genuinely surprised. Her robes seemed too big for her petite frame, and yet she carried an aura of authority that wasn't an act. Judge Nakamura sat down on the bench, shuffled some papers around for a moment, then took a hard look at Gary. He felt as if her eyes were drilling holes in his skull, and it seemed to make his headache worse. Finally, she banged hard on the desk with her gavel.

"This hearing is now in session!" she announced and stated, "I have read your brief. You are charging the defendant with conspiracy to commit murder, aiding and abetting of a terrorist, hate crimes, destruction of evidence, and obstruction of justice!"

"Yes, Your Honor!" confirmed the prosecutor.

"That's quite the litany of charges, but your brief was skinny on evidence. I expect to see a lot more of that today!" said the Judge and motioned, "present your case!"

"Thank you, Your Honor! The defendant and the shooter met in the lobby of Branch #37 just moments before the shooting. We have video footage of that, and we believe that the defendant let Mr. Fields into the building at that time. The defendant knew the assailant, knew what Mr. Fields was about to do, and hid in the basement of Branch #37 until the deed was done.

The defendant's personal laptop and the phone appeared to be wiped of all incriminating evidence, but we found numerous messages on his work computer to Mary Jenkins - the same Mary Jenkins specifically targeted by Mr. Fields. Furthermore, the defendant had several failed relationships, none lasting more than a few months, supporting that Mr. Hastings, just like Mr. Fields, has deep misogynist tendencies. In addition, the defendant continues to obstruct justice by refusing to give us access to his social media accounts. This is clearly an attempt to hide his extremist views. In summary, the prosecution believes that the defendant conspired with the assailant or perhaps hired the shooter outright to commit a hate crime! Mr. Hasting is as culpable in this horrible act, if not more so, as Mr. Fields was!" summarized the prosecutor confidently.

"Counsel, there was nothing in your brief about soliciting a hitman. The police report on Mr. Fields concluded that he acted alone, driven by rage and indoctrinated by online bigotry. Has that changed? Will the prosecution present evidence for these new developments today?" wondered the Judge.

"Your Honor, this is an ongoing investigation, and we are still looking into the defendant's financial transactions!" replied the District Attorney.

"Aha. While it is customary and prudent at these hearings to give the prosecution some leeway in building its case against the defendant, you cannot add new charges until you find something actionable!" the Judge reminded him.

"Yes, Your Honor!" relented the prosecutor.

"The Counsel for the defense may respond!" announced the Judge.

"Thank you, Your Honor! My client worked at Branch #37 for 15 years, he was a good employee, and he got along with his coworkers and superiors. As the attendance record showed, Mr.

Hastings was present at the annual office meeting, but he excused himself to use the bathroom, made his way downstairs, used the facilities, washed his hands, and returned to the office area. My client did not return to the meeting because he felt ill, so he emailed his supervisor in that regard, then left the branch office and drove home. It was not until later that day that my client learned from the news on TV that a shooting had happened at his workplace! Even the prosecution agrees on this chain of events!" stated Gary's attorney.

"Objection! We believe the defendant knew about the shooting before it happened!" barked the District Attorney.

"Sustained! Counsel, do not second-guess the prosecution!" warned Sharon Nakamura.

"Understood, Your Honor!" apologized Mr. Huntsman and observed, "let's look at the charges one at a time. The prosecution claims that the defendant knew the assailant. But all they verifiably know from the video recording is that my client and the assailant were crossing paths in the foyer of Branch #37 for approximately five seconds. When that happened, there was no interaction between Mr. Hastings and Mr. Fields – no words were spoken, no hand signals and no eye contact was made!"

"Objection, Your Honor! The defense does not know what happened outside the view of the camera!" interjected the prosecutor.

"Overruled! Neither do you!" replied the Judge and shook her head.

"There are no phone calls, no letters, no emails or text messages, no mutual associates, no common locations that Mr. Fields and my client have visited in the past, nothing that would indicate that my client ever knew that Mr. Fields existed!" continued Mr. Huntsman.

"Objection! Mary Jenkins was a mutual associate of the defendant and Mr. Fields!" interrupted the prosecutor.

"Sustained! However, I expect the prosecution to prove that connection beyond the obvious!" answered the Judge and added: "Continue, Counsel!"

"The prosecution claims that Mr. Hastings was hiding in the basement when the shooting happened. But the evidence corroborates my client's version: the cleaning crew confirmed that the men's room's trashcan had been emptied the night before. Forensics found only one item in the wastebasket: a paper towel with the defendant's DNA on it. As my client said, he washed his hands after he used the facilities," said Mr. Huntsman and continued, "Furthermore, the prosecutor speculates that my client enabled the assailant's entry to the building since no card key was found on Mr. Fields body. But the camera footage shows that my client never got close to the receptionist desk, nor were his fingerprints found on the switch that triggers the front door. My client maintained that the receptionist had left the doors unlocked for the catering service, and the bakery has confirmed that arrangement."

"Objection! The defendant couldn't have known that!" interjected the prosecutor.

"Sustained! Explain that, Counsel!" ordered the Judge.

"My client worked at Branch #37 for 15 years. For the last ten years, the office has used the same catering service to deliver donuts and refreshments after the annual meeting. Indeed, my client wasn't explicitly informed of this arrangement, but it was self-evident: with all employees, including the receptionist, gathered at the conference room upstairs, the bakery had no way to deliver the goods unless the front door was left unlocked for that time" explained Malcolm Huntsman.

"Was that company policy?" inquired the Judge.

"No, it was not, and corporate security confirmed as much. But they conceded that the policy was not always strictly enforced by every branch office," explained Gary's attorney.

"I see," acknowledged Judge Nakamura and motioned, "continue!"

"The prosecution points out that the defendant never contacted the authorities when he learned about the shooting at his workplace. That is true because my client believed that he had no useful information for the police, and he still believes that. My client also values his privacy, and he admits that he wanted to avoid media attention. That is not a crime!" proclaimed Mr. Huntsman.

"Objection! Perhaps not a crime, but it is certainly very suspicious!" interrupted the prosecutor.

"Overruled! Show some restraint, Counsel!" warned the Judge.

"The prosecution asserts that Mr. Hastings wiped his phone and computer of incriminating evidence. However, they have shown no proof that such destruction of evidence ever happened. No software or hardware was found that could do such a thing. My client insists that nothing was wiped because such evidence never existed!" stated Gary's attorney.

"Is that true?" asked the Judge, the question directed at the prosecutor.

"Cyber Crime has not finished analyzing all of the defendant's electronic devices. We found additional computer components, USB drives, and other gadgets at his residence!" replied the prosecutor evasively.

"Counsel, the absence of evidence cannot be evidence! The defense doesn't have to prove that it didn't exist; you have the burden of proof that it did. Do I have to remind you of this basic principle we've all learned in first-year law school?" asked Judge Nakamura rhetorically and then added, "the defense may continue!"

"The same holds true for the prosecution's claim that my client refused to give law enforcement access to his social media accounts. My client readily surrendered his email account and pin to his cellphone, and no incriminating evidence was found there. But he cannot grant access to social media accounts that do not exist! As I said earlier, my client values his privacy, and again, that's not a crime!" remarked Mr. Huntsman.

"Objection! In this day and age, everybody has some kind of social media account!" countered the prosecution.

"Overruled! I don't have one either, Counsel!" said the Judge and asked, "did law enforcement check with the various social media platforms if Mr. Hastings has accounts with them?"

"Yes, Your Honor, we checked!" confirmed the prosecutor, seemingly unwilling to say more.

"And?" questioned the Judge and raised her eyebrows.

"There are dozens of Gary Hastings listed, and of course, there is also the likely possibility that he signed up under a false name! Since the defendant refuses to give us access, we cannot examine them yet, but Cyber Crime is working on it!" elaborated the District Attorney.

"As of this moment, can you prove that the defendant has social media accounts? Yes or no?" the Judge demanded to know, very sternly.

"No, Your Honor!" admitted the prosecutor grudgingly.

"That's what I thought!" observed Judge Nakamura and stated, "continue with the defense!"

"The prosecution claims that the defendant is a hateful misogynist. As proof, they offer the depositions of two women who were at one point or another in a relationship with my client: Amy Leong called him a boring cheapskate who didn't appreciate her enough, and Janice Alvarado complained that the defendant loved his dumb cats more than her, but a third woman, one Rebecca Morrison, my client's most recent girlfriend, praised Mr. Hastings a kind and principled man. There is likely resentment over unhappy relationships in the testimonies of Ms. Leong and Ms. Alvarado, but I fail to see the misogyny here!" stated Gary's attorney.

"Does the prosecution have additional evidence? Did the defendant threaten, abuse, or beat these women?" asked Sharon Nakamura.

"We cannot be certain, Your Honor! We have the names of three more women, but we were not able to take their statements yet!" stated the prosecution.

"I'm a woman, in case you haven't noticed, and I too fail to see the misogyny in these depositions! At this very moment, do you have anything else to support your claim that the defendant hates women?" quizzed the Judge pointedly.

"Not at the moment, Your Honor, but we will have it as soon as we can access the defendant's social media accounts!" informed the prosecutor.

"Counsel, I warn you: this might work for QAnon or certain Presidents, but doubling down on utter nonsense will not be tolerated by this court!" said the Judge harshly, and Gary sensed that the woman was getting aggravated, "Counsel for the defense, please wrap this up!"

"I will, Your Honor. The prosecution's most outlandish claim is that my client, like Mr. Fields, was pursuing some kind of sexual relationship with Mary Jenkins. Over the course of the five years that my client and Ms. Jenkins were both employed at Branch #37, these two coworkers exchanged 53 emails in total. I have printed all of them out and could submit them as an exhibit if the court wishes. All of them were friendly and courteous but strictly professional and exclusively work-related. Even by the wildest stretch of the imagination, my client never had personal relations or pursued them with Ms. Jenkins!" concluded Malcolm Huntsman.

"I'm almost afraid to ask…," remarked Judge Nakamura sarcastically, "…does the prosecution have any evidence that the defendant pursued Mary Jenkins?"

"Your Honor, Mary Jenkins was a beautiful woman, and the defendant is single. Does it not strike the court as suspicious that the defendant has never shown any interest?" questioned the prosecutor. Even Gary could tell that the man was desperate now.

"Counsel, do you think I'm a fool, or are you intoxicated? Either way, I'm this close to holding you in contempt! Are you seriously arguing that the defendant was trying to get into Mary Jenkins' panties by acting professional and NOT showing any interest?" exclaimed Sharon Nakamura angrily and advised, "it is better if you don't answer that! The defense may finish up!"

"In conclusion, my client has no prior convictions and is not a registered sex offender. By all accounts, he was a good, courteous employee without any red flags. Unlike his 29 coworkers, my client was spared on that fateful day. Maybe he should have paid more attention to that unknown man in the foyer, and perhaps it was a mistake not to contact the police after he learned of the tragedy. But that was not a crime! My client is only guilty of being very lucky to be alive, nothing more!" summarized Mr. Huntsman.

The agony and shortness of breath had made it hard for Gary to follow the proceedings, but he was impressed by his new attorney. The man was eloquent and convincing. Just then, he experienced a very painful coughing fit, which attracted the Judge's attention again.

"Thank you, Counsel!" said the Judge, and added while looking at Gary, "before we continue, the police report doesn't mention that defendant resisted arrest, yet it seems to me he is injured and can barely sit upright. Why is that?"

"The injuries are accidental or self-inflicted!" informed the prosecutor.

"Did someone look at the defendant?" asked the Judge.

"That did not seem necessary," remarked the Counsel, but the Judge wasn't satisfied with that at all.

"Mr. Hastings, you are under oath, so answer me truthfully: did you inflict those injuries on yourself?" inquired Judge Nakamura. Gary struggled to stand up before he responded.

"Your Honor...," interrupted the prosecutor.

"I'm talking to the defendant; you can make your point later, Counsel!" countered the Judge and waved him off.

"No, Your Honor!" rasped Gary. He feared that he would pass out at any moment now.

"Tell me what happened!" insisted Judge Nakamura.

"I complied with the arrest, but I was kicked in the ribs while I was laying on the ground, and now I have trouble breathing. Then I was shoved hard into the door frame of the police van. That's how I got the injuries in my face!" reported Gary truthfully.

"Do you believe it was accidental?" questioned the Judge.

"No, I do not!" answered Gary, wheezing hard. Mr. Huntsman looked at him, concerned.

"Your Honor!" interrupted the District Attorney once again.

"Shut up, Counsel!" yelled Sharon Nakamura, and then asked Gary in a much softer voice: "you look pale, Mr. Hastings - do you need medical attention?"

"Thank you, Your Honor, but I believe I can manage!" replied Gary bravely, but he wasn't sure if he really could for much longer. Judge Nakamura didn't seem to be too sure either, but then she continued the proceedings, and Gary was grateful that he could sit down again.

"The prosecution's entire case is built on the camera footage that showed the defendant crossing paths with the assailant in the foyer of Branch #37. I saw the video, and it is not convincing. So far, you have failed to provide any other evidence to support any of the serious charges you have filed. If you have a silver bullet left, use it now, Counsel!" emphasized the Judge impatiently.

"As I said before, this is an ongoing investigation, but we cannot allow a dangerous predator, a terrorist, to be let loose on the public. That's irresponsible and inexcusable! We must uphold law and order, Your Honor!" exclaimed the prosecutor forcefully. Judge Nakamura just looked at him with disdain and shook her head.

"I cannot remember a time when the prosecution had failed more miserably than you did today! You never had a case against the defendant, but you stubbornly tried to pull one out of your rear with speculations and plain bullshit! I know you are a better attorney than that, so I wonder if this case had more to do with your political ambitions than with justice. Either way, do not come into my courtroom again so unprepared!" growled the Judge, and her gavel came down hard on the desk.

"Please rise!" ordered Sharon Nakamura and announced her decision: "All charges are dismissed! The defendant is to be released immediately, and all his belongings must be returned to him!"

"We demand a new hearing!" yelled the District Attorney angrily.

"You do that, Counsel! Good luck!" replied the Judge dismissively.

"Thank you, Your Honor!" rasped Gary relieved, visibly swaying on his feet. Then he spat out a wad of blood and collapsed on the courtroom floor.

Gary woke up in a hospital bed. He felt sore all over, and his head was hurting. A nurse was adjusting the drip on his IV. Gary had no idea how he got here or how long he was out.

"What happened?" rasped Gary, his throat parched and scratchy.

"Ah, you are finally awake!" noted the friendly nurse and added, "you collapsed at the courthouse with a punctured lung. But don't worry, you will recover!"

"Oh," replied Gary and asked, "how did I end up here?"

"We see a lot of things at this hospital, but your arrival was something else!" said the nurse and explained, "you were still handcuffed and dressed in that orange jumpsuit when the EMTs brought you in. But a Judge in full robes was riding with you in the ambulance, and she completed your admission to the hospital personally. The Judge didn't leave until the doctors assured her that you would recover!"

"Wow!" mumbled Gary, unsure what to make of that.

"Are you related to her?" asked the nurse curiously.

"No, not at all; I've never met Judge Nakamura before today. I was arraigned on serious charges, but fortunately, she dismissed them. Then I passed out!" recounted Gary.

"Yesterday! You have been here since yesterday, Mr. Hastings!" corrected the nurse and added with a smile, "you must have made quite the impression on that Judge. She asked us to inform her when you regain consciousness!"

"Am I free to go?" asked Gary slowly.

"No, we will keep you here for at least another day. Your injuries were quite serious, and we are still monitoring your concussion, too!" the nurse informed him.

"Sorry, I meant something else…," mumbled Gary, and the nurse nodded at him.

"The police came by and chained you to the bed. They even posted an armed guard in front of the door. But they are gone now, some legal stuff about an injunction and a hearing being denied!" mentioned the nurse as she adjusted the headrest on Gary's bed.

"I don't understand?" wondered Gary confused.

"The news is all over it, Mr. Hastings. At first, they said you conspired with that horrible man who killed all those people, but now they are saying that you were a political scapegoat and abused by the police. Did you really get those injuries from the cops?" inquired the nurse.

"I'm afraid so!" confirmed Gary.

"I'm sorry, Mr. Hastings. Sometimes it seems as if the police isn't any better than the criminals!" remarked the nurse quietly.

"Some of them, but not all!" replied Gary, thinking of Detective Harris, who helped him get a competent attorney.

"If it's any consolation, the Chief of Police has resigned, several cops are suspended, and the District Attorney is under investigation. His poll numbers are way down, and that slimy jerk probably won't get elected now!" laughed the nurse, but then she cautioned, "there will be time to sort that all out, but for now, you should rest and get well again! Use the buzzer if you need anything!"

"Before you leave, could I get some water, please!" begged Gary.

"Of course, but drink slowly!" advised the nurse and held a glass of water to his lips. He drank deeply until the glass was empty.

"Thanks, and please inform Judge Nakamura that I'm very grateful for what she has done for me!" requested Gary and smiled at the nurse.

"You can tell her yourself! She said she would stop by when you are awake!" laughed the nurse and added, "now get some rest, Mr. Hastings!"

Gary was lying in bed for a while, staring at the ceiling and sorting his thoughts. While he was a little apprehensive about seeing that tough lady again, he was also eager to thank the Judge for her help. Gary could not imagine where he would be now or if he would even still be alive without her intervention. Then he looked at the small desk next to the bed and saw his cellphone. He took it and checked his messages. Someone must have leaked his number because there were hundreds of them, and his voice mail was full, too! He scrolled through the text messages but didn't read any of them until he found one from Becky.

Gary, what have you done? Now everybody knows that we have dated, and the police came to my work to question me. Do you have any idea how that reflects on me? This might be my ruin! How could you do that to me?!?

He was hurt, but Gary understood Becky's anger. She had worked tirelessly on her career, and it meant everything to her. Gary was genuinely sorry that her association with him caused her grief. He scrolled further to see if she had sent anything more recently.

Gary, I saw the news, and I'm really happy for you. I heard that you were hospitalized? Are you alright? Leila and Misha are OK, but they miss you! Please let me know when you can pick them up!

Gary put the phone down and closed his eyes. He resolved to call Becky as soon as he felt better. Gary wanted to thank her for her kind words to the police. All in all, this was not a bad day: he was a free man, Becky wasn't mad at him anymore, his cats were OK, and he would recover from his injuries. Gary smiled a little just before he fell asleep again.

It has been nearly four weeks since Gary was discharged from the hospital. His ribs were still hurting, but the swelling in his face was gone, and only a small scar remained above his left eye. They had just finished dinner, and Gary was sitting on the couch, watching the evening news with Misha on his lap. There had been another shooting today. This time, the assailant was a high school student. He had used his father's guns to kill a teacher and several of his classmates. Gary changed the channel, but all the news stations reported the shooting, so he just turned the TV off. Once again, he felt numb and couldn't bring himself to care. With enough repetition, human beings can get used to the most horrible things, thought Gary and exhaled loudly.

"Gary, you can tell me the truth now! What happened at Branch #37?" asked his girlfriend as she sat down next to him and took his hand in hers.

"Everything I have said was true!" replied Gary quietly.

"But?" she wondered and raised an eyebrow.

"But I omitted something: when I returned to the office area, I was not feeling ill. I went back to the conference room, but I didn't enter because I saw the bullet holes in the door. Some of my coworkers weren't mentally stable, so I feared that one of them had snapped, and that's when I felt sick! I didn't want to get shot, I didn't want to see the carnage, I didn't want to get interrogated by the police, and I didn't want the inevitable media circus! So, I rushed back to my desk, sent an email to my supervisor, and left the building. I just wanted to get away as far as I could!" divulged Gary and sighed deeply.

"In a perfect world, I would berate you for not disclosing that, but we don't live in such a world. Nothing you have omitted would have changed a damn thing anyway, and I might have done same under those circumstances!" she remarked consolingly.

"Thank you! It is good to get that off my chest finally!" said Gary relieved. He truly felt liberated, and he was grateful to have someone he could trust in his life.

"Come, let's call it a night. You have to get up early for the deposition in front of the Grand Jury! Besides, I might know of something that will cheer you up...," she said and winked at him suggestively. Gary grinned broadly, gently removed Misha from his lap, and stood up. Then, he suddenly scooped up the small woman from the couch and carried her in his arms to the bedroom.

"Yes, Your Honor!" he said respectfully, and Sharon giggled like a schoolgirl!

2. THE JOURNEY

Kelly was looking forward to this trip. She had planned and postponed it several times. First, it was work, then her divorce, then the pandemic, and finally a broken arm. But now, she was ready, more than ready, for an extended vacation!

The flight was on time, which Kelly took as a good omen. She put her magazine away and boarded the plane. After Kelly had stored her luggage in the overhead compartment, she sat down and took a deep breath. Her vacation was about to start, and she was happy and relaxed. Kelly had kept the first part of her itinerary open for some leisurely sightseeing, but she would spend the last part of her journey at the home of an old friend from college. Kelly hadn't seen her in years, and she was very much looking forward to catching up with her. The seat next to her was still empty, and Kelly hoped it would remain so, but now a tall man was tucking away his bag above the vacant seat. Oh well, no luck, she thought.

"Hello, I'm Kelly!" she greeted him friendly as the man sat down next to her.

"Pleasure to meet you, Kelly; I'm Hagen!" responded the man politely.

"I'm pleased to meet you too, Hagen!" said Kelly and asked, "that's an unusual name!"

"German mythology, the Nibelungen saga!" explained Hagen as he opened his leather briefcase and took out a laptop.

"Wagner's opera! Are you German?" wondered Kelly.

"Oh no, but my father was!" replied Hagen and added humorously, "I wish he would have picked a different name because

Hagen von Tronje wasn't exactly a nice guy!"

"So, what do you do, Hagen?" asked Kelly; by the looks of him, she suspected that he was an attorney.

"Oh, I fix up the house, play with the cats, tend to the garden, and that kind of stuff!" elaborated Hagen nonchalantly.

"I meant your profession!" remarked Kelly and chuckled.

"Retired, of course!" answered Hagen, as he was fiddling with the mouse of his computer.

"Aren't you a bit too young to be retired?" questioned Kelly. She wondered why he didn't want to give her a straight answer.

"I take that as a compliment! I retired as soon as it was financially feasible. I'm lazy, you know?" stated Hagen and smiled disarmingly.

"Somehow, I don't believe that!" laughed Kelly.

"It's true!" insisted Hagen and asked, "but tell me, what are you doing for a living, Kelly?"

"I'm a psychologist," replied Kelly.

"Oh, then I better watch what I'm saying!" remarked Hagen. Kelly knew that he was joking, but something in his voice indicated to her that there was also some truth. She looked at him oddly.

"That was a joke, Kelly, probably a bad one!" apologized Hagen and added, "I would have said the same if you were a judge or in law enforcement!"

"I'm not offended. But usually, people just ask me about my crazy patients or want some free therapy!" mentioned Kelly.

"I bet they do, and I can imagine that you could tell them some stories, but you won't because that would be unethical!" observed Hagen.

"Indeed!" replied Kelly and asked, "what did you do before you retired?"

"Oh, just scientific stuff!" deflected Hagen and asked, "so, what's it like to dive into people's minds, learn all their dark secrets and twisted emotions?"

"Psychology is a job like any other, but it can be challenging!" answered Kelly.

"I think it would also be fascinating! The human mind is so complex!" stated Hagen excitedly.

"It can be, but it can also be sad, and...," said Kelly, but left her sentence incomplete.

"And?" inquired Hagen curiously.

"Disturbing, revolting, scary even!" admitted Kelly and slightly shook her head.

"Given the right incentives, all of us are capable of unspeakable evil - no devil needed!" agreed Hagen, as he was looking for a place to store the airline blanket. Kelly thought that was a harsh assessment of humanity, but she found herself agreeing with his point of view to some extent.

"If you don't need the blanket, might I have it, please?" asked Kelly and explained, "I tend to get cold on these long flights!"

"Oh, of course, Kelly!" assented Hagen readily and handed it to her.

"Thank you!" she said with a smile and wrapped the blanket around her legs.

The flight crew prepped for take-off, and Kelly strapped the safety belt around her waist. Hagen did the same, and a few minutes later, the engines roared, and the big plane lifted off the runway. Kelly was excited, the long-awaited journey had begun, and she was determined to enjoy every bit of it. Meanwhile,

Hagen opened his laptop after electronic devices were permitted again, clicked on a text file, and started typing. Kelly noticed that he was very focused on his work.

"I thought you were retired?" questioned Kelly and pointed at Hagen's laptop.

"Oh, this is just for fun!" explained Hagen and stopped typing.

"Sorry, I didn't mean to interrupt you!" apologized Kelly and asked, "what are you writing?"

"Books and short stories!" noted Hagen and added humorously, "but it's just a hobby, sales are abysmal, I'm no Orwell or Hemmingway!"

"What kind of stories?" asked Kelly curiously.

"All kinds! Fiction, science fiction, mystery, some philosophy, and even some non-fiction once in a while. Whatever I feel like writing!" elaborated Hagen and offered: "Would you like to read one?"

"Oh, no, thank you. I'm on vacation; I have to read a lot at work!" Kelly declined politely. She wasn't sure why she rejected his offer because she would have liked to see one of his stories to understand better who this man was.

"No problem, you are not missing much; they are not that exciting!" remarked Hagen and grinned at her. Somehow that made her even more curious. Hagen returned to his writings, and Kelly looked at the screen, deciphering the words. But the font was too small and the laptop too far away for her to see clearly. A moment later, a stewardess stopped by and offered refreshments. Hagen interrupted his work and looked at Kelly.

"Since you are on vacation and I'm retired, would you care to join me for a drink, Kelly?" he asked.

"Oh, yes, that would be nice!" replied Kelly, a little unsure at first, but then she said, "Long Island Ice Tea for me, please!"

"Good!" said Hagen, placed her order, and got gin tonic for himself. Then he paid for both of them, but Kelly objected!

"Hagen, thank you, but I can pay for my own drink!" she insisted. She probably would have accepted a free drink from a stranger in a bar, but not in this setting.

"It was my invitation, and since I'm getting you drunk, I can at least pay for the damage!" countered Hagen with a grin and handed her the cocktail. She relented, took the glass, and smiled at him a little. For the next hour, they chatted about their travel plans and the various places they had visited in the past. Then they talked about art, music, history, and social developments. They touched on a lot of different topics. Kelly found it very easy to talk to this man, and they seemed to share similar views. A few minutes into the conversation, Kelly discovered that Hagen was brilliant and highly educated. Not only was she surprised by his knowledge and depth, but she genuinely enjoyed the intellectual challenge to keep up with this man. Eventually, the discussion circled back to her work.

"Hagen, can I ask you a personal question?" wondered Kelly and smiled at him.

"Oh sure, I don't have taboos!" said Hagen, friendly.

"Are you gay?" asked Kelly bluntly.

"What makes you say that?" inquired Hagen and raised his eyebrows.

"You don't act like a typical man, at least not an American man!" noted Kelly.

"What is so different about me?" wondered Hagen.

"You are polite, respectful, and you have good manners – no inappropriate innuendo, no bragging, no false bravado! You are eloquent but soft-spoken, and you use high-brow vocabulary, but more importantly, you talk to me as an equal, not condescendingly, because I'm female. You are also well-dressed and groomed, and there is nothing crude or exaggeratedly masculine about you!" summarized Kelly. When she heard herself talk, she wondered if Hagen would think that she was an overly opinionated lesbian feminist now. It wasn't going the way it should!

"Ah, so you are saying I'm not a savage? I take the compliment!" replied Hagen and grinned at her.

"I guess so," conceded Kelly and apologized, "I'm sorry, Hagen, I didn't mean to offend you; please forgive my nosiness!"

"I have been asked that question several times in my life. Of course, in my younger years, they didn't call me gay; they had much cruder terms for it!" remarked Hagen.

"I'm sorry!" apologized Kelly again, unsure what else she could say.

"Don't be, Kelly! I'm not gay and not even the slightest bit curious!" laughed Hagen. Kelly was surprised and embarrassed that she had asked Hagen about sexuality in the first hour of meeting him and even more ashamed that she had questioned his masculinity.

"In the name of fairness, I'm a normal, heterosexual woman!" declared Kelly stiffly, trying to smooth over her slipup. Hagen nodded and chuckled but didn't verbally respond to that. He turned to his computer and typed a few lines. Kelly glanced at the laptop again, but she still couldn't make out any of the words.

"Did you ever have therapy, Hagen?" inquired Kelly a moment later. Immediately, she questioned her judgment. Why would she ask a stranger something so personal?

"Just once, and it wasn't entirely voluntary. I went to a marriage counselor with my wife!" disclosed Hagen and stopped typing.

"You are married?" asked Kelly, and there was a hint of disappointment in her voice, and she didn't even know why it was there. Hagen wasn't her type!

"Not anymore, because that was about 20 years ago," clarified Hagen and added, "the therapist told me that I was insane!"

"That's not what any therapist would say!" contradicted Kelly.

"That one did, but I didn't mind!" disagreed Hagen and remarked, "in a twist of fate, it was my ex-wife who suffered from paranoid delusions. She joined a cult, and eventually, her violent, anti-social tendencies got her institutionalized! I'm not sure if she has gotten better; I've not talked to her since!"

"That's terrible!" claimed Kelly compassionately. She was fully aware of how difficult it was to deal with someone who suffered from violent mental illness.

"Did you ever try therapy again?" wondered Kelly. Hagen might be perfectly content and sane, but now she implied that he needed therapy! It baffled her why she was so forward and disrespectful to a total stranger.

"No, and it would be too challenging!" replied Hagen and shook his head.

"Why challenging?" quizzed Kelly. She knew that people had a thousand reasons why they didn't want to see a therapist, and she was curious to see which one was Hagen's.

"We would have to establish a common ground first, and that takes time!" said Hagen thoughtfully.

"Common ground?" pondered Kelly and wrinkled her forehead. That didn't sound like anything she had heard before.

"Let's say we want to talk about traveling to the other side of the globe. But you believe the Earth is round, while I'll insist that it is flat! Can you see the problem?" asked Hagen and pointed at the display that showed the plane's progress superimposed on an image of Earth.

"Sort of, but the belief that the Earth is flat isn't that common, Hagen!" countered Kelly.

"OK, then let's say we want to talk about social matters: for example, you believe that the government should support education, but I say that the government is really a secret cabal that rapes and eats children in the basement of a pizza parlor, and there are millions more like me who believe that!" stated Hagen and concluded, "so, you will try to convince me with facts, science, history, reason, and logic, but I will reject it all because I believe you are trying to indoctrinate me with fake news. You and I have no common ground, so our dialogue will rapidly descend into pointless name-calling but will accomplish little else!"

"I sincerely hope you don't actually believe that!" remarked Kelly briskly and observed, "yes, I can see the problem, but that's not how therapy works!"

"If you were my therapist, first we would have to establish common ground before we could even have a dialogue!" postulated Hagen, and asked, "you talk about concepts such as love, happiness, loyalty, honesty, family, compassion, etc., do you not?"

"Yes, I do!" confirmed Kelly, still not sure where this was leading.

"But these concepts are nebulous and subject to interpretation! Fortunately, you hold personal definitions of these terms that are similar enough to most of your patients' definitions, and because of that, you have intuitively established common ground. Hence, the therapy can progress, and you will be able to help them!" continued Hagen and took a sip from his gin tonic.

"But your definition of love, happiness, honesty, and such is very different?" wondered Kelly.

"Precisely, Kelly!" concurred Hagen and concluded, "so, we would have to agree on a common language first, and that's not easy or fast!"

"Intriguing!" admitted Kelly and added, "I'm pretty good at reading people, it comes with the job, but you are an enigma, Hagen!"

"I am? Will you give me a free psych evaluation now? That would be amazing!" gushed Hagen and smiled at her broadly.

"Do you want me to?" wondered Kelly slowly.

"Of course! And don't hold back, I can take it!" insisted Hagen excitedly.

"I should never attempt this after I've known someone only so briefly...," warned Kelly, but she was secretly looking forward to the challenge.

"Pretend you are profiler for the FBI! You are not helping but exposing me!" encouraged Hagen. Kelly hesitated for a moment longer, but then she nodded and began her analysis:

"You self-depreciate, and most people who do that have low self-esteem because they doubt their worth. But you self-depreciate for the opposite reason: your self-esteem seems unshakable! You self-depreciate so that others can relate to you!"

"But you don't have an exaggerated sense of self-worth, you don't seek admiration, you don't blame others for your mistakes, and you possess empathy! In fact, this whole time, you are trying to deflect from yourself, and that's inconsistent with a narcissistic personality disorder!"

"You have paranoid tendencies. For example, when I told you that I'm a psychologist, you became guarded, and it wasn't a joke! You believe that I might find something out and use it against you! However, your mistrust isn't just rooted in fear of imaginary danger; there is something real behind it!"

"You have obsessive-compulsive tendencies: your briefcase is neatly organized, your wardrobe is impeccable, even the desktop on your computer looks immaculate! You have meticulously prepared for functionality and efficiency, and you use expensive quality items, but nothing about you is flashy. You are not vain but like to be in control."

"On the surface, you seem like a people pleaser: you allow others to make decisions, you are mindful of your words, you are helpful and almost submissive. So far, you have catered to me more than some dates I've had, yet I don't think you are sexually interested in me. Therefore, a dependent personality disorder is unlikely."

"You said I shouldn't hold back, and I could tell that you meant that. That's quite unusual! Most of my patients, most people in general, are apprehensive about my findings and often have difficulty accepting them! You, however, are amused by it, and frankly, you don't seem to care if I praise or criticize you. That would indicate a schizoid personality disorder, but you don't appear shy or withdrawn."

"You are brilliant and educated. You know that you are not like most people, and you probably have known that since childhood, but you either don't care or are at peace with that. You mimic socially acceptable behavior and do it exceedingly well, but you would prefer solitude so that you can focus on the things that are important to you - and other people are not on the list!"

"You are charismatic, deceptive, and manipulative. You might call yourself retired, but you are independently wealthy, yet money has very little value to you. You are appalled by ignorance and generally resent society, perhaps humanity, but you don't care enough to change it, or you believe it is futile to try."

"You are a functional sociopath, Hagen!" concluded Kelly and looked at him.

"Thank you, I'm thoroughly impressed, Kelly!" acknowledged Hagen and bowed his head a little.

"Now I feel terrible, and I don't really know why I did this! I'm no better than that therapist, who called you insane!" apologized Kelly and shook her head. She couldn't believe that she had labeled his friendly man a sociopath! What had gotten into her today?

"I'm not upset at all! As you said, I don't care if you praise or criticize me, but I always appreciate honesty," replied Hagen softly.

"But I analyzed and objectified you in a manner that would only be suitable for a scientific paper or a criminal investigation!" noted Kelly and insisted, "it is not how I treat my patients!"

"Your profession requires that you show just enough empathy to reach your patients, but not so much as to get dragged into the vortex of their mental turmoil!" stated Hagen and cautioned, "it is a perilous tightrope walk between compassion and aloofness, and any misstep could have serious consequences, for you or your patients!"

"I never thought of it like that, but you are not wrong!" agreed Kelly. She was impressed by Hagen's level of understanding, and now she felt even worse about her analysis, "Hagen, I cannot possibly be correct about everything I've said!"

"Perhaps not everything, but there was enough truth in your analysis that I'll forego the rebuttal! The delivery was brief and precise, free of unnecessary ballast. I've learned something, and for that, I thank you, Kelly!" said Hagen appreciatively and observed, "but now that you have a better idea who I am, I completely understand if you prefer not to continue our conversation!"

"I've insulted you, Hagen! I should ask you if you still want to talk to me, not the other way around!" argued Kelly in disbelief.

"In that case, let's keep talking, Kelly!" answered Hagen with delight, and Kelly quickly nodded her agreement. She thought it was strange that Hagen forgave her so readily, but she was also pleased that he did.

"I had to profile a serial killer once: he was easy, but you are something else!" remarked Kelly, and then she asked: "Why were you not honest with me?"

"I'm not honest with anyone, except with myself!" confirmed Hagen and added jokingly, "and maybe with my cats!"

"But why?" wondered Kelly.

"Deception is the most human of all our traits! It rules every aspect, almost every moment, of our lives! We constantly lie to each other and ourselves – sometimes for good reasons, sometimes for bad ones, and often for no reason at all!" proclaimed Hagen and confessed, "Kelly, I have manipulated you into giving me the psychological evaluation, but I didn't do it to make you feel terrible. In fact, I thought you might enjoy it – and I believe you did!"

"No...," Kelly started to disagree, but she stopped because she knew that Hagen was right.

"You were dishonest when you said psychology is a job like any other. Sure, you like to help people, but you are in this profession for a much deeper reason: when you study other minds, it gives you insights into your own!" continued Hagen.

"I have to admit that's true!" confirmed Kelly.

"On a much smaller scale, I also realized that you lied to me when I asked if you wanted to have a drink. You only agreed because you didn't want to offend me. My glass is empty, but your cocktail is still untouched," said Hagen and pointed at her glass, "lastly, you declined reading my short stories, but I've noticed that you glance at my screen every time I work on it."

"Son of a bitch!" blurted Kelly out, but then she laughed, "OK, I see your point, Hagen!"

"Against common belief, honesty is rarely well-received! That's why you weren't honest, and that's why I'm not honest! Ultimately, that's why we all mimic socially acceptable behavior, as you put it!" concluded Hagen and smiled warmly at her.

"Return the favor! Analyze me!" challenged Kelly and drank from her cocktail. She enjoyed talking to this man, and she didn't mind that he had exposed her little lies.

"I cannot, Kelly!" said Hagen seriously.

"I believe you could analyze me better than I could do it myself!" insisted Kelly confidently.

"Perhaps, but I cannot, and please don't make me!" begged Hagen somberly. Kelly noticed that this was a touchy subject for Hagen, but she had no idea why.

"Hagen, I didn't mean...," said Kelly softly and briefly touched his hand on the armrest.

"It's no problem, Kelly," replied Hagen and smiled at her again.

"Let's do an experiment!" suggested Kelly, upbeat, and then she proposed, "for the rest of this flight, can we try to be completely honest with each other? Think of it as a game of truth-or-dare, but we will only stick with the truth!"

Kelly had no idea why she had suggested this, and she almost regretted her words as they came out of her mouth: perhaps it was just a whim, maybe she wanted to learn more about this man - or was there something else?

"No dares, huh?" wondered Hagen and remarked, "it would be fun for me, but it's a long flight, and I'm not so sure if you would really like that, Kelly!"

"Then I have only myself to blame!" countered Kelly and

changed the subject, "you mentioned that you write about philosophy?"

"You remembered! Philosophy and psychology both center around the human mind. But their methods and goals are very different!" explained Hagen and elaborated, "you study the mind because you want to help people cope with their lives. I study it because I want to find universal truths, and what I discover is often incompatible with your work!"

"Why do you think it conflicts with my work?" wondered Kelly.

"Let's say you have a suicidal patient," stipulated Hagen and asked, "you would discourage that by emphasizing all the things that make life worth living, would you not?"

"Yes, of course!" confirmed Kelly.

"Meanwhile, I would quote Shakespeare's Macbeth: *life is a tale, told by an idiot, full of sound and fury, signifying nothing!*" explained Hagen and added, "and then they'll jump!"

At first, Kelly looked at him aghast, but then she started laughing out loud until some of the other passengers noticed and looked at her strangely.

"With that philosophy, why haven't you jumped yet?" questioned Kelly humorously.

"Because then I wouldn't have made your lovely acquaintance!" answered Hagen and smiled at her.

"Ooooh, so smooth, so charming!" replied Kelly, giggled, and shook her head.

The stewardess came by and delivered their meals. Hagen only took a salad and a cup of coffee, but he asked the stewardess if she could microwave his plastic meal container. At first, the young woman said that she couldn't, but Hagen worked his charm on her, and a few minutes later, he had a warm, home-cooked meal.

"You brought your own dish?" asked Kelly while eating her alfredo pasta.

"Yes, I'm not too fond of airline food! It gives me heartburn. Would you like to try?" asked Hagen, but Kelly shook her head.

"You offer me your food? Are you the second coming of Alfredo Ballí Treviño?" asked Kelly jokingly, pretty sure that Hagen wouldn't understand the obscure reference, and so she was genuinely impressed when he did!

"No, Clarice, I'm not Hannibal, and I don't intend to harm you," said Hagen and smirked at her.

"Hannibal never harmed Clarice!" countered Kelly with a big grin on her face.

"That's true, but the thought of consuming human flesh is still revolting to me!" laughed Hagen and added, "it's just salmon, not brains, I swear!"

After finishing the meal, Kelly wanted to get some toiletries from her bag. She was standing on her tippy toes, trying to get her luggage out of the overhead compartment. Hagen noticed and stood up.

"Oh, let me help you with that!" he offered.

"Hagen, I'm not your date. You don't have to do that!" said Kelly forcefully. She wanted to set some boundaries so that Hagen would not be misled, but this came out more aggressively than she had intended. All the more, she was surprised that Hagen took it in stride.

"But I like you, Kelly!" proclaimed Hagen and added, "this has been the most interesting conversation I've had in a long time!"

"You need to talk to more people!" laughed Kelly.

"I rather not, but I enjoy talking to you, and that's the truth!" said Hagen and looked at her.

"Why don't you want to talk to people?" wondered Kelly.

"Simple, I get bored easily, and then I either have to be rude or suffer through their babble, their little lies, and diatribes. I couldn't imagine doing your job, not for all the money in the world!" divulged Hagen.

"You get bored because they don't stimulate your mind. Your dates are not smart enough, is that it?" questioned Kelly.

"Perhaps. But you are, and I love that!" replied Hagen and smiled at her broadly.

"Hagen, are you hitting on me?" asked Kelly seriously.

"You said that I wasn't sexually interested in you! Are you retracting that now?" wondered Hagen and raised an eyebrow.

"Hagen…," said Kelly, but he interrupted her right away.

"Sorry, that wasn't fair. Now I'm sexually interested in you, Kelly!" admitted Hagen bluntly: "Truth or dare, without the dare, remember?"

"You are manipulative, Hagen!" scolded Kelly and insisted, "there is no way that could ever happen!"

"Probably, but what I said is still true, and you haven't turned me down yet!" noted Hagen.

"Fine, I find you intriguing! Happy?" divulged Kelly and rolled her eyes.

"Yes, with that out of the way, let me help you with your luggage," maintained Hagen with a smirk.

"Thanks!" replied Kelly and shook her head. Maybe Hagen was right, and this experiment was more challenging than she thought it would be?

"Why?" asked Hagen after taking Kelly's luggage from the overhead compartment.

"Why what?" Kelly returned the question as she was rummaging through her bag.

"Why are you attracted to me?" questioned Hagen curiously.

"Hagen, you look fine, but you are not my type! Let's not talk about this anymore!" remarked Kelly defensively because she started to feel cornered.

"You didn't answer the question, Kelly!" Hagen reminded her.

"You see this as a conquest, don't you? It's a long flight, and you are bored, so you use your impressive intellect and charm to ensnare me!" claimed Kelly tersely. Was she ready to pick a fight with Hagen?

"Nothing could be further from the truth, Kelly, and I doubt I could ensnare you even if I wanted that! But I warned you that you might not like that much honesty. Should we stop the experiment?" offered Hagen softly, and she had to think about that for a moment.

"No!" insisted Kelly determinedly and asked, "why are you suddenly interested in me?"

"Your intelligence, of course, and your smell!" explained Hagen.

"My perfume?" wondered Kelly.

"No, your scent!" corrected Hagen.

"Am I sweaty or something?" wondered Kelly, a little self-conscious.

"It's nothing like that, Kelly! But I believe that smell is a good indicator for compatibility with another person!" postulated Hagen.

"Seriously? You must have an incredible nose!" observed Kelly.

She had never heard of such a thing.

"I do, and it's not a gift, more like a curse. The world is pretty stinky!" explained Hagen and chuckled. She had to smile, too, but then she got serious again.

"That's not real, Hagen! Do you imagine that you have a super-power?" insisted Kelly pointedly. Unless it was obnoxious, she had never paid much attention to how a man smelled.

"Oh, but it is real, and you can verify it. A tiny percentage of the population is born with a heightened sense of smell. Usu-ally, these folks end up being famous chefs, food critics, or wine tasters. An even smaller group of people can detect odors that go unnoticed by everyone else!" explained Hagen.

Kelly made a mental note to check that later, but she had no reason to believe Hagen was lying. It was a fascinating idea, and Kelly couldn't stop thinking about it.

"Scent...," she mumbled, and the word suddenly triggered powerful desires in her, but Kelly had no idea where these emo-tions originated.

Hagen got another cup of coffee from the stewardess. Kelly no-ticed that Hagen treated the stewardess with kindness and re-spect, and the young woman enjoyed the attention. Whenever she passed by their seats, she would give Hagen a bright smile and ask if he needed anything. Kelly went to the restroom after the meal. When she returned, Hagen was typing on his laptop again.

"Hagen, are you currently in a relationship?" she asked as she was sitting down.

"I'm not, and I haven't been in one for a while!" answered Hagen and stopped typing.

"Why not?" questioned Kelly.

"Not too many women are interested in dating a sociopath, even a more-or-less functional one!" explained Hagen humorously.

"Oh, come on, that's a blatant lie! With your charisma, manners, and appearance, you could be with a different woman every night! Just look at our stewardess!" observed Kelly and looked at him expectantly.

"Of course, it was a lie!" admitted Hagen readily and added quite seriously, "Melinda is a sweet girl but a little too young for me!"

"Melinda? That's her name? Did you get her number, too?" gasped Kelly. She was outraged, but she didn't even know why. There was no way Kelly would have any relations with Hagen, so why would it bother her if a stewardess was flirting with him?

"No, I didn't ask for her number!" laughed Hagen and returned to Kelly's previous question, "the truth is that I'm very picky!"

"That I can believe! I have no idea what your expectations are, but I guess it can't be easy for anyone to meet them!" speculated Kelly and added provocatively, "a pretty face, big boobs, and a tight butt just won't do it for you: the woman would also have to smell right, whatever that means!"

"Who says I don't appreciate physical attributes?" questioned Hagen and blatantly undressed her with his eyes.

"Stop it!" warned Kelly playfully. But now, she was amused, not offended.

"Most importantly, the woman has to be intelligent. To me, there is nothing sexier than that!" observed Hagen with a bit of smirk, and asked, "so, are you currently in a relationship?"

"Would it matter to you? Would you not be interested in me if I were in a relationship?" asked Kelly pointedly.

"It would change nothing at all. My desires would be at the mercy of your decision either way!" replied Hagen.

"So, you would sleep with me, even if I'm married?" inquired Kelly.

"Yes. The question is would you sleep with me if you were married?" asked Hagen in return.

"I would not, and I also wouldn't if you were in a relationship!" stated Kelly formally.

"I accept that you wouldn't want to mislead your partner, but why would it matter to you if I was seeing someone?" wondered Hagen.

"I might destroy your relationship or hurt your girlfriend or wife," explained Kelly.

"You would not destroy my relationship or hurt another woman; I would be risking that with my decision to sleep with you!" corrected Hagen.

"I suppose that's true, but I would still feel bad about it," mused Kelly, but she had to admit that Hagen had a point.

"You are still evading my question, Kelly - are you in a relationship?" inquired Hagen again. Kelly knew that she was stalling, and it took her some time before she answered.

"I'm divorced. I had a couple of flings after that, but I'm not in a relationship!" recounted Kelly and sighed a little.

"That didn't come easy, and I wonder why?" questioned Hagen and looked at her.

"You were right, Hagen. This experiment is harder than I thought," admitted Kelly and divulged truthfully, "under the right circumstances, I would sleep with you even if both of us were married!"

"Does it hurt to admit that?" inquired Hagen curiously.

"I'm disappointed in myself," conceded Kelly with a frown.

"I'm not. I'm impressed with you! You stick with the experiment, even when it gets uncomfortable!" praised Hagen.

"Did you expect me to give up?" wondered Kelly, a little hurt that Hagen didn't believe she could play this game.

"Yes. I didn't think you could handle it. Most people cannot, but you try, and that shows strength and character!" lauded Hagen.

Suddenly, Kelly felt anxious. It came with no warning. It was as if she was trapped in a tiger cage, and the big cat had just noticed her. She was trying to suppress that feeling, but her heart was beating faster and faster.

"Did you drive your ex-wife to insanity?" asked Kelly nervously and changed the subject.

"You ask that question out of fear. Why?" wondered Hagen.

"I don't know, I suddenly feel inferior to you, like your prey!" stammered Kelly, clutching her blanket so hard that her knuckles turned white.

"You are not inferior, and you don't have to fear me, Kelly. I swear I will not harm you physically or mentally!" promised Hagen sincerely. Kelly wiped beads of sweat from her forehead with her hand.

"Answer my question!" urged Kelly irrationally, and her breaths became labored.

"No, I did not. But I wasn't as supportive as I should have been. When my ex became very ill and unpredictable, I was still young and didn't know what to do. In the end, I chose the easy way out and divorced her!" elaborated Hagen calmly, and then he just watched her in silence. Slowly, Kelly regained her composure.

"Do you have panic attacks often?" asked Hagen softly after Kelly seemed to have weathered the storm.

"No, this was only the second time in my life. The first time was the day when my dad died!" disclosed Kelly and finished her drink. She was disappointed when the glass was empty, and Hagen noticed that.

"I'm sorry if I triggered it. I suspect my personality has strange effects on people sometimes," remarked Hagen. He pressed the call button for the stewardess.

"I thought that I was trapped in a cage with a tiger. You were the tiger, and you were about to devour me! I didn't have actual delusions, but that's how it felt!" recounted Kelly and shuddered a little.

"Ah, rest assured, this tiger just wants you to scratch him behind his ears. He'll purr like a kitten if you do!" replied Hagen humorously. Kelly pictured that scene in her mind, and surprisingly, it helped her. Her caresses turned the vicious predator into a big pussycat, and that made her smile. The stewardess came, and Kelly ordered a shot of tequila and a beer.

"Do you regret what happened with your ex-wife?" asked Kelly after she downed the shot. Kelly knew that alcohol wasn't a good remedy for what she had experienced, but she just didn't care.

"It was a long time ago, and I have come to terms with it!" concluded Hagen and asked, "how did your marriage end?"

"Of all the questions, I hoped you wouldn't ask that one!" sighed Kelly, praying that it would not trigger more anxieties.

"Kelly, experiment or not, if it's too stressful, just don't answer!" warned Hagen. Kelly noticed that he was genuinely concerned for her well-being, and she appreciated that, but she was determined to press on.

"No!" she blurted out, but then she admitted, "when I proposed that we are completely honest, I expected that I would have the upper hand because of my training. I thought I could find out more about you while I remain bulletproof. It turns out to be the other way around, but I don't regret that!"

"Perhaps you need a little therapy yourself?" speculated Hagen and smiled fondly at her.

"I do, and believe it or not, you might be the only person who can give it!" conceded Kelly.

"I bet you know many capable colleagues who could do a much better job than me!" claimed Hagen.

"No, that's just it! I cannot see another therapist. I know all the questions, mechanics, and little tricks to get a patient to open up. I would just defeat or evade their attempts to help me!" maintained Kelly and sighed.

"Understood! I'm a stranger, and we will go our separate ways in a few hours. You can tell me anything you want to get off your chest, and I won't judge you, Kelly!" promised Hagen with a smile.

"What if I have killed somebody?" she whispered.

"I still wouldn't judge you or report you to the police!" assured Hagen. Although Hagen wasn't bound by doctor-patient confidentiality, Kelly sensed that he would keep his promise, and that made her relax a little.

"I didn't kill anybody, but I cheated on my husband with a former patient. He found out and left me! And I still don't even know why I did it!" disclosed Kelly and added with a sigh, "I have never told this to anyone, not even my ex-husband. I kept lying to him until the end!"

"Contrary to societal norms, human beings are not monogamous, Kelly!" replied Hagen after she had finished talking.

"So, you approve?" questioned Kelly and raised her eyebrows.

"I neither approve nor disapprove. Sometimes the biology takes over, and all our morality and principles are reduced to rubble!"

remarked Hagen quietly.

"I don't like that!" exclaimed Kelly with resentment in her voice.

"The explanation or the fact that you are human?" wondered Hagen and smiled a little.

"Both!" insisted Kelly forcefully and asked, "if you were my husband, what would you have done?"

"I would have asked you to tell me the truth, and once you did, I would have forgiven you!" explained Hagen.

"Just like that?" Kelly blurted out incredulously.

"Just like that!" confirmed Hagen calmly.

"You wouldn't feel betrayed? You wouldn't be jealous?" Kelly demanded to know.

"You are my wife, not my possession! You are an adult, capable of making your own decisions. If you decide to sleep with someone else, all I would ask is that you are honest about it!" elaborated Hagen.

"Fascinating! From my experience, only people with dependent personality disorder act that way: they will forgive everything not to lose the person they depend on, but you are nothing like that, Hagen!" observed Kelly, but then she added with a sigh, "my ex-husband was a good man, but he was jealous, even when there was no reason. If I had told him that I had an affair, he would have divorced me anyway."

"Jealousy is the combination of mistrust and possessiveness, and neither is a good basis for a relationship. I suspect that your marriage would have failed sooner or later, regardless of your affair!" speculated Hagen.

"That's kind of you to say, Hagen!" replied Kelly, but she doubted his explanation.

"You knew that your husband was jealous when you married him, did you not?" asked Hagen.

"I suppose I've noticed that already when we were dating," confirmed Kelly.

"You thought his jealousy was an expression of his love, his commitment and caring. In exchange, you allowed yourself to be owned by him. Many, if not most people, would make that mistake," stated Hagen thoughtfully.

"You have never been jealous, Hagen?" wondered Kelly.

"I might have been when I was younger, but I know better now: if you love someone, you set them free!" remarked Hagen and smiled at her again.

"Deep and philosophical! Society disagrees with you, but I can't say I do," concurred Kelly and added, "I guess I'm just a confused chick, hung up on guilt and remorse! God, I remind myself of some of my patients!"

"If you say so, but we both know that's not true!" replied Hagen. Instinctively, Kelly sensed that Hagen was right, but she wasn't ready to admit that yet.

"Tell me about your relationships?" Kelly encouraged him and changed the subject.

"First, define the term, Kelly!" requested Hagen.

"The times you felt like you had a partner in life!" explained Kelly.

"Very well, and what would you like to know about my relationships?" asked Hagen and looked at her expectantly.

"You don't like open-ended questions?" wondered Kelly.

"I recognize that open-ended questions are a tool of your trade, Kelly. But I prefer precision; it cuts down on the noise!" explained Hagen. Kelly realized that Hagen used words like tools. To him, every word had a purpose and shouldn't be wasted needlessly on idle chit-chat.

"OK, how many relationships have you had?" inquired Kelly.

"Oh, perhaps a dozen or so," estimated Hagen.

"Lost track?" teased Kelly and smirked at him.

"Never kept track!" countered Hagen and grinned back at her.

"How and why did they end?" asked Kelly more seriously.

"You already know about my ex-wife, but all my other relationships ended for a variety of different reasons," explained Hagen.

"Do I smell a lie?" speculated Kelly, pretty sure that Hagen had omitted something.

"You are observant! No, it wasn't a lie, but it was not the whole truth either," confirmed Hagen and admitted, "ultimately, the relationships ended because of me, but I'll let you guess why!"

"Hmm, we are going back to something we talked about earlier," said Kelly and stated, "you got bored with the women. They failed to keep your interest because they weren't your intellectual equals!"

"I'm not proud of that, but that is the truth!" acknowledged Hagen with a nod.

"I'm going a step further, but please stop me if I'm crossing a line," said Kelly and proclaimed, "you have retired for the same reason, and you prefer solitude over dealing with idiots and by idiots, I mean mere mortals like me!"

"Ouch, I'm arrogant and elitist!" summarized Hagen humorously and observed thoughtfully, "Kelly, you are quite good at reading me – but you are positively not an idiot, or this conversation would have ended about five minutes after take-off!"

"Thanks, but I feel I haven't even scratched the surface. I could do years of research on you, Hagen!" suggested Kelly and chuckled.

"Well, you have about three hours more, so hurry up!" joked Hagen and winked at her. She looked at him for a moment before she continued.

"You are not arrogant and elitist, Hagen!" noted Kelly quietly. Those labels appeared to fit nicely on the surface, but she was sure that Hagen didn't think of himself as superior. As ridiculous as that seemed, Kelly started to believe that Hagen genuinely was a superior version of sorts!

"And you are no simple, confused woman, Kelly!" replied Hagen and maintained, "your turn to tell me about your relationships!"

"Very well, and what would you like to know about my relationships?" asked Kelly, intentionally echoing the exact words Hagen had used earlier. Hagen noticed and grinned broadly at her!

"I had nine relationships in my life, beginning with my first boyfriend at the age of 13. Yes, I started early!" recounted Kelly and added, "They ended because I stopped being in love with them, that's all!"

"Why did you stop being in love with them?" wondered Hagen.

"I wish I could say something profound, but it was just the sex. It didn't satisfy me anymore, so I moved on," remarked Kelly and added, "and yes, I'm that shallow!"

"The sex didn't satisfy you because you were bored with your partners, and you were bored with them because they failed to stimulate your mind," postulated Hagen and added softy, "and that is also the real reason why you cheated on your husband."

"How could you even know that?" gasped Kelly, but sensing some truth in Hagen's words.

"I'm just guessing, but am I wrong, Kelly?" asked Hagen and stipulated, "You can forgive me for being arrogant and elitist, but not yourself. You prefer to be called shallow because that's more acceptable in this society!"

"Hagen…," Kelly started saying, but then she stopped. Hagen had terminated his relationships because they didn't fulfill him anymore, but she had done the same. He ended them because his partners were not smart enough, and she ended them because they didn't satisfy her in bed, or so she thought. Kelly recalled every one of her past relationships. Most of the men she had dated were good people, highly skilled, successful professionals, and by societal norms, they have been her equals or more. But all of them were somewhat limited, and Kelly had found those limitations early in the relationships. She couldn't help comparing her former dates to Hagen, and intellectually, it was not even close!

"Embrace who you are, don't fight it!" suggested Hagen, observing her attentively. His words contradicted everything Kelly believed in and the advice she gave to patients with marital problems: one was supposed to make an effort to understand the partner, focus on the commonalities and constructively work out the differences, be loyal and committed, and communicate effectively, not walk away out of boredom! But what if no common ground remained, and there was no meaningful communication left to have because the partner was simply too limited? Why should she care if society disapproved? Why should she sacrifice her happiness for an exercise in futility?

"This is not how I envisioned my vacation to start!" blurted Kelly and laughed a little.

"You expected that we would exchange a few meaningless pleasantries, then you would watch a movie or take a nap while I would work on my laptop. At the end of the trip, we would say goodbye and safe travels, and never waste another thought on it again," speculated Hagen.

"Yup!" agreed Kelly, "instead, I'm having a conversation like none other with a total stranger!"

"Is that good or bad, Kelly?" quizzed Hagen expectantly.

"Good, definitely good!" stated Kelly quickly and added, "consciously, I suggested that we try this experiment because I wanted to learn more about you. But now I believe that I suggested it so that I could learn more about myself!"

"Talking to me, a stranger whom you will never see again in your life, has one tremendous advantage: I'm a virgin canvas!" postulated Hagen.

"You need to explain that, Hagen!" urged Kelly, although she suspected that she already knew.

"Think about your mother, or a sibling, or a friend you have known all your life. There are things you have never told, things you cannot tell, things you should have said but didn't, things you said that you regret, and things that weren't true. Over the years, all the countless lies, big and small, have created a painting on that canvas, and it would be hard to change and nearly impossible to erase now. You cannot have a free and honest conversation anymore because there is too much baggage attached!" observed Hagen and paused for a moment to collect his thoughts.

"There are no lies between us, Kelly. Even before we started the experiment, you were refreshingly open: you asked me if I was gay, you asked if I had therapy, and you gave me a brutally honest psych evaluation! You could do that because we have no baggage yet, the canvas is blank, and that's what you needed to have an honest dialogue. That's why you proposed the experiment to me!" concluded Hagen.

"You are right; I needed this, and there is no way I could have talked to anyone else like that!" agreed Kelly and asked, "Hagen, I know that you don't want to analyze me, and I respect that. But your opinion has become very important to me: please tell me, what do you think of me?"

"I will say only this: you excel at reading others, but you fail at reading yourself!" said Hagen and clarified, "oh, I'm sure you have analyzed and categorized your personality, but you still don't know who you are. You are not alone, Kelly; most people never figure that out in their lifetimes!"

"Have you figured it out?" asked Kelly curiously.

"It's work-in-progress until the day I'll die!" replied Hagen.

"Have you figured me out?" she inquired next.

"That too is work-in-progress, Kelly!" said Hagen and smiled fondly at her.

"Please, keep working on it, even if you'll never tell me what you found!" begged Kelly, and on a whim, she took Hagen's hand in hers. She held on to it for a while, and he let it happen.

"Hagen, why do you not want to tell me? Is it that bad that you are afraid I might be upset with you?" wondered Kelly quietly. For a moment, Hagen didn't reply and just looked at her thoughtfully.

"Earlier, we talked about the differences between psychology and philosophy. I quoted Macbeth, and you laughed a lot…," explained Hagen with a sad smile on his face. It took Kelly a moment to grasp the gravity of Hagen's words.

"Oh my god, that actually happened!" she gasped and squeezed Hagen's hand tightly, "say no more, Hagen, I'm so sorry that I've asked!"

"Don't worry about it!" replied Hagen in a neutral voice. He took his hand back and typed a few sentences on his laptop. Kelly was worried that she might have lost him with her stupid question. She was trying to think of something to improve the situation, but her mind was not cooperating. She turned on the little TV screen and scrolled through the movie listings. Hagen was still typing, paying no attention to her. She turned the screen off again, sipped on her beer, and started playing with the miniature crucifix on her necklace.

"Do you believe in God, Hagen?" she asked absentmindedly. Hagen stopped typing and looked at her once more.

"No, I don't, but I like your antique necklace. I noticed it right away. Is it an heirloom?" asked Hagen. Kelly was pleased that Hagen was talking to her again, but he didn't seem as personal as before.

"Yes, it is from my grandmother. I've had it since I was a little girl!" explained Kelly.

"Are you Catholic?" inquired Hagen, turning back to his computer to finish a sentence.

"No, I'm not religious, and I don't know if I even believe in God!" disclosed Kelly, wrinkles on her forehead.

"You seem preoccupied. What's the matter, Kelly?" wondered Hagen as he closed his laptop. Kelly took a moment before she answered.

"I've hurt you, Hagen. I didn't mean to, but that doesn't matter. Now I fear that I've lost you, and it weighs on me more than I care to admit!" disclosed Kelly uncomfortably.

"You didn't lose anything, Kelly!" he assured her consolingly and reached for her hand. Her face lit up when he did, and she was so relieved.

"We are holding hands, Hagen!" she laughed out loud.

"It seems that way. Good thing or bad one?" quizzed Hagen.

"Such a small gesture...," she noted, and then she leaned over and confessed quietly, "but it is the nicest thing that has happened to me in a long time. Thank you, Hagen!"

"You are welcome, Kelly!" agreed Hagen fondly. He took her hand and kissed the back of it. She let it happen and watched in amazement. After a moment, she moved her lips very close to his ear.

"It will never happen, but now I'm ready to fuck your brains out!" whispered Kelly, giggled, and shook her head.

"Conquest complete!" teased Hagen with a smug look on his face.

"Oh, you son of a bitch, I knew it!" cursed Kelly and playfully elbowed him in the ribs.

"I was just kidding, of course!" laughed Hagen and added softly, "I feel the same, Kelly!"

Relieved and exhausted, Kelly decided to take a brief nap before the plane was scheduled to land, but she tightly held on to Hagen's hand. Before she dozed off, she asked one last thing:

"Hagen, why was this experiment so much easier for you than it was for me?" asked Kelly sleepily.

"I have practice, but you bravely jumped in the pool unprepared!" noted Hagen with a smile.

"Is it because you don't deceive yourself, but I'm mired in a million little lies?" wondered Kelly, although she already knew that it was.

"Yes, Kelly, but being honest with oneself isn't easy and often painful, so don't beat yourself up!" replied Hagen encouragingly.

"I wish I could be honest all the time...," she mumbled, closed her eyes, and drifted off to sleep.

Kelly and Hagen were waiting at baggage claim in silence. After they had deplaned, Hagen had thanked her for the wonderful time, and she said something similar to him. She felt in her gut that the fairy tale had ended, and reality had retaken its rightful place. The bags came out of the chute, and the carousel started to rotate. Hagen's bag came first, and he picked it off the conveyer belt. He waited until Kelly's big suitcase passed by and helped her lift it off the carousel. Kelly extended the handle on the luggage and pulled it behind her as she walked away without another word. Hagen did not follow, and she was relieved that he didn't. The fantasy was over, and Kelly was determined to keep walking and never see this strange, creepy man again. She was almost to the exit of the baggage claim area when she stopped. Don't turn around, she reminded herself sternly...and then Kelly turned around!

"Are you coming?" she yelled and waved in his direction. Hagen smiled, nodded, and started jogging to catch up with her.

Kelly had a great vacation! She saw exciting places, met new people, and caught up with her old friend. Three whole weeks of rest and relaxation did wonders for her body and mind, but today was her first day back at the office. No patients were scheduled yet because she had to catch up with the paperwork first, and there was a big stack of mail, mostly bills, waiting for her. One stuffed envelope, in particular, caught her attention. She opened it and pulled out a book. It was by some unknown author, and she suspected it was a promotional gift of sorts. On a whim, she opened the cover and saw a handwritten dedication. She read it and almost dropped the book: it was from Hagen, and he specifically told her to read one particular chapter. He had even left a marker on the appropriate page. Kelly flipped to that page and started reading the first few lines.

The story was about a psychologist who met a stranger on an airplane! The names were changed, and nothing in the chapter could identify her, but Kelly knew immediately that the story was about Hagen and her. She sat down by her computer and eagerly read the whole thing nearly to the end. Kelly was in shock! Not only had Hagen documented their encounter in exact detail, but he had written it from her point of view. The emotions and thoughts he had attributed to her in this play were so precise as if he had read her mind! Throughout their brief journey together, Hagen must have analyzed her thoroughly, yet unnoticed, gathering the right clues from her every word and slightest reaction. On the one hand, Kelly admired his exceptional awareness and power of observation, and she was even a little envious of his talents. But on the other hand, it left her feeling naked, vulnerable, and anxious. When she got to the last page, she couldn't believe what she was reading:

When Kelly opened the envelope, she didn't pay much attention to the book inside, but she opened the cover page and noticed Hagen's dedication on a hunch. She was surprised and went to the chapter he had marked for her. After reading a few sentences, she recognized that it was their story! Kelly finished the entire chapter, unsure how to feel about it. Hagen had refused to analyze her when they were on the plane, but this went beyond any psychological evaluation Kelly had ever read. Hagen had guessed her thoughts and emotions more accurately than it should have been possible. A part of her was angry at him, and another was surprised and scared, but yet another part remembered their encounter very fondly.

All this was eerie and impossible! Yes, Kelly was angry at him! Angry that Hagen had published this without her consent, and she resented that he was able to read her so quickly and effortlessly. But then her thoughts went back to their conversation: it had been incredibly liberating to talk to someone without any deception! Kelly recalled the night in the hotel, Hagen's touch, his embrace, and how exhilarating it was to make love to him. But mostly, she remembered his scent, and once again, that triggered powerful emotions in her.

Kelly read the dedication once more. It was lovely and eloquent, but it became clear to her that Hagen viewed their encounter as two ships passing in the night. Suddenly, something inside her rebelled at that notion! She quickly closed the book, looked at the back cover, and noticed the author's email address.

"Predict this, you son of a bitch!" she cursed to herself as she was entering it on her computer, "I'm not finished with you yet, Hagen, not by a longshot!"

How dare you, Hagen!

I've trusted you with some very personal stuff, and you published it for the world to see! When I called you a sociopath, I was too kind because you are also a scary creep! You have deceived and manipulated me, and you are exploiting my problems for your gain! Do you know no shame? I hope the book sells well because I'm seriously considering litigation!

For a moment, Kelly hesitated, but then she sent the angry email to the address on the back of the book. She sat at the computer for a long time and stared at the screen. Her feelings were a convoluted mess, but thanks to her training, slowly, she regained her composure. The anger faded, but the anxiety was still there. Hagen was brilliant and perhaps dangerous, and Kelly might have just made a fatal mistake. But she knew that Hagen's personality wasn't violent. Most likely, he would probably be amused by her tirade if it had any effect on him at all. Finally, the anxiety subsided and made room for another, kinder emotion.

"I won't sue you, Hagen. Please, just respond...," mumbled Kelly to herself sadly as she turned off her computer.

Hagen read the message only a few hours after Kelly had sent it. He was surprised that she contacted him but not that she was angry. Although his intentions were for her to have a record of their memorable encounter, Hagen knew from the start that it was risky. For the first time in as long as he could remember, he was unsure what to do next, so he didn't respond to Kelly's email right away.

He called his attorney and checked if Kelly had an actual legal claim against him. The lawyer assured him that there were no grounds for criminal or civil charges against Hagen without any personally identifying information in the story. Even if Kelly went through with a lawsuit and succeeded, damages would be awarded according to the book sales. But in the past, none of Hagen's literary efforts have returned any profit worth mentioning, and it wouldn't be any different with this new publication. The worst-case scenario was that Hagen would have to remove the story from the book and compensate Kelly with a few dollars. He could live with that, but Hagen decided to go one step further. Hagen instructed his attorney to transfer all the book's rights into Kelly's name. He signed the documents and included a brief note before returning them to his lawyer the next day.

Kelly had checked her email every day, but Hagen had not responded. Perhaps the email on the back of the book was wrong, or was Hagen so offended by her message that he ignored it? Maybe even worse, had he already forgotten about her? The post office had just dropped off today's mail, and Kelly sorted through it until she found a manilla envelope from a law firm. She opened it and pulled out a few legal documents. Kelly glanced at them, but they didn't seem to make much sense. Then she noticed Hagen's handwritten note, read it, and then she cried, and she couldn't stop crying!

Kelly, I sincerely apologize!

Our encounter was extremely important to me. I wanted to create a permanent record of it for you and me. It was not my intention to anger or scare you, but I was mistaken, and I realize that now. My books don't sell well, and this one probably won't either, but all proceeds will go to you from now on. Of course, I know that won't make up for the trust I have violated. - Hagen

Kelly instructed her office assistant, Maria, to cancel all her afternoon appointments. She was in no condition to see any patients; instead, she was pacing restlessly in her office. Finally, Kelly sat down at her computer. She wanted to respond to Hagen, but she didn't know what to write. At first, Kelly wrote another furious email but then erased it. Then she wrote one that wasn't quite as angry, but it was still not right. Then Kelly typed one that was more forgiving but discarded that one as well. In the end, she settled for only five words.

Hagen, can we meet, please?

She grabbed a box of tissues, dried her eyes, and stared at the computer screen. Very soon, a response arrived in her inbox.

Of course, Kelly. Please let me know when it is convenient for you, and I'll make the travel arrangements.

Kelly had no idea where Hagen lived, but the law firm's address implied that he must be located in a different state. Kelly quickly wrote a response that included her phone number.

Just come, and text me when you are at the airport!

Only a few minutes later, another email arrived with Hagen's itinerary.

I'll be there tonight!

When Hagen came out of the gate, Kelly was already waiting for him. She wasn't sure what to do when she saw him. Hagen smiled at her, and Kelly spontaneously gave him a big hug. She held onto him for a while, but then she suddenly backed up and slapped him hard across the face! The passengers passing by looked at her strangely, but she didn't care if she made a scene in public.

"I guess I deserved that!" mumbled Hagen and touched his burning cheek.

"You son of a bitch!" growled Kelly, but then she said in a much softer voice, "I missed you!"

"I missed you too, Kelly!" admitted Hagen quietly and looked at her sadly. She didn't respond, but she took his hand, and they started to move away from the gate.

"Are we still honest with each other?" asked Kelly hesitantly as they were walking down the long corridor to baggage claim.

"If you want that, Kelly!" consented Hagen and Kelly nodded at him.

"Hagen, I loved your gift. It angered me, and it scared me, but I loved it!" said Kelly and admitted, "I wrote that nasty email because I wanted to see you again!"

"I wanted to see you too, Kelly, but I didn't think that would ever happen!" said Hagen and added, "we parted on the best possible terms. I wanted to cherish that memory forever. That's why I wrote it down!"

"I understand, and I'm glad that you did," concurred Kelly and asked, "but why did you think you could never see me again?"

"So many reasons, Kelly...," replied Hagen and stopped walking. They were now in an airport area that wasn't that crowded or noisy.

"I want to hear all of them!" insisted Kelly and turned to face him.

"Kelly, I'm a sociopath, and you were absolutely correct about that!" admitted Hagen and added somberly, "I'm not easy to get along with, contrary to what you might believe, so I thought it best not impose on you any further. You have your own burden to carry, and I shouldn't add more weight to that!"

"So, you decided to ride off into the sunset without asking me first, you son of a bitch?" argued Kelly.

"What was I supposed to ask you, Kelly?" asked Hagen sadly.

"Well, at least ask for my number, address, email, or something!" insisted Kelly.

"You didn't ask for mine, and I don't blame you," countered Hagen.

"Hagen, I wanted to so badly, but I thought...," admitted Kelly but didn't finish her sentence.

"You thought what?" questioned Hagen and raised his eyebrows.

"I didn't want to be the next girl who bores you until you cut her loose!" divulged Kelly and cast her eyes down.

"Surprise! You are the first girl that doesn't bore me, Kelly!" laughed Hagen loudly.

"Ah, there is that charm again. Of course, I don't believe a word you say, Hagen!" countered Kelly and looked at him again.

"You should believe it because it is true. I'm still sticking to our game!" observed Hagen.

"Hagen, I'm flattered, but...," replied Kelly, unsure what to say to that.

"Kelly, I would marry you, right here and now!" said Hagen quite seriously.

"Now that's definitely a lie!" laughed Kelly. Hagen didn't answer; he just looked at her fondly and went down on his knee.

"You are kidding? Oh my god, you are serious! Hagen, I...," stammered Kelly, but then she closed her eyes, took a deep breath, and just said: "Yes!"

"Perfect! Now that you are my fiancée, let's get my luggage and grab a drink to celebrate?" asked Hagen and kissed her gently.

"You are the most amazing, unpredictable, crazy son of a bitch

I've ever met!" exclaimed Kelly joyfully, then she kissed him deeply and said, "I love you, Hagen!"

"And I love you, Kelly!" proclaimed Hagen, started walking again, and added with a wink, "but remember, I'm just marrying you for the free therapy, and boy, will you have to give me therapy!"

"That's OK; I'm just marrying you for your money! I'll be an expensive wife!" joked Kelly and asked humorously, "on that note, where is my ring?"

'You get what you pay for!" conceded Hagen and apologized, "oops, the ring! That's a problem with spontaneous proposals, but we'll fix that very soon!"

"I don't need no ring, Hagen, but promise me something important!" replied Kelly but added thoughtfully, "you will teach me how to be candid with myself, and we will never stop playing our game. I don't ever want any baggage between us!"

"I will, Kelly!" promised Hagen and quipped, "and you will let me know when I need to step it up in bed, preferably before you look for greener pastures?"

"Yes, but I don't think you have to worry about that, Hagen. I still want to fuck your brains out, now more than ever!" giggled Kelly and gently poked him in the ribs.

"I thought I wasn't your type? I remember you were implying that I was gay?" mused Hagen as he took his luggage from the carousel.

"True, the brilliant philosopher sociopath with the incredible sense of smell wasn't on my list!" laughed Kelly and added fondly, "but now he is the only one on my list!"

"That's very sweet, Kelly!" replied Hagen with a warm smile. Kelly sensed that he wanted to say something else, but he never did.

Hagen had booked a hotel at the airport. Kelly tried to persuade him to stay at her place, but Hagen mentioned that he might have to leave on short notice. The hotel room was luxurious, and Kelly didn't mind staying there for the night. Tomorrow was Saturday, and she had no plans for the weekend, so this might double as a bit of a getaway too. They barely made it into the room before they tore each other's clothes off. Hagen was more sensual, but Kelly was running on raw lust. Their lovemaking was as wild as it was quick. Afterward, Kelly needed a few minutes to catch her breath while Hagen gently ran his fingers through her messed-up hair.

"It was so easy, so natural," muttered Kelly finally.

"What was?" wondered Hagen.

"I only know you for 24 hours, and that's being generous, but because we were honest with each other, it was so easy to say yes. I have no doubts, no second guesses. I'm just happy!" admitted Kelly and smiled at him broadly.

"Wait until you hear me snore!" laughed Hagen and Kelly had to giggle.

"I'm serious! I dated my ex for over a year before we decided to marry, and even then, I wasn't one hundred percent sure," recounted Kelly and raised her eyebrows.

"The length of time doesn't matter that much. We may have learned more about each other in a few hours than a couple that has been married for 30 years!" remarked Hagen in response.

"Why does everybody lie all the time, if honesty makes life so much easier?" asked Kelly, but then she answered the question herself, "I guess we lie because we are afraid – afraid of rejection, criticism, embarrassment, loss, and conflict, and the reasons just keep coming."

"I think so too, Kelly!" concurred Hagen and warned, "but we still have a lot to learn about each other!"

"I know, and I realize it won't always be easy," assented Kelly and added sincerely, "but I'm looking forward to it; I really do!"

"It will be unequal because I will need you a lot more than you will need me," observed Hagen and added humorously, "you are the sane one in this relationship, Kelly!"

"I'm not so sure if I'm sane, Hagen!" replied Kelly slowly and admitted, "I'm not even sure what sanity is anymore!"

"We all have some darkness inside of us!" concurred Hagen thoughtfully.

"Hagen, I want to tell you a secret. I studied psychology because of something that happened when I was very young. My grandmother killed my grandfather. She confessed to me on her deathbed, and I have no idea why she told me that, but it changed everything for me!" divulged Kelly.

"How old were you, Kelly?" wondered Hagen.

"I was eleven," noted Kelly.

"Were you close with your grandmother or your grandfather?" asked Hagen next.

"I liked them both, but I didn't see them that often. My grandparents lived far away, and it was a long drive to get there. They had four children and a bunch of grandchildren. I was just one of many!" elaborated Kelly.

"How and why did she kill him?" questioned Hagen.

"She poisoned him," disclosed Kelly and added, "but all she said was that she wanted him gone!"

"Was he abusive or very ill?" wondered Hagen.

"No, my mother always said that they had a great marriage, and my grandfather was strong as an ox until he suddenly died. The coroner never did an autopsy and determined a stroke was the cause of death. I was just seven years old when we went to his funeral!" elaborated Kelly.

"Did your grandmother give you that antique crucifix when she confessed?" asked Hagen and pointed at Kelly's necklace.

"Yeah, how did you guess that?" wondered Kelly in surprise.

"I sensed from the moment I've met you that you had a special connection to that necklace, but I didn't think it was a murder...," answered Hagen somberly. It seemed to Kelly that he wanted to say more.

"You are so observant, Hagen. It's eerie!" exclaimed Kelly and asked, "do you know why she killed him or why she chose me to confide?"

"I don't have superpowers, so I cannot even speculate why she killed him, but I believe I know why she told you. Even back then, you were probably the most sensitive family member, and she was compelled to clear her conscience before she died!" responded Hagen, and Kelly noticed that he was unhappy now. No, not just sad; he was enraged, barely able to contain it, and Kelly wasn't sure why.

"After that happened, I lost a lot of weight because I was so afraid that I might get poisoned, too. It wasn't until a year later that I could normally eat again. I haven't taken this necklace off since my grandmother gave it to me. I sleep with, I shower with it, and I even have sex with it," disclosed Kelly softly and looked at Hagen. His face was hard, and his eyes were cold, and it frightened her a little. Suddenly, he reached for the necklace, tore it off Kelly's neck, and tossed it in the wastebin. Kelly wasn't hurt, but she was startled and a little upset, but now Hagen just looked at her sadly.

"You will not have to carry that yoke any longer!" he said solemnly and kissed her on the forehead, "I cannot undo what has been done to you, but I won't allow that to happen again!"

For a moment, Kelly was unsure what to do or say. She reached for her neck, and it felt strange that the necklace wasn't there anymore, but she wasn't angry at Hagen.

"Hagen, what would you have done if you were there when my grandmother confessed?" wondered Kelly finally.

"I would have killed her, Kelly!" said Hagen with no expression in his voice, and then he explained, "not because she murdered your grandfather, but because she burdened a child with that selfish confession!"

Instinctively, Kelly knew that Hagen meant it! She had patients who had spoken of killing before. Sometimes, it went so far as to exceed the limits of the doctor-patient confidentiality, and it had frightened her a great deal. Kelly was sure that Hagen could kill someone and would do so without hesitation or remorse if the need arose. But strangely, this didn't scare her at all. She realized then that she could do the same under the right circumstances. In a way, it felt natural that Hagen was protecting her, and she was shielding him by all means necessary.

"I should be scared of your words, Hagen, but I understand, and I appreciate!" replied Kelly and avowed, "I promise, I will protect you just like you would have protected me because I sense you carry a burden as well."

"You are also very observant, Kelly," acknowledged Hagen and added quietly, "But we'll save that for another time!"

"Thank you for being so honest and so caring, Hagen!" remarked Kelly and looked at him fondly.

"I will take our marriage very seriously!" promised Hagen.

"Because you want to make up for what happened with your ex?" wondered Kelly.

"I admit, that's a part of it," replied Hagen and nodded.

"Hagen, I know how terrible some mental illnesses can get. You were powerless to help her!" observed Kelly.

"Yes, I know that now. I couldn't help my ex or protect her from her demons. But I'll be there for you!" promised Hagen and added with a smile, "When we get your ring, we'll also get you a new necklace, one with happy memories attached!"

"I'd love that, Hagen!" exclaimed Kelly happily and said, "but I want a simple ring and necklace, nothing pricey or too fancy!"

"I thought you wanted to be an expensive wife?" wondered Hagen and grinned at her.

"Oh, you'll pay the price, but it won't be money!" threatened Kelly and wrapped her legs around him.

This time, lovemaking was gentle and much slower. Kelly enjoyed every caress, every touch with strangely heightened awareness. She could smell Hagen's body, and she liked the scent of his cologne, but she wished she could smell him the way he could smell her. Kelly felt calm, safe, and very happy when they had finished.

"Hagen, what do I smell like?" asked Kelly curiously after a few moments.

"Good! Your scent is just right, but it's hard to describe, Kelly!" explained Hagen thoughtfully.

"Try!" insisted Kelly with a yawn because she was exhausted from the sex now.

"I don't know how. You smell like... my wife?" wondered Hagen quietly and winked at her.

"Charmer! You just got laid twice. Are you trying for more?" chuckled Kelly and added with some regret in her voice, "I wish I could share that experience with you, Hagen!"

"Kelly, we need to talk...," said Hagen quietly a minute later. Kelly heard the words but didn't respond because she was already drifting off to sleep.

It was Saturday evening, and Kelly wasn't just happy. She was blissful. Aside from a few quick meals and a couple of showers, Kelly and Hagen had spent the whole day in bed. Hagen was her perfect match in every way. Her talks with him were profound, empathic, and intellectually stimulating. They were so in sync that she found herself finishing his sentences, or he finished hers just as often. She loved how Hagen seemed to know how to charm her or make her laugh with just the right words. Kelly had always been sexually curious. She had many fantasies but rarely acted on them because she feared her former lovers would perceive her as deviant. But she had no inhibitions with Hagen, and Hagen responded almost intuitively to all her desires. Kelly had lost count of how many times they had joined, but her cravings were still insatiable, and Hagen's stamina seemed to be limitless!

"Hagen, we were destined for each other! It is almost too good to be true!" gasped Kelly. Her body was still trembling from the last climax.

"You already know why that is, Kelly!" replied Hagen softly and kissed her breasts.

"Yes, because we are completely candid!" concurred Kelly joyfully, slowly starting to breathe normally again. Hagen was watching her for a while but didn't say anything.

"Kelly, we have to talk...," he stated pretty seriously after a few minutes.

"Hagen, not now, please. I'm enjoying this too much!" replied Kelly and closed her eyes. She wanted to talk to Hagen, but something inside her suddenly didn't want to hear what he had to say. Kelly found that odd, but she dismissed it right away, and Hagen didn't press on.

It was Sunday afternoon, and Kelly and Hagen went to the airport mall after a late lunch. They stopped at a fancy jewelry store, and Hagen encouraged Kelly to look for a ring and necklace. The shop was pricey, and Kelly felt a little guilty about shopping there. She was never much for jewelry, but eventually, Kelly found a plain platinum band and a matching choker that she liked. She tried it on, and Hagen approved with a broad smile. The band needed to be corrected for her finger size, but the manager promised that the adjustments could be made within a few days. Hagen paid for the merchandise, and Kelly instructed the store to send the finished goods to her office. After that, they strolled through the mall for a bit longer, had a drink at a bar, but very soon, they found themselves back in the hotel room for more lovemaking. Kelly couldn't think of another time in her life when she had been as happy as this weekend!

Early Monday morning, Kelly went back to work. She felt recharged and joyful when she entered her office. Her office assistant, Maria, was already there. Kelly grabbed a cup of coffee and informed Maria that the jewelry store would stop by later this week to drop off a gift from her fiancée. The woman looked at her strangely, but Maria nodded and said she would take care of it. Kelly was busy all day, and for the first time in a while, truly enjoyed her work. The hope she could instill in her patients made it worthwhile. Little by little, they were getting better, and that reward was much more important to her than any monetary compensation.

When Kelly left the hotel room in the morning, Hagen promised to pick her up after work and take her to a nice restaurant for dinner. She was very much looking forward to it. But after her last client had left, Hagen still hadn't come by to pick her up. Maria had gone home as well, and Kelly was waiting impatiently in her office. She checked her text messages and emails, but there was no word from Hagen. It was getting late, and Kelly decided to drive back to the airport. Perhaps Hagen had misunderstood and was waiting for her there? Hagen had given Kelly a key card, so she went straight to his room. He wasn't there, and his luggage was gone too. Kelly almost panicked, but suddenly she saw a note on the little table by the window.

Kelly, something urgent came up, and I needed to return home. I will be back soon, but then we have to talk! Love, Hagen

Kelly read the note and was relieved. But she wondered what Hagen wanted to discuss. Did he have a dark secret? Was he married? Broke? Had he killed someone? Kelly was going through all the worst-case scenarios in her mind, but she didn't care about any of them except for one: was Hagen terminally ill? That thought scared her, but he seemed very healthy and vibrant, so she doubted that was the case.

After a few moments, she decided to leave the hotel room, but as she was closing the door, it occurred to her that Hagen couldn't have known that she would return here. It would have made more sense to call or text her on her phone. She went back inside to the little table. Hagen's note was gone, and only a pristine notepad with the hotel stationery remained. Did she toss the paper in the trash? She looked in the basket, but it was empty. Kelly checked her purse next, but the note wasn't there either. That was odd, but she wasn't too worried over a misplaced message.

Of course, Kelly was disappointed that Hagen had left so abruptly, but she knew that life could thwart the best plans, so she wasn't too concerned. When she got back to her car, she decided to send Hagen a quick text from her phone. But the messages Hagen had sent to her when he had arrived at the airport were no longer there. Kelly doubted that she had deleted them. First the note, now the messages – Kelly suddenly felt uneasy. Initially, she would go home, but now she decided to return to her office. The drive from the airport to her office was short, but dread was mounting inside her with every mile, and she didn't even know why.

When she got back to her office, Kelly ran to the bookshelf and removed the book Hagen had sent her. She opened the cover, but there was no dedication from him. It was just a promotional message from a publishing company in cursive print. She went to the page Hagen had marked. She recognized the mark as one of her own sticky labels. The story was about a woman who met a man on an airplane, but it was not their story, just an excerpt from a cheesy romance novel. Kelly flipped the book over and checked the email address printed on the back. She rushed to her computer and opened her mail. Kelly saw that she had sent several messages to that address, but the responses were not from Hagen, just notifications that her emails were undeliverable. She searched for the envelope with the legal documents on her desk. She took out the paperwork and read it carefully when she found it. It wasn't a transference of royalties but an extension of the lease for the office. The attached note was not from Hagen but Maria, instructing her to sign off. Desperately, Kelly checked her bank statements and credit card expenditures next: Kelly had paid for the room at the airport, and she had purchased the ring and necklace at the jewelry store!

Kelly knew that the human mind had a powerful imagination from her professional experience: delusions, hallucinations, and even nightmares could be frightfully real. But this real? She could still feel Hagen's touch on her skin, hear his voice, and smell his aftershave. She had sex with him about a million times this weekend, and there is no way it could have felt so good if it was just an illusion!

Kelly's world shattered! She sat down at her desk and stared at the blank screen of her computer. She tried to recall how she had met Hagen. But now, the details became fuzzy. She remembered the plane, she could recollect her panic attack, but the man sitting next to her wasn't Hagen. He wasn't a man at all but a frail old lady, and suddenly she recalled how the friendly stewardess had paid extra attention to the elderly woman for the entire flight. Suddenly, Kelly's phone rang, and it jerked her away from her discombobulated thoughts. She jumped out of her chair, ran to get her purse, hoping that it was a call from Hagen, explaining everything that seemed so wrong now. But it wasn't Hagen.

"Hey honey, how was the trip?" asked Matt and added, "Was the flight OK? I know you are a little anxious about flying."

"It was perfect!" Kelly heard herself saying.

"Listen, I have to stay here for a couple more weeks. You know how it goes when you work for an eccentric sheik. Every day he wants to add or change something!" explained Matt and claimed happily, "but the building will be a real beauty!

"I see," replied Kelly monotonously.

"Are you alright?" asked Matt after noticing that Kelly wasn't very talkative.

"Just tired from work, and it's late over here!" answered Kelly.

"Oh yeah, the time zones, sorry! OK, I got to run, but I'll call you again soon! Love you!" remarked Matt and quickly hung up.

Kelly was numb. Nothing made sense anymore. Matt had divorced her nine months ago when he found out that she had cheated on him. Did she cheat on him? Kelly wasn't sure anymore. She kept staring at the vase with the plastic flowers on the windowsill for at least an hour, but slowly, her thoughts started to come back together. Suddenly, she picked up her phone and called her mother.

"Kelly!" exclaimed her mother when she picked up, "I haven't heard from you since the holidays! Do you have any idea how late it is over here?"

"Mom, is there a history of mental illness in our family?" asked Kelly, ignoring her mother's complaint.

"Of course not!" replied her mother briskly.

"Did grandma and grandpa have a good marriage?" inquired Kelly next.

"Yes, yes. Your grandparents were very happy. Why do you ask?" wondered Kelly's mother.

"Was there ever anything odd about Grandma?" questioned Kelly.

"No, but she was under a lot of stress. Grandpa wasn't the easiest man to get along with, and she had to raise all four of us kids!" replied her mother.

"What was different about her?" asked Kelly.

"Sometimes, she got a little confused, forgot a few things, or had problems talking straight, and...," answered her mother, hesitant to say more.

"And?" Kelly demanded to know.

"...and once in a while, she would see things that weren't really there, but it was just exhaustion from not sleeping right!" admitted her mother reluctantly.

"She had delusions, hallucinations?" questioned Kelly.

"How can you say this? She wasn't crazy!" replied her mother briskly, and then she explained, "Grandpa loved her and us kids, but he had trouble showing it. He never talked much and was a little disconnected, just like most men of his time. Sometimes that wore her out, but they had a good marriage, and they never fought!"

"Do you remember Grandma's last day?" Kelly asked her mother.

"Of course, I do! You were the last person to talk to her. You spent the whole evening in her room, and she gave the crucifix to you!" observed her mother and added sadly, "the next morning, she was gone."

"That evening before she died, she confessed to me that she had poisoned Grandpa! She said that she wanted him gone. Then she gave me the necklace!" stated Kelly.

"How can you say such a terrible thing?" gasped her mother and insisted, "she gave you the necklace because she loved you!"

"Do you remember that I wouldn't eat for a whole year after that?" questioned Kelly.

"Yes, because you grieved!" acknowledged Kelly's mother.

"I never knew her that well. We didn't visit very often!" countered Kelly.

"OK, maybe it was just puberty? These things happen when you grow up!" remarked her mother and asked dismissively, "you never said anything about being afraid of poison! Where do you get those awful ideas?"

Kelly had to admit that her mother was right; she had never talked about her fear of getting poisoned. But in that instant, she finally realized why: her mother had prepared all the meals during her childhood. Kelly had loved her father, and his death had been devastating to her, but she never trusted her mother!

"That's ridiculous; I lost 30 pounds! It wasn't puberty, Mom!" disagreed Kelly, but her mother completely ignored her comment.

"You should have married that nice boy, Tom, who took you to the prom. His mother is in my church group! Be a good wife, have kids and a family!" her mother berated her.

"I wanted a career and meet someone I love, not be bred like livestock!" replied Kelly agitatedly.

"It is a woman's place; it is what God intended you to be!" argued

Kelly's mother piously.

"Your God, not mine!" retorted Kelly defiantly.

"Watch what you are saying! I don't know why your father let you go to college! See what all that education got you? Now you are turning on your own family!" spat her mother into the phone and added accusatorily, "my mother was nothing like those deranged people you see every day! You don't know how hard it is to raise children; you don't even have any!"

"Grandma had schizophrenia," concluded Kelly and thought to herself, "and so do I!"

"That's a lie, Kelly!" exclaimed her mother loudly, and just before she abruptly ended the call, she added, "I won't talk to you again until you are ready to apologize!"

Kelly's entire existence was suddenly put into question. She knew that schizophrenia could be hereditary and often skipped a generation. But now, she had no idea what was genuine in her life and what had just been her imagination. Worse yet, she knew nobody she trusted to verify key events or fill in some blanks. It terrified her beyond anything she had ever experienced before. Her heart rate skyrocketed, she broke out in cold sweat, and every muscle in her body was paralyzed. For what seemed like an eternity, she suffered through another panic attack, worse than any of the previous ones, and this time without Hagen's soothing presence. When it finally subsided, Kelly quickly drank several shots of vodka, then went to bed without even taking her clothes off and cried herself to sleep.

For the next two weeks, Kelly was in a trance. She did her work, but she felt like a fraud. Her patients had mental ailments, but in Kelly's mind, she was downright crazy. She had no right to help them because it was her who needed help! Kelly researched treatment options and medications, and she considered getting help. But a big part of her didn't want help; it wanted Hagen and nothing else. The thought about losing the love of her life was too painful to bear, and so, Kelly decided that she would live with her disorder if that meant that she could see Hagen again someday.

Matt had returned from abroad today. Kelly had left the office early to go home and meet him. She prepared a nice dinner for the two of them. While they were eating, Matt was going on and on about his architectural projects, only interrupted by quizzing her about other men Kelly might have had contact with while he was gone. Not once did he ask her how she was doing, so Kelly didn't pay much attention to her husband, just gave mono-syllabic responses or occasionally nodded when she thought it was appropriate. After the meal, Kelly made some drinks. As she was mixing the alcohol, she took a capsule out of her pocket, opened it, poured the powder into Matt's glass, and stirred the concoction. Matt was dead by morning. Kelly calmly called the police and surrendered peacefully. She confessed right away that she had poisoned Matt, expressing honest remorse. In her mind, Kelly didn't want to kill him; she just saw no other way. The sub-sequent psychological evaluation confirmed what she already knew. The trial was swift, and reasons of insanity suspended the manslaughter verdict.

Kelly had been institutionalized for six months now. Only Maria, her former assistant, visited her a few months after she was committed. Maria wanted to give Kelly the ring and necklace, but the mental hospital confiscated the jewelry. But they talked for a little while, and Kelly appreciated the visit. Kelly's family had never visited, and she knew that they would never come to see her. She considered writing letters to her mother, brother, or some of her cousins, but she realized they would not respond. Kelly assumed that it would be taboo to talk even amongst them-selves about her. The mental illness was a much greater stigma for her family than the crime she had committed.

At first, the orderlies kept Kelly heavily sedated, but since she was considered non-violent and complied with the treatment, they had finally allowed her out of her cell. It was a warm, pleasant spring day. Kelly was sitting on a bench in the small park on the hospital grounds, watching a blue jay in one of the big oak trees. Suddenly, a man sat down next to her. Kelly didn't look at him, and neither spoke for a while.

"I tried to tell you, Kelly," said Hagen finally.

"I know. You kept all your promises. You were always honest, and you taught me how to be honest with myself," replied Kelly and admitted, "I knew that you were not real, but I just couldn't let go."

"This sounds strange, but I wish I were real. I would have protected you!" Hagen assured her.

"I know that too, Hagen!" remarked Kelly and smiled. It felt wonderful to hear his voice and sense his presence once again.

"Why did you kill him, Kelly?" asked Hagen after a while.

"I wanted you and nobody else," Kelly said slowly, and then she echoed the words of her grandmother, "I just wanted him gone!"

3. THE PROPHET

Peter Wells had always enjoyed the ocean. Something was soothing about the smell of the sea, the sounds of the waves, and the view of a seemingly endless body of water expanding to the horizon. The cruise ship was clean, the service exceptional, the weather perfect, and Peter felt thoroughly relaxed and at peace.

It was a welcome change from the dreadful last few months. After 20 years of marriage, Peter's wife Anna suddenly told him she was moving out one day. She had hooked up with one of her clients from work. Peter had no idea and was completely blindsided! But there was no point in fighting the inevitable, and with only slight hesitation, he agreed to an amicable divorce. They had no children, so that simplified matters greatly, as did the fact that they had always separated their finances. After buying his wife out with a lump sum, Peter kept their modest suburban home. She had no use for it since she moved to an impressive estate. Anna was a successful attorney, and her income outpaced his wages from the research institute by a considerable margin, but, although entitled to financial support, Peter outright declined that.

The weeks after Anna left were hard for Peter. Try as he might, he missed her a lot. Peter and Anna weren't the most social people, but they had quite a few common friends. Now, Peter found out that these friends had been only hers all along. Without a companion, children, friends, or relatives living nearby, the house felt too big and empty. Still, Peter much preferred a clean break, a tabula rasa, over a drawn-out, messy and painful process. So one day, Peter found an ad on the internet for this cruise and booked it on a whim. He reasoned that he needed a change of scenery to figure out what he would do next in his life.

Today was the 6th day of the cruise. It started with a headache, but after a good cup of coffee and some relaxation in the jacuzzi, the rest of the day had progressed splendidly. Earlier, Peter had made evening reservations for a little French bistro on the starboard side. The hostess welcomed him and swiftly guided him to his table when he arrived at the restaurant. But there was a mix-up with the reservation, and two ladies already occupied it. The hostess profusely apologized for the mistake, but Peter seemed out of luck tonight since no other tables were available.

"Oh, just join us!" insisted the woman with the jet-black hair and smiled warmly at him.

"I appreciate that, but I shouldn't be intruding!" retorted Peter politely.

"Nonsense! Grab a chair. We went on this vacation to meet new people!" added the blonde lady with piercing green eyes.

"Thank you!" replied Peter and sat down while the hostess rushed to get another set of silverware.

"Peter Wells," he introduced himself.

"Nice to meet you, Mr. Wells. I'm Janet, and that's Cassandra!" said Janet.

"A pleasure to meet you as well, and please call me Peter!" he replied. Peter was never a good judge of age, but he estimated the women to be in their mid or late thirties, certainly a little younger than himself. While both were slender and well proportioned, they looked strikingly different: Janet was petite with short straight black hair, while Cassandra was rather tall and sported long blonde curls, but Peter couldn't help noticing that both ladies were very easy on the eye.

The food was great, and the dinner conversation was even better. These two women were as sophisticated as they were entertaining. They talked about the cruise, their jobs, and life in general well after they had finished dessert. And they laughed so much! But eventually, Peter noticed that Janet was glancing at the clock on her cellphone.

"I'm sure you have other plans tonight, so I will not keep you any longer!" observed Peter politely, stood up, and added, "but I very much enjoyed the dinner and your company!"

"So did we, thank you! You are a charming man, Peter, but we have tickets to a show at the ship's theater. That's why we have to cut this a bit short!" explained Janet.

"You will see a lot more of us in the next few days, perhaps more than you care for...," added Cassandra cryptically. Janet seemed a little embarrassed by her friend's words and glanced at her disapprovingly.

"Well, I'm certainly looking forward to that. Enjoy the performance and have a good night, ladies!" replied Peter and bowed his head a little.

The next morning, Peter woke up by someone knocking on his cabin. He put on a bathrobe and opened the door. Janet was smiling at him broadly.

"Hi, Peter! Since your cabin is just a few doors from ours, I thought I stop by and invite you to join us for breakfast. Cassie is already waiting for us in the dining hall!" revealed Janet happily.

"Oh! Sure, if you can give me a minute to get dressed?" asked Peter and added, "I tend to sleep in on vacations!"

"Me too! But Cass is an early riser, and once she gets going, there is no way to keep sleeping!" laughed Janet and offered, "take your time, Peter. I'll wait outside."

"No, please come in and have a seat; it will be just a minute. I'll skip the shaving – another perk of being on vacation!" mentioned Peter and grinned at her.

"Ah, the ruggedly handsome look? Why not!" giggled Janet and sat down by the little table in the cabin.

The breakfast was good. Peter had second's and third's, not because he was that hungry, but because he enjoyed spending time with these two lovely ladies. But finally, Cassandra got up from the table.

"I have an appointment for a massage and spa treatment now, but you kids have fun!" mentioned Cassandra as she was leaving the table, and then she divulged, "I'll see you both before the ship runs aground. I'm not looking forward to that hovel of a hotel where they'll dump us after the evacuation!"

Janet looked worried, but Peter was just confused by Cassandra's words. Will the ship run aground? It was supposed to arrive at the next port in the afternoon, but they would not disembark until the following day, and there was no overnight stay scheduled at that destination. Peter was trying to wrap his mind around Cassie's strange remarks, but his thoughts were suddenly interrupted when the cruise director announced over the intercom that dolphins were racing the ship at the bow.

"Oh, I want to see that!" exclaimed Janet and jumped off her seat. She grabbed Peter's hand and almost dragged him out of the dining room.

Janet and Peter spent the next few hours together. First, they watched the dolphins, then they strolled through the ship's casino, and then played whack-a-mole in the arcade, laughing as if they were kids again. Finally, they rested in the sunshine by the pool.

"We will get burned by the sun if we wait here for Cass!" warned Janet and handed Peter a bottle of sunscreen from her purse: "Could you put that to my back and shoulders, please?"

"Of course!" assented Peter. Then he squirted some lotion into the palm of his hand and applied it to Janet's back. He was gentle but swift and took care not to touch her in inappropriate ways. He returned the sunscreen bottle to Janet and laid down on his lounge chair again when he had finished. Janet quickly applied some more sunscreen to her front, arms and legs.

"OK, your turn!" declared Janet after she had finished.

"Thanks, but I think I'll be fine," replied Peter with a smile.

"No, you will be in pain, so turn around now!" ordered Janet jokingly, and Peter obediently rolled on his stomach. Janet's touch felt good on his skin, and she took her time applying the lotion. It was almost a massage, and Peter secretly didn't want her to stop. But eventually, she had finished, and Peter sat up again. Janet looked him in the eyes for a long moment. It was an odd look, not exactly romantic, and Peter didn't know how to feel about that: was he supposed to kiss her, was she going to kiss him, should he expect to get slapped across the face now, or did he just have some dirt on his cheek? Finally, the moment passed, and Janet just smiled a little, turned away, and laid down on her lounge chair, leaving Peter unsure of his feelings: he barely knew this woman at all, but she was funny, sweet, and genuine, and if Peter was honest with himself, he had to admit that he was already infatuated with Janet.

Cassandra found them again in the early afternoon, and they all sat down by the pool bar. Peter bought the drinks while Janet ordered a big bowl of delicious shrimp salad for them to share. Suddenly, the whole ship jerked, and the empty salad bowl went flying off the table. Janet spilled a drink in her lap, and Cassie almost fell off her chair. Similar things happened to other passengers all around them. A bell sounded the alarm. The captain announced that the ship had run aground a few moments later, but there was no immediate danger. As a precaution, all passengers were ordered to return to their cabins and strap on their life vests, then proceed in an orderly fashion to the designated evacuation zones, leaving all luggage behind aside from small items that could be carried on their persons. They would be transported to shore shortly, while the ship would undergo inspection and repair.

Peter, Janet, and Cassandra made their way below deck to the cabins, but that took some time because the elevators had been disabled, and the stairs and hallways were crowded with frazzled, anxious people. Peter exchanged his shorts and sandals for sweatpants, sneakers, and a fresh shirt. Then he donned the life jacket, secured it, grabbed his wallet, cellphone, and water bottle. A few minutes later, Peter was out the door and went to Janet's and Cassie's cabin to meet them. He found their cabin door open, knocked on the frame, and entered. The women were struggling with the life vests, and Peter quickly assisted. Janet carried a small duffle bag, and Peter added his few items to the content.

They were met by a chaotic scene when they got to the evacuation zone! Alarms were sounding, children were crying, and crewmembers were shouting orders. It was a logistical nightmare to evacuate thousands of people from a ship this size. Finally, they were herded into the lifeboats. Their small vessel was cramped, and Cassie almost had to sit on Peter's lap while Janet held on to their meager belongings.

"Do you know where they are taking us?" wondered Janet when their boat was lowered into the water.

"First to the port, then we will have to wait around for a couple of hours before they bus everyone to various hotels. We will have adjacent rooms at the Imperial Palace!" informed Cassie and added with disdain, "but don't let that fancy name fool you; it's more like the emperor's latrine!"

"How do you know this, Cassie?" asked Peter, wondering how Cassandra could be so confident when even the crewmembers seemed to have no idea.

"I just do!" declared Cassie, seemingly unwilling to say more. But then, Peter remembered that Cassandra had predicted these events over breakfast already, and suddenly, he got the strangest feeling about the pretty blonde woman pressed against his shoulder.

The boat ride only took a few minutes because the big ship had been very close to shore. When they landed at the piers, they were greeted by heat, humidity, and the smell of decaying fish. It was a stark contrast to the pleasant temperatures and fresh sea breeze onboard the cruise ship. Peter already didn't like this place. A crewmember ordered them to gather at a designated area and remain there until further notice. Peter was happy that he brought the bottled water along because the heat was almost unbearable. Janet, Cassie, and Peter had finished it long before a bus finally arrived to take them to their next destination.

It was getting dark when they arrived at the hotel. Even with Cassie's warning, Peter was ill-prepared for the desolate state of the building. The lobby's décor was in shambles, and the place positively stank of urine. A grumpy old man with a stained clipboard walked up to their group of passengers and assigned them their quarters while two seedy-looking individuals watched a boxing bout on a small TV in the lobby. As Cassandra had predicted, she and Janet got room 304, while Peter stayed in the adjacent room, number 305. Naturally, the elevator was broken, so they had to take the dirty stairs to the third floor. When Peter entered his room, he just shook his head. The first thing he noticed was the foul odor of vomit and stale cigar smoke, and then he found that the lock on the door didn't latch at all. The carpet was so stained that it was hard to say what its original color might have been. The lamp by the bed didn't work, and the bathroom was downright filthy with roaches scurrying over the broken floor tiles. But at least the bed was a decent size and seemed to have clean sheets. Peter was grateful for that because he was tired and exhausted from all the day's excitement.

He stretched out on the bed, and despite the heat, humidity, and stench, he fell asleep almost immediately.

It was three o'clock in the morning when Cassie suddenly burst into his room, dragging Janet behind her. Both women only wore bathrobes and flip-flops.

"Wake up, Peter!" she shouted.

"Woah, yeah…I'm awake!" mumbled Peter, disoriented, and asked, "what the heck happened?"

"Sorry, Peter. Nothing happened!" claimed Janet calmly and added with a snort, "Cassie just had another epiphany. But she won't tell me what it is, go figure!"

Peter sat up in the bed and looked at the two women. Janet sat down on one of the chairs by the little table, but Cassie was standing up straight, wringing her hands, with an anxious look on her face. Then she looked sternly at Janet.

"Jan, did you sleep with Peter this afternoon?" inquired Cassandra with urgency in her voice.

"What kind of question is that, Cass? I'm happily married, remember?" retorted Janet briskly.

"We both know that's not true, and you didn't answer my question!" insisted Cassie.

"Can we please not discuss my relationship in front of strangers?" barked Janet and added snidely, "besides, three o'clock in the morning isn't the right time to be jealous. I saw how you looked at Peter!"

"That doesn't matter right now, and you still haven't answered the question!" Cassie pressed on.

"We just had a great time, for heaven's sake! But, no, I haven't slept with him!" responded Janet exasperatedly.

"You were supposed to!" mumbled Cassie, looked at Peter, and asked: "Is that true?"

"Uhm, yes, of course, that's true," confirmed Peter and opined, "I think you have some explaining to do, Cassie!"

"Do you believe that I can see the future or possible futures?" Cassie directed the question at both of them.

"I know you all my life, Cass. Most of your visions have come true, so I guess I believe it even though I still don't understand it," admitted Janet and shrugged her shoulders.

"And you, Peter?" inquired Cassandra.

"I only know you for about 36 hours, but your predictions were accurate thus far...," replied Peter, stopping himself before he said more.

"But?" questioned Cass with her eyebrows raised.

"But I don't believe in fortune-tellers, Cassandra. I think this is either coincidence or remarkable intuition. Or you are exceptionally aware of your surroundings. Or perhaps a combination of all of those things processed by a mind highly skilled in deduction?" speculated Peter.

"Tactful words, Peter, but I'm not Sherlock Holmes. Just call me crazy or a freak, as most people do!" remarked Cassandra dryly and asked, "but tell me, how could I have known that the cruise ship would have mishap? How did I know that we would be stranded in this roach-infested place?"

"True, I don't have a good explanation, but that doesn't mean that you are a prophet," countered Peter, but then he added with a friendly smile, "but for argument's sake, let's say you are – that still doesn't explain why you wake us up at this godawful hour and ask about our sex life."

"In a few hours, an asteroid will crash in Africa. There will be significant death and destruction!" proclaimed Cassandra somberly.

"OK, that's very disconcerting, but what does that have to do with Janet and me?" wondered Peter. The scientist in him immediately worried about the size and speed of this asteroid. If it was big enough or fast enough, Africa wasn't that far away!

"The cruise ship runs aground. Then, either just before or right after that, you sleep with Janet. Then, finally, the asteroid falls to Earth. In that order!" declared Cassie.

"But why is that significant?" Janet chimed in.

"Because this is a fixed chain of events, an anchor point for all possible futures! It must happen or…," explained Cassandra.

"Or what?" questioned Peter cautiously.

"Or the branches will break, and futures become invalid!" emphasized Cass with a worried look on her face.

"Alright, but why would that be so terrible?" asked Peter, but then he answered his own question: "Oh, I understand now: if the futures become invalid, you cannot predict them anymore!"

"This isn't about me!" insisted Cass emphatically and elaborated, "yes, I won't be able to predict anything for a while, but that's not a problem because eventually, new possibilities will open up again. But if there is a hole in the flow of time, anything can happen, and whatever happens will not be pleasant. I have seen the possible futures for you, Janet, me, and the whole world. Most are painful, horrible, and downright abysmal even, but a few inspire hope. Without that hope, we are lost, and the world will be lost, too!"

"Cassie…," interrupted Janet gently.

"No! You must sleep with Peter right now!" demanded Cassandra in a raised voice.

"Do you really want me to strip down and fuck a stranger at three o'clock in the morning in this shithole of a place while you watch?" questioned Janet sarcastically.

"Yes, and please hurry!" confirmed Cassandra, seemingly oblivious to Janet's sarcasm.

"Cass, that's bizarre, even for you!" laughed Jane and Peter had to chuckle a little.

"Do you not like each other?" asked Cassie with some doubt in her voice.

"I like Peter – as a friend!" said Janet and emphasized that last word.

"I like Janet, and I like you too, Cassie. You are both attractive, bright, funny, and kind!" admitted Peter and added, "but even if the fate of the world hangs in the balance, I can't just sleep with Janet on command!"

"Why not?" Cassandra demanded to know.

"That's not how I function! Sex happens in my mind first; if it doesn't happen there, it will never happen in my pants!" laughed Peter, a little frustrated that Cassandra didn't seem to understand that.

"But you are a man, you are not in a relationship, and you are not gay!" contradicted Cassandra stubbornly.

"Does that mean I can just sleep with any woman whenever it's called for?" asked Peter, slightly upset now, "I'm a man, not a savage!"

"I didn't mean to insult you, Peter. I thought it would be no problem for any man to do the physical act?" speculated Cassandra.

"It might be possible for most men, but not for me. Sorry Cassandra, even if Janet agrees to this, it will not happen!" stated Peter firmly, and then he changed the subject somewhat: "There are over 7.5 billion people on this planet. At any given moment, hundreds of thousands of them have sex somewhere in the world. So why would it even matter if I sleep with Janet?"

"This one time, only you and Janet matter, that's all I can tell you!" countered Cass, but Peter sensed that she was holding something back, and Cassandra could tell that Peter had noticed.

"Cassie, can you please leave us alone for a few minutes?" begged Janet suddenly.

"Yes, but don't take too long!" warned Cassie, exited the room swiftly, and closed the door behind her.

For a moment, Janet and Peter were silent. Peter was putting on a T-shirt while Janet was examining the back of her hands.

"Cassie and I went to elementary school together," stated Janet and added, "one day in winter, we were sitting in class when Cassie suddenly asked to go to the restroom. After she got permission from the teacher, she stood up, walked over to my desk, took me by the hand, and we left the classroom together."

Peter listened attentively, but he did not interrupt Janet's story.

"But we didn't go to the restroom. Instead, Cassie took me outside the building to the little playground where the slide and swings were. She sat on one of the swings and beckoned me to sit on the one next to her. I was cold and worried that we would get in trouble with the teacher, so I urged her to go back inside. But she was holding on tightly to my hand and said that we could not do that!" continued Janet. She paused for a moment to collect her thoughts.

"We were sitting on the swings, holding hands, for about half an hour. Then, suddenly, the fire department and several ambulances showed up, sirens blaring! Five children and the teacher had died. A faulty heater had vented carbon monoxide into the classroom," concluded Janet and emphasized, "Cassie saved my life that day!"

"That's sad, fortunate, and remarkable, all at the same time!" observed Peter.

"A few years later, she predicted that my dad's car would break down and catch fire. She envisioned that both of us would be admitted to the same college; she told me that I would meet Jake there and that we would get married. But on my wedding day, she disclosed to me that my marriage would fail!" revealed Janet and added, "I was in love with Jake and so mad at Cassie that I wouldn't talk to her for a whole month. Of course, in the end, she was right yet again. My marriage has been over for years now. Ever since Jake started drinking a lot, I just haven't been able to come to terms with that."

"I see," said Peter, subdued.

"When we booked this cruise, Cassie predicted that I would meet a tall, handsome, older gentleman with impeccable manners, and he would be my life's true love!" maintained Janet and added, "…and she thinks that's where you come in, Peter!"

"A stunning, almost eerie story!" acknowledged Peter. Now he understood the strange look Janet gave him when they were sunbathing by the pool. She tried to figure out if Peter was the man Cassandra had prophesized.

"I swear it is all true!" avowed Janet.

"But I'm sure you could meet other tall, handsome, older gentlemen with impeccable manners on this journey!" remarked Peter humorously and quipped: "Can Cassie predict the Lotto numbers too?"

For a minute, Janet didn't say a word. Peter got a little concerned that he might have offended Janet with his joke, but then she looked straight at him again and sighed.

"Cassie had a boyfriend, and she loved him very much. He knew about her...talents," disclosed Jane and continued, "one day, he asked her for the Lotto numbers. She knew what would happen, and so she refused to tell him, but he was persistent, and eventually, she relented."

"What happened?" asked Peter curiously.

"Bob won over 60 million dollars!" noted Janet and added, "but then he left her and went on drinking, whoring, and gambling sprees for several years. Then, when the money was all gone, he blew his brains out in a shitty hotel, just like this one. Cassie was devastated and never fully recovered from that!"

"I'm so sorry to hear that. What an awful no-win situation that must have been for Cass!" noted Peter and sorely regretted that he had joked about the lottery.

"Please, whatever happens, you cannot tell Cass that I entrusted you with this, and you can never ask her for Lotto numbers; it would kill her!" begged Janet.

"Of course, I won't. I'm neither greedy nor callous!" Peter reassured her.

"I know," concurred Janet and asked him very seriously: "Do you believe now that Cassandra can predict the future?"

"I'm a scientist and hence skeptical by nature, but I have to admit that this is quite compelling, even more so if that asteroid hits Africa in a few hours!" said Peter slowly.

"But you still doubt my words," noted Janet and sighed.

"No, I believe everything. But I wonder if the conclusions you are drawing are accurate," corrected Peter and proposed: "please do not be offended, but may I play the devil's advocate for a moment?"

"Go ahead! I won't be offended, I promise!" Janet assured him.

"Is it possible that Cassie's predictions can be explained in other ways? For example, did her boyfriend simply pick the correct Lotto numbers on his own? Was she alarmed by a bad smell coming from the furnace in the elementary school? Did Cassie know that your father's car had problems? Did she notice your husband's affinity for alcohol, or was she aware of other character flaws? Is Cass now trying to set us up because she wants you to be happy? Perhaps Cassie is just very good at reading people, and she is manipulating us like a magician doing card tricks?" speculated Peter and looked expectantly at Jan.

"I have asked myself the same questions a thousand times for as long as I know her!" admitted Janet and continued, "I could doubt some of the examples I've given you, but not all of them, and there are many, many more. Cass is honest, brutally so, not a trickster. Besides, you were there when she told us that the cruise ship would get stuck on a sandbar, and we would be evacuated to this crappy hotel. She even recalled the name of this dump! How could she know that in advance?"

"Yes, I cannot refute that!" conceded Peter.

"Trust me, that asteroid will crash, and Cassie isn't working for NASA!" insisted Janet forcefully.

"If it does, I will be a believer, although it will probably consume the rest of my life to figure out how Cassie's ability works," admitted Peter and thought about this for a moment.

"Did Cassandra ever tell you how her ability works?" inquired Peter.

"I've asked her that question for the last 30 years now, but she never gave me a straight answer. I believe she knows, but she isn't ready to tell me!" replied Janet and shook her head and added, "Sometimes I think she is afraid to say too much!"

"If her gift is real, I can understand her hesitation," concurred Peter and then changed the subject, "Jan, where do we go from here?"

"I don't know, Peter. Cassie is a good person, despite what you might think of her now. I love her dearly, and if she thinks this is so important, I would be a fool to ignore it!" replied Janet and then asked a little embarrassed, "When we first met did you want to...well, you know?"

"I wasn't lying earlier. You are lovely, Janet, and we had a wonderful time today, shipwreck notwithstanding," said Peter and smiled at her, "but I haven't fantasized about making love to you if that's what you are asking?"

"I did, almost immediately after I saw you," revealed Janet bluntly, "but I hoped that Cassie would be the one because she deserves someone like you!"

"I don't know what to say to that, Jan!" uttered Peter, caught off guard. Janet got up from her chair, unbuttoned her bathrobe, and let it slide down from her shoulders, exposing her naked figure.

"Was it true that you can't have sex on demand?" she asked slyly. Peter was stunned by this bold move, but he also admired Janet's physique for a moment before he responded.

"You are beautiful, Jan! But what I said earlier was true...," answered Peter slowly; however, his sentence was cut short as Cassandra entered the room again without knocking. She glanced at her naked friend and put a tall bottle of tequila on the table.

"It won't work that way, Janet," she mentioned nonchalantly and opened the bottle, "I found something to drink, but there are no clean glasses anywhere. So we will have to chuck it straight from the bottle!"

"Cass!" gasped Janet, quickly picking up her bathrobe from the floor to cover herself. Cassandra ignored Janet's exasperation and turned to Peter.

"I know what she told you, and I know that you don't believe it, but I wasn't listening at the door!" maintained Cassie and drank some tequila. She made a face as she swallowed the strong drink. Then she handed the bottle to Peter.

"I would prefer a cup of coffee, but this will do!" said Peter and held the bottle up as if he was toasting the two women before he drank.

"Cass, I'm sorry that I talked about Bob," apologized Janet, distraughtly looking at her friend.

"Don't be, Jan. It is time that I got over that!" replied Cassie without emotion.

"Are you sure, Cassie?" asked Jan, clearly worried about her friend.

"Yes, I'm sure, Jan., I'm crazy enough the way it is; I don't need irrational guilt to make it worse!" disclosed Cassandra and cast her eyes to the floor.

"Cassandra, you are not crazy, and your talents – whatever they might be - are truly remarkable!" interjected Peter. He still didn't believe in fortune-tellers, but without a doubt, Cassandra had a fantastic gift that could not be readily explained in scientific ways.

"I wish so much that it was just parlor tricks, Peter!" replied Cassie and sighed, "the weight...."

"...must be crushing you!" Peter finished her sentence compassionately. Cassie looked at him and nodded sadly. Peter collected his thoughts for a moment before he spoke again.

"Your parents have named you aptly!" he said quietly, his remarks directed at Cassandra.

"Huh?" wondered Janet, unsure about Peter's cryptic comment.

"Cassandra of Troy - condemned to see the future, and she always spoke the truth, yet nobody would believe her!" elaborated

Peter and Cassandra gave him a slight nod.

"Greek mythology!" explained Cass and continued, "Jan, I didn't tell you how my ability works because the time wasn't right. But now it is because Peter is here, and he is a scientist."

"You waited all these years for this moment?" gasped Jan incredulously, and Cass nodded her head.

"I have studied everything I could ever find on prophets, psychics, and soothsayers. Trust me, it's all bullshit!" declared Cassandra bluntly and added, "but then I looked at physics, and I found a few things that might explain my gift, or curse, a little better. I read scientific theories that propose the existence of an infinite number of parallel universes. None of it can be proven, but at least there is some math to back it up."

"Yes, I have read about that, too. But how does that relate to your ability?" wondered Peter as he was raptly listening to Cassandra's explanation.

"I believe that I cannot predict the future but experience episodes where I see glimpses of different universes. These universes are similar to ours but not identical, especially not with respect to time flow. I witness the outcome of an event as it happened there, but before it happens here," explained Cassie and added, "I call the different possible outcomes I can see the branches of the future!"

"How do you sort this all out?" questioned Peter in amazement.

"Very, very carefully! Jan is right; I'm afraid to say too much because navigating the different futures or universes is like walking through a minefield. Some futures look great at first but end horribly! So I have to be cautious with my predictions and the path I choose because any misstep can have grave consequences," admitted Cassie somberly and added, "I know both of you have more questions, and I will answer them all as best as I can when the time comes, but tonight we must hurry!"

"Wow, that was way over my head, Cass! But I'll read up on it as soon as we get back home because I have to know what makes my best friend tick!" promised Janet humorously, and Cassandra grinned at her in response.

"Yes, a stunning and fascinating explanation, Cassandra, and I can't wait to hear more!" lauded Peter and added, "true, it cannot be proven and might never be proven, but it is not magic either!"

"Thanks! Peter, you already suspected earlier that I didn't tell you everything. I shall amend that now: not only do you have to sleep with Janet promptly, but you also have to sleep with me as well. All of that must happen before the asteroid strikes, so time is short!" explained Cassie in a matter-of-fact voice. Janet almost spat out the tequila she was drinking that moment, and Peter's jaw dropped open.

"That's how it is going to be: Jan and I will share you, and if we follow that possible future, all three of us will be happy for a long time to come!" declared Cassie, but then she added, "but for now, just think of it as a drunken threesome on a wild vacation if that's easier for you. It might even be fun!"

"Cass, you are my best friend, my sister in a sense, and we did a lot of things together, but we never…," Janet blurted out quickly, but she didn't finish the sentence.

"…shared a man?" questioned Cassandra and completed Jan's words.

"Yeah!" acknowledged Janet hesitantly.

"Wrong, we already did that," corrected Cassandra.

"What do you mean?" gasped Janet in surprise.

"I slept with your husband the night before your wedding. Peter was right: I predicted that your marriage would fail not because I saw the future, but because I knew Jake's character!" disclosed the blonde woman truthfully. That admission must have been difficult for Cass, which in turn had a profound effect on Peter. Now he was convinced that Cassandra was no charlatan!

"Oh my god, why didn't you tell me that? I would have called it off!" exclaimed Janet in shock.

"You were so in love, you wouldn't have listened, and I would have lost you!" explained Cassandra, and Peter nodded slightly in agreement. Janet pressed her lips tightly together, and Peter suspected that she also realized the truth in Cassie's words.

"Did you seduce him?" asked Janet finally with a bit of suspicion in her voice.

"No, he came to my place after his bachelor party, supposedly to talk about the wedding. Jake was drunk and got pushy. I let it happen!" elaborated Cassandra.

"But why?" inquired Janet incredulously.

"My talents, as you call them, come and go. I couldn't see your future at that time, but I needed to find out who Jake really was!" disclosed Cassie and grimaced.

"Did you sleep with him more than once?" wondered Janet, now more curious than upset.

"Only that one time, but not for lack of trying on Jake's part, even after you two were married," concluded Cassandra and sighed deeply.

"That bastard! That settles it! When I get back home, I will divorce him!" cried Janet, tears streaming down her cheeks, but after a few moments, she calmed down again and asked, "Cass, you slept with my husband, and I don't know if I should thank you or be furious?"

"That's easy, Janet: Cassandra is your guardian angel!" noted Peter solemnly.

Janet looked at him for a moment, then she got up and hugged

Cassandra fiercely. Cass returned the embrace, glanced at Peter over Janet's shoulder, and silently mouthed the words *thank you* to him.

For the next half an hour, they were chatting about other things, mainly the horrible conditions in this hotel, while drinking tequila until the bottle was finished. Peter suspected that he would regret later that he ingested so much of the cheap booze. Finally, Janet got up, dropped her bathrobe again, staggered naked to the bed, and sat back down next to Peter. She turned on the radio that was part of the alarm clock. Surprisingly, it was working, perhaps the only thing that functioned in this awful place. Jan tuned the radio to a soft music station. Then she put her hands on Peter's cheeks and kissed him deeply. Cassie watched them and nodded.

"Right, it's time to get down to business!" she said, disrobed, and joined them on the bed.

The mattress was a little cramped with three bodies on it, but it wasn't uncomfortable. Jan was lying on one side, Cassandra on the other, while Peter was sandwiched in the middle. He could smell the faint odor from Jan's shampoo in her hair, and he felt Cassie's breath brushing against the back of his neck. Janet's firm butt pressed against his loins, and Cassie gently caressed his chest. Physically, Peter had not felt this good in a long time. Here he was, in between two beautiful, kind women who were willing and eager to sleep with him, and he liked both of them a lot! He imagined that most men would do anything to be in his place right now.

Yet, Peter was caught between rejection and acceptance: all he could think of was how absurd, surreal, and impossible this whole situation was. There was no scientific evidence that clairvoyance existed: all the so-called prophets have either been flat-out wrong or so vague that their words could be interpreted to fit any possible future. Cassandra told him that he must hurry and fuck on demand to save the world. She promised happiness if he did and warned of impending doom if he didn't. Even if that was indeed the case, and he only had Cassandra's word for that and no other proof whatsoever, was a future worth saving if it meant that he had to prostitute himself for that?

On the other hand, despite his doubts, he was very fond of Cassandra, although he had known her only for a little while. Peter had never met anyone remotely like her: she was an exceptional woman with a true gift, and her explanation for the ability had some basis in actual science! Peter's mind was racing, and he now regretted that his judgment was so clouded from all that alcohol. Then, suddenly, the radio station interrupted the music for an important announcement. A few minutes ago, a sizeable asteroid had crashed on the coast of Angola.

"Damn! We are too late!" exclaimed Cassandra in desperation.

Peter woke up with a splitting headache. The light hurt his eyes, so he kept them shut for now. Peter felt sore and remained motionless in the bed for a while longer. That damn tequila, he thought. He tried to recollect what had happened last night, but a few pieces were missing. Peter remembered lying in bed with Cass and Jan and how good it felt to have their bodies next to his. He recalled that he was trying to figure out if he should have sex with them or not. Did he do it in the end? Peter couldn't say either way because the last thing he could conjure up in his mind was the announcement on the radio about the asteroid strike in Africa. If he had slept with them, what does that mean now? Was it just an alcohol-induced threesome, as Cassie had suggested, or was he now in some sort of love triangle? And if he didn't sleep with them, were they disappointed or upset with him? Or perhaps even worse, have Cassie's dire predictions come true already? Peter opened his eyes and sat up in the bed. It was then that he realized that he wasn't in that awful hotel anymore but back at his cabin onboard the cruise ship.

"Oh crap, how did I get here? I must have completely passed out from the booze!" muttered Peter to himself.

He was concerned that he might have embarrassed himself in front of Cass and Jan. Worse yet, they might have had to drag him back to the ship. No more tequila for a long time, he vowed. Peter got up, popped a couple of pills for the headache, and took a long shower. After he toweled off and put on some clothes, he felt a little better. Peter decided to go to Cass and Jen's cabin to apologize for last night. If he was lucky, maybe they could fill some of the gaps in his memory too. A few minutes later, Peter knocked on their cabin door. For a while, there was no response, but then the door finally opened.

"Hello, Janet!" Peter greeted her with a friendly smile.

"Yes, I'm Janet. Are you with the crew?" asked Janet expectantly.

"Uhm, no...," replied Peter, befuddled.

"Then who are you?" questioned Janet with some irritation in her voice.

"I'm Peter. I just came to check on you and Cass after last night...," he explained slowly, but he saw no recognition in Janet's eyes.

"Peter? I don't know you, and I have never seen you before!" interrupted Janey tersely and added, "listen, you are acting very creepy; please leave before I have to call security!"

"Of course, sorry!" stammered Peter as Janet slammed the door shut.

Peter stood in front of the closed cabin door for a good minute, dazed and confused. On the one hand, he was ashamed and felt like a fool, but on the other hand, his mind couldn't reconcile what had just happened with the events of the last few days. Finally, Peter turned around and headed back to his cabin. He went straight to the little coffee machine by the sink when he entered. Peter hadn't used it thus far because he could get coffee in the dining area and because he suspected that this instant brew wouldn't be very tasty. But right now, he needed some caffeine to wake up and think straight.

Peter was a scientist, and as such, he was trained to solve riddles with critical thinking. If the last two days were just a dream, vivid and exquisitely detailed like none he had before, Janet's reaction would be perfectly normal because she really wouldn't know Peter at all. But if it was a dream, how could he have known her name and cabin number? Before they had met at the bistro, Peter was utterly unaware that Jan and Cass even existed. Peter sipped on his coffee and concluded that a dream could not be the answer he was looking for here.

But that left only one other, less pleasant alternative: Janet knew him but pretended not to! Perhaps because she and Cassandra simply wanted a sexual adventure with no other strings attached. However, if he hadn't slept with them, Janet might be disappointed and rather not be reminded of that failure. Alternatively, she might be agitated that he had misbehaved in his drunken stupor or that they were forced to drag his unconscious body back to the ship. Peter couldn't say which of these scenarios was the most likely because of the gaps in this memory, but they all seemed equally plausible. Sadly, Peter would have to live with that uncertainty because he would never find out the truth, nor would he be able to apologize for his behavior if it had been improper.

Somewhat satisfied with this analysis, Peter finished the coffee and tossed the paper cup in the wastebasket. He resolved to avoid Cassandra and Janet for the rest of the trip, but he had to admit that he would miss their charming company. Peter was about to leave his cabin to get some fresh air on deck when someone knocked on the door. He opened it and was very surprised!

"How do you know us? Why did you come to our cabin? Tell

me the truth!" demanded Cassandra sternly. Peter looked at her dumbfounded. His hypothesis must have been wrong, and once again, his mind was thrown into turmoil.

"We had a pleasant dinner at a bistro, then you and Janet went to a play afterward. The next morning, we had breakfast together, and while you had a massage, Janet and I watched some dolphins. We met with you in the afternoon for a snack, then the ship ran into a sandbar, and we were evacuated. We spent the night in the hotel from hell, and finally, an asteroid devastated the coast of Angola early next morning!" recalled Peter and added somberly, "of course, I know how that sounds. I came to your cabin because I truly thought I had met you and Janet before. My mistake!"

"That's the most unusual, elaborate pickup line I've ever heard. Are you sure you are not omitting anything else?" inquired Cassandra sharply and raised an eyebrow at Peter. He felt that her striking green eyes were drilling holes into his skull. This situation was so humiliating that he wished the ocean would rise to swallow him up, right this second!

"I'm mortified, and I don't know what's wrong with me, but I wasn't trying to pick up on you. So I sincerely apologize, also to Janet, and I promise I won't bother you again!" said Peter formally, bowed his head a little, and slowly closed the cabin door, but Cassandra quickly reached for his hand and stopped him.

"Check your calendar!" she suggested softly.

"My calendar?" repeated Peter slowly, unsure what Cassandra implied.

"Yes, check it!" insisted Cassandra and pointed at Peter's cellphone. He took it out of his chest pocket and switched it on. It took him a moment to comprehend what he saw.

"It is just the 6th day of the cruise!" he gasped.

"That's right. Janet and I will have dinner at the French bistro tonight. But now I shall make the reservation for three people," replied Cassandra nonchalantly.

"I'm so confused!" gasped Peter, staring wide-eyed at Cassandra.

"I was cruel to you, and I'm sorry. But now you know how I feel almost every day of my life!" apologized Cassandra with a bit of a sigh, and then she added consolingly, "the events you've recounted have not happened yet."

"You believe me?!? I just don't know what to think anymore...," mumbled Peter incredulously.

"You have been given a second chance, Peter. Don't think! Just feel, act, and let it happen – all of it, even the parts you have omitted from the chain of events. Especially the parts you have omitted!" emphasized Cassandra and winked at him knowingly, "we will see you later tonight!"

4. THE RESEARCHER

Miriam Jennings loved research! From early childhood on, she explored, experimented, and discovered. So it surprised nobody in her family that Miriam would study science and make a successful career out of her passion. She was only 35 years old, but she held two doctorates and a master's degree in three different fields and had published dozens of scientific papers. But Miriam wasn't much for theory or teaching, although she has given many guest lectures at renowned universities. No, her approach to science has always been hands-on, and that was just what MindMelt International was looking for!

The company was only a tiny startup, but Miriam had eagerly accepted the job as a group leader. It was generously compensated with many additional perks. But it was the immense potential that made Miriam enter employment at MindMelt International: nearly half of all Americans, and many, many more people worldwide, were suffering from mental illness at one point or another in their lifetimes. This company attempted an innovative approach involving neither drugs, therapy, institutionalization, nor draconian medical intervention.

The funding was staggering but a little mysterious. A company of this size, barely a few months old and without any marketable products, shouldn't have nearly a billion dollars in its coffers. But the company founder, Jack Garson, was a venture capitalist with an MBA from an Ivy League school. He was highly regarded in the financial community, albeit with a reputation of ruthlessness. But Miriam didn't worry too much about where the money was coming from, only how it could help the millions of poor people who were stricken by mental ailments.

Her small, diverse team was exceptional, not just by their qualifications but also their dedication to the project: Neville Prescott was a neuro-radiologist; Hans Melzer, an electrical engineer, specialized in implants and prosthetics; Li Zeng, an outstanding programmer; Matt Goldstein, a renowned psychologist; Kathy Helms, a biology professor, and Gupta Vidal, a statistician. They also employed nearly two dozen assistants, graduate students, and interns. But all in all, there were less than 30 people on the payroll, not counting security and janitorial services, but Jack promised that they would get more help very soon.

The general public believed that mind reading and mind control were firmly placed in the realm of science fiction. They couldn't be more wrong! Mind reading and mind control existed right here and now and worked quite well, and the critical technology was a century-old: electroencephalograms (EEG) have been used to examine the human brain since the 1920s. Capturing and analyzing brainwaves was old news, but with enough computing power, the patterns could now be deciphered as well. In 2013, researchers were able to move a rat's tail with just the power of their minds, and flying a mind-controlled drone has been an actual sport since 2018. The contestants would wear EEG headsets, the signals were transferred to the drone, and then the drone's electronics responded to the commands. In 2019, scientists had decoded brain waves and translated them into actual words using a powerful AI. MindMelt International combined all this existing research and added the newest, most advanced equipment and computing power. The preliminary results were astonishing, and the potential for healthcare was enormous!

The project, dubbed *Mindfulness*, was progressing to everyone's satisfaction. The company has reached the first and most significant milestone in a few short months: designing and building an experimental chamber to test volunteers' mental abilities and responses. This chamber was shielded from all outside radio interference and had a myriad of sensors on the inside to receive or transmit radio signals from and to the brains of a test subject. For now, the chamber was just a somewhat claustrophobic prototype because aside from a tiny window in the door, it was fully enclosed and not much bigger than a broom closet. Inside was a plain chair where the volunteer could sit down comfortably and an intercom to communicate with the operator on the outside. Essentially, the chamber was a big EEG unit encompassing the entire body instead of placing various electrodes on the test subject's head.

When the chamber received the signals from the brain, it would simply save the wave patterns in digital form just like any EEG could. A volunteer would be given a stimulus, such as sounds, smells, tastes, textures, and various visual cues, and whatever mental response it triggered would be recorded for further analysis. But the chamber could also send previously saved and modified wave patterns to the volunteer's brain, which was the groundbreaking part of the project! For example, if a volunteer was shown pornography, it triggered arousal, and the corresponding brain waves were recorded. Then the same wave pattern was transmitted to the next volunteer, and the effects were re-recorded. Upon careful comparison and statistical analysis, Miriam's team had concluded it was possible to use the chamber to instill not just arousal but many different emotions in a test subject. By now, the team had compiled a sizable library that covered almost all possible human emotional responses.

But the chamber could do even more! Some volunteers were given cue cards ranging from simple geometrical shapes to cartoon representations of natural things to actual photos depicting complex environments. When the volunteer looked at the picture, the brain waves were recorded and subsequently analyzed via computer algorithms. The results were astonishing! For example, if the volunteer looked at a photo of Paris, the software could decipher that so well that the researchers had no trouble recognizing the Eiffel tower. But perhaps the most impressive feature was this: when the scientists gave written paragraphs or verbally read a text to the volunteer and measured the mental responses, they found that a computer could recreate the information from the thoughts of the test subject and could do so nearly without flaws in the translation. The only limitations left were the refinement of the software, the sensitivity of the recording equipment, and the processing power of the computer system!

Today, Miriam was supposed to meet with her boss, Jack Garson, to discuss future projects. However, Jack was a busy man, and he postponed last minute, but he still found time to stop by Miriam's office just before lunch. Jack was usually a level-headed guy, but today he seemed somewhat excited.

"Miriam, we need to be able to treat the minds of those who are not willing to undergo the procedure!" proposed Jack eagerly.

"Jack, we cannot force people!" contradicted Miriam. She was slightly offended that Jack would suggest such a thing, but Garson wasn't deterred and explained his reasoning.

"Think of this: a mass shooter or a terrorist is about to kill a bunch of people. If we had a remote way to change his mind, wouldn't that be a blessing?" questioned Jack and raised his eyebrows.

"I suppose, but this is a slippery slope, Jack!" replied Miriam unconvinced. Still, Jack made a point worth considering, but Melissa, Jack's personal assistant, knocked on the open office door before Miriam could do that.

"Mr. Garson, His Highness' emissary is waiting for you!" informed the woman.

"Oh yes, on my way! Thanks, Melissa!" said Jack and got up in a hurry, but before he left Miriam's office, he added, "I have to run, but think about our conversation. It is vital for the project and the company!"

"I will, Jack!" promised Miriam and closed her office door after Garson had exited.

Jack had left the room in a hurry, and he had forgotten his tablet on Miriam's desk. It was still unlocked, and Miriam took a quick look. An excel sheet was left open. It was the ledger of the company's impressive funding. Miriam had suspected that at least some money had come from military contracts, so she wasn't surprised to have her suspicions confirmed. But this assortment of financial donors was the who-is-who of totalitarian regimes, questionable democracies, big corporations, super-rich individuals, and even organized religion! The last one surprised Miriam a bit, but she realized that compulsion would be ideal for ensuring unwavering faith in an unprovable god. Miriam scrolled down the long list, and it made her stomach turn! She clicked on a few other files on the tablet, and one, in particular, affirmed her worst fears:

Project Mindfulness

Phase 1: Develop a technology to remotely influence the minds of individuals, groups, and population segments to suppress dissent and uprisings, instill resolve in police and military, overrule moral objections to commands, elevate the productivity of the workforce, increase the efficacy of advertisement, solidify religious faith, sway votes in elections, and extract information from uncooperative subjects. This technology can also be used to determine a given test subject's intellectual capacity and aptitude from childhood onward.

Phase 2: Develop a technology to override consciousness and take complete control of a person remotely. Concurrently, develop adequate safeguards against the technologies of Phase 1 and 2 for VIP customers.

Phase 3: Expand the reach of Phase 1 and 2 technologies to a global scale by integrating them into a secure satellite network.

Miriam turned the tablet off, left her office, and discreetly placed the device on a table in the reception area outside the view of the security cameras. She didn't want Garson to suspect that she had read what was on it. When Miriam returned to her office, she closed the door, sat down, and for a long time, she was just staring at her empty coffee cup on the desk. Miriam knew that all aspects of Phase 1 were already a reality. They had proven more than once that they could read at least parts of a volunteer's thoughts. They could also measure the cognitive abilities of the test subjects, and the researchers could elevate or suppress their mood. Perhaps they couldn't reliably extract specific information yet, but it was only a matter of time and computing power. With enough money, their technology could certainly be scaled up to influence a protest, a stadium, or even an entire city.

Thanks to Hans Melzer's tireless efforts, Phase 2 was also progressing beyond the proof of principle: Hans was already able to control a rat's movements at will with just the power of his mind. Of course, the rat was still implanted with a clunky interface connected to a myriad of wires, but again, it would only be a matter of time until this technology could be miniaturized, connect wirelessly, and work in humans. Miriam wasn't an expert on satellites, but she suspected that Phase 3 could also be achieved in due time and with enough resources. So, Miriam's enthusiasm for this project was draining out of her rapidly! Now, she didn't know what to do. Should she quit her job? But if Miriam did that, someone else would replace her, and that person might not object to these despicable goals. But if she continued her work, she would be directly responsible for a new type of slavery, one that might very well encompass almost all of humanity. Miriam knew that she couldn't live with herself if that happened.

"I have to sabotage the project," Miriam mumbled to herself, although she had no idea how to do that yet.

Of all her colleagues, her subordinates really, she liked Hans Melzer the best. The German engineer had the same passion for the project as she had. He was also refreshingly open and honest, and she enjoyed talking to him at work and over their lunches. Miriam needed a confidant, and Hans was probably the only one of her coworkers she could fully trust. So she sent him a quick message to meet her for lunch at the small bistro around the corner from their work. A moment later, Hans replied that he would be there.

After the waiter had brought their food, Miriam told Hans what she had seen on Jack's tablet. Hans continued to stir his soup with a spoon for a long time but didn't say anything. Miriam was beginning to think this had been a mistake, but finally, the German engineer looked at her again.

"Miriam, who is not getting along in our group?" asked Hans cryptically.

"Well, that's easy: Kathy and Matt always butt heads!" she laughed and elaborated, "Matt wanted to finish the project yesterday, but Kathy likes to put the breaks on it with all her ethical concerns!"

"In the past, I've sided with Matt because I want to finish up so that we can start helping people," replied Hans thoughtfully.

"But...?" wondered Miriam, unsure what the German man implied.

"But now I think our technology will be abused, and Kathy was the first victim!" stated Hans and sighed.

"What do you mean?" Miriam demanded to know.

"I finished and tested the new modifications of the shielded chamber on Monday. It worked fine, and it is ready for the volunteers tomorrow. I left around 8:00 PM to get dinner on my way home before the restaurant closed. When I got back the next morning, someone had used the chamber," Hans informed her. Miriam was concerned because nobody was supposed to access the sensitive machinery without Hans being present.

"Who?" she asked.

"I don't know who operated the equipment. Whoever did it meticulously wiped the procedural logs, but they forgot about the operational log. It shows that the chamber was active from 10:02 PM Monday evening to 1:16 AM Tuesday morning," observed Hans.

"Oh my god, that's over three hours! We never activate it for more than a few minutes when we test the volunteers. We have no idea what prolonged exposure can do to the brain; it could be hazardous!" gasped Miriam, now genuinely worried.

"As I said, I don't know for sure who operated it, but I know Kathy was inside the chamber!" elaborated the German engineer.

"Kathy? How do you know that?" inquired Miriam, disturbed by this new information.

"I found a scrap of pink fabric underneath the chair. Nobody else wears pink but her. Also, I believe she wasn't in the chamber voluntarily. When I checked the electrodes, I found a piece of a zip tie, one much bigger than the type I use for the wiring!" noted Hans and wrinkled his forehead.

"Wow...," exclaimed Miriam incredulously. She wanted to ask more questions but then let Hans finish his thoughts first.

"When I got in on Tuesday, I saw that the dials weren't the way I've left them. The chamber electrodes had been switched from reception to transmission. I don't know what else they have done to Kathy, but the last the settings they used were those for arousal!" said Hans.

"Arousal?" wondered Miriam, not sure why anyone would use that particular setting.

"Yes, and it worked. I came in on Tuesday before the custodians had cleaned up, and I saw a used condom in the trashcan by the sink!" concluded the German man.

"That's rape! Or something like that! Hans, this is abhorrent!" blurted Miriam exasperatedly.

"Don't look behind you, Miriam. Matt and Kathy are having lunch together at the table in the corner. Go to the restroom, take an inconspicuous look at them, and tell me what you saw when you get back!" instructed Hans. Miriam got up and walked to the restroom to wash her hands. When she got back a few minutes later, she was visibly trembling.

"Kathy is spoon-feeding Matt with dessert! Kathy is married, but they act like lovers!" whispered Miriam with worries in her eyes.

"And just last Friday, they were yelling at each other in the meeting!" added Hans and concluded, "Miriam, they brainwashed her!"

"Oh my god!" gasped Miriam and asked fearfully, "do you remember who was still in the building when you left Monday evening?"

"Neville Prescott was still working on the MRI, but his technician left at the same time as me. Kathy and Matt were in their offices, and there was light upstairs, so I believe Jack was still working, too," recollected Hans and added, "and one of our buff security guards was seeing me out the door!"

"So, just Jack, Matt, Kathy, Neville, and the guard?" verified Miriam.

"Yes, I believe so!" concurred Hans.

"Neville is absentminded and aloof. He gets so engrossed in the work that he forgets our meetings!" observed Miriam and added, "but I don't think he is in on this!"

"Agreed. The guy is as smart as he is asocial, but he wouldn't take part in something like that!" concurred Hans and suggested: "We could ask him if he saw or heard something on Monday, but I doubt we will get anything useful because he just isn't aware of his surroundings."

"I will try anyway," replied Miriam.

"Miriam, I didn't sign up for what happened to Kathy and what you found on Jack's tablet!" stated Hans firmly and declared, "you will have my resignation by tonight!"

"No, Hans!" exclaimed Miriam quite loudly, but then she whispered, "you cannot resign! I thought the same thing, but we must stop this from the inside!"

"Miriam...," Hans started saying, but Miriam interrupted him.

"Hans, please! I need your help! I cannot do this alone!" she begged.

"But how can we stop it? If we go to the police, they'll never get a search warrant for Jack's tablet, and they wouldn't believe that Kathy was brainwashed and raped either," countered Hans and added, "she would probably tell them how much she is in love with Matt now!"

"True, and this is so scary! But we have to do something, perhaps sabotage the technology?" proposed Miriam.

"But how?" questioned Hans and noted, "Sure, we can throw a few wrenches in there to slow it down, but as it is, you and I could be replaced quite easily now. Any third-rate engineer or scientist could finish our endeavors!"

"I know...," mumbled Miriam and said firmly, "I'll think of something, Hans! Please, don't resign!"

"OK, Miriam. I stay for now, but this goes against everything I believe in!" remarked Hans and got up.

"Thank you, Hans. I understand you so well, but we will find a solution!" insisted Miriam as she followed him out of the restaurant.

"I hope so," said Hans with doubts in his voice as they walked back to the office.

After lunch, Miriam found Neville Prescott in his lab. He was tinkering with the MRI equipment when Miriam entered, but he didn't seem to notice her until she spoke up.

"Hello, Neville! I lost my bracelet in the hallway on Monday evening. It's not very valuable, but it is a family heirloom, and I'm fond of it. I remember you were still here when I left. Did you find it by any chance?" lied Miriam.

"Regretfully not, my dear! I left around half past nine that day, and I'm afraid I didn't notice anything in the hallway!" replied Neville jovially. It sounded odd, but of course, Miriam had worked with Neville long enough to know that it was just the way the British man talked.

"Was anyone else still here?" inquired Miriam.

"Jack was driving off the lot when I exited the building. Perhaps he fetched it?" wondered Neville. But, of course, it would make sense that even this absentminded man would notice Jack Garson's fancy Lamborghini. So, Garson wasn't here when the chamber was running at 10:02 PM. But, of course, that only left Matt and the security guard as suspects.

"OK, I will ask him, too!" she responded with a friendly smile.

"No problem, Miriam. Maybe you ought to check with Matt and Kathy, too. I seemed to recall that they were still here when I left, but don't take my word for it, I'm not the most observant guy!" replied Neville and gave her a thin smile. Miriam had to suppress a giggle, but now she was pretty sure that Neville wasn't part of what had happened that day.

"Thanks, Neville! I'll see you later at the meeting!" she said.

"Cheers!" replied Neville and promptly turned his attention to the equipment again.

When she left Prescott's lab, Miriam briefly considered questioning the security guard, but she couldn't remember which one of them was on duty that Monday evening. Also, she didn't like these gruff, bulky men who never spoke a word. If she was frank, they scared the heck out of her! Miriam stopped by Hans' office and informed him that only Matt and the guard were in the building when the chamber was active. Hans confirmed that it was his suspicion all along that Matt had been the culprit. Miriam went back to her office and sat at her desk for a while. The group meeting wasn't going to start for another 30 minutes, and she decided to call her ex-boyfriend to ask for a favor. John and Miriam hadn't parted on the best terms, but John was a highly-skilled computer engineer despite all his faults, and that's just what she needed right now.

"Miri, that's a surprise…," said John after he picked up the call.

"John, I need a favor!" replied Miriam, straight to the point.

"You dumped me, and now you are asking for favors?" wondered John and chuckled.

"I didn't call to rehash our relationship, but I dumped you because you used me to hack into a server and stole sensitive information! I got in trouble, but I kept my mouth shut. If I hadn't, you would be in prison right now!" summarized Miriam and added firmly, "you owe me, John!"

"Fine, what do you want?" asked John after a moment of hesitation.

"I'll send you a list of names, and I want you to find out whatever you can about these people," elaborated Miriam.

"You want me to do a simple search? You could just google them, you know!" laughed John.

"No, I need more than that! Quite literally, the fate of the world might depend on it!" urged Miriam.

"Miri, you are overly dramatic again. I always hated that about you!" complained John.

"I'm not overly dramatic this time! Please do this for me, and be very, very careful!" warned Miriam and added, "these are dangerous people!"

"Sure, send me the list, but encrypt it first, and I'll get back to you in a few days," remarked John and insisted firmly, "but then we are even, OK?"

"Yes, then we are even, John!" agreed Miriam quickly.

Two days later, Miriam got a text message on her phone.

Miri, for old time's sake, let's meet at the restaurant where we had our first date. Tonight at 7:00 PM?

John was a lot of things, but he wasn't a romantic. Miriam knew that he wanted to meet because he must have gotten some results for her. She quickly replied yes, deleted his message, and looked at the clock. It was already 6:00 PM, and the restaurant was pretty far away from MindMelt. She powered off her computer, put her coat on, left her office, and locked the door with the security code. On her way out, she noticed that the entrance was now guarded by two hulking security guards, one of which carried an automatic rifle. They looked at Miriam suspiciously but didn't stop her from leaving the building. When she got to the restaurant, John was waiting in front of it, smoking a cigarette. Another habit Miriam didn't like about him, but she wasn't going to complain about it today.

"Walk with me," said John and extinguished his smoke.

"What did you find?" asked Miriam.

"Here, take this. But don't use it at work!" replied John, and slipped a USB drive into her purse.

"Anything suspicious?" wondered Miriam.

"I'm sorry that I called you overly dramatic," apologized John and explained, "only four people on that list are who they claim to be!"

"Who?" Miriam demanded to know. She had included every single person in the building, including the guards and custodians. But she could hardly believe that only four people out of 39 employees at Mindmelt were genuine!

"Yes, the German guy, the British doctor, his technician, and you! Everyone else has fake or sanitized identities, with ties to all kinds of governments, corporations, and even criminal organizations!" said John and added, "your boss is shady on every level! Did you know he met that Syrian dictator in person?"

"Wow, but I can't even say I'm surprised," answered Miriam and shook her head.

"Your security guards are not your average mall cops either. These guys work for a private military contractor, and all of them are former special forces – Green Barrettes, Navy Seals, Delta Force, and so on. Heck, not even your janitors are who they claim to be!" elaborated John.

"What about Kathy Helms?" inquired Miriam.

"She really is a full professor at a university in Michigan...," noted John slowly, unsure if he should say more.

"But?" pressed Miriam.

"She also works for a watchdog organization on the hush. You know, the kind that ferrets out corruption and unethical conduct in government and industry," explained John.

"So that's why they brainwashed her!" exclaimed Miriam.

"Wait, what?" asked John, confused, and stopped walking.

"Kathy was our conscience. She always reminded us of the moral implications of our research. But now, she just agrees with everything and is madly in love with Matt Goldstein!"

"Matt Goldstein is missing and presumed dead for the last two years. So whoever this guy is, he isn't Matt Goldstein!" corrected John and asked: "Brainwashed? Be honest, Miri - does this mind control stuff really work?"

"Yes, and much better than you think!" replied Miriam with a sigh.

"Damn!" cussed John and warned, "Miri, I still hate how it ended between us, but you have to get the hell out of there before you get hurt. MindMelt International makes my little server hack look like a prank!"

"I can't, John! I have to stop what they are doing, or all of us will be brainless puppets very soon!" insisted Miriam desperately.

"Shit! If mind control works, you weren't lying about the end of the world!" conceded John and asked, "could you go to the police?"

"No, there is no way they would ever believe me. Worse yet, there are no laws against messing with someone's mind! No laws mean that there will be no arrests and no prosecution!" explained Miriam and divulged, "this imposter Matt Goldstein forcefully brainwashed Kathy with our technology, then he raped her, and now she is doting over her assailant. There is no doubt that he'll get away with it!"

"Miri, I cannot help you any further. If they find out that I snooped around, I'm as good as dead, and you will be too!" warned John and stated seriously, "this is too big to leave any loose ends!"

"I know that now, and I'm very sorry that I dragged you into this!" apologized Miriam and added, "John, forget that we ever talked, and if you never hear from me again, you know why!"

"I know I was a jerk, but I sincerely hoped we could patch things up between us. But now, I think I'll accept a job offer on the other side of the country, just to be far away from here. Please be safe, Miri!" replied John somberly and gave her a firm hug. Then he quickly got into his car and drove off.

The following day, Miriam emailed Jack to let him know that she would be late for work because she wanted to check something at the library. Then she called Hans and told him to meet her in a community college computer lab nearby. When Hans got there, Miriam showed him the profiles John had compiled.

"Unbelievable! Nobody is who they claim to be, and nobody can be trusted!" gasped Hans when they scrolled through the files together.

"Only you, Neville, his assistant Agnes, and me," concurred Miriam and wondered, "do they represent competing factions, or are they all united in evil?"

"Who knows, but it doesn't matter: none of these people should have access! Imagine if a drug cartel uses our technology to get more people hooked on their poison!" contemplated Hans and shook his head.

"We can't go to the police, so we will have to stop them at their own game!" suggested Miriam cryptically.

"What do you mean?" wondered Hans.

"It's just a thought, but what if we use our technology to turn these awful people into good ones?" proposed Miriam.

"We would be no better than they are, Miriam!" protested Hans and shook his head.

"But we would quite possibly save the world!" insisted Miriam firmly.

"Yes, I know what you mean, but still…," replied Hans, sighed deeply, and added, "I will think about it. But, for now, we should keep quiet and play along!"

"Right, and maybe slow things down as much as we can!" agreed Miriam.

"Yes, the chamber will undergo some unscheduled repairs for the next two weeks. Perhaps you should cancel the volunteers, Miriam?" suggested Hans and winked at her.

"Got it! We will have to adjust the schedule promptly!" concurred Miriam and grinned at him.

When Miriam got to her office later that day, she immediately knew that someone had searched it. To the casual observer, everything would appear just the way Miriam had left it the day before, but one small but crucial detail was different: Miriam was lefthanded, yet her empty coffee mug was now on the right side of the computer monitor. Miriam checked her drawers and file cabinets but could not find anything amiss. She looked at the door lock and number keypad, but nothing indicated tampering. MindMelt International had no IT department yet, but Li Zheng also handled all the computer access and networking issues as the lead programmer. Miriam knew that only Li could reset the codes for the office door locks. Therefore, he must have searched her office or facilitated the search for someone else. This development was alarming, and Miriam feared that she was already being watched. She talked to Hans about it, and the German engineer was worried as well, but there was very little they could do other than be extra careful.

Kathy was missing without excuse at the next group meeting,

and Miriam worried about that. Kathy was very busy juggling her job at MindMelt and her work at the university. But in the past, she had always informed Miriam when she would be missing time. Jack was also not present today, but Miriam knew that her boss often had to entertain important visitors, so his absence was not unusual. Hans reported that the testing chamber had to go offline for repairs and essential upgrades. The team was disappointed, but Hans convinced them that the safety of the volunteers should not be compromised. Just as Li Zheng was the makeshift IT department, Hans ran facilities as a side job. In that function, Hans announced that the city's fire department would send an inspector very soon. To comply, Hans would have to check all the smoke detectors, safety equipment, and fire extinguishers in the office and laboratory areas. Suddenly, Jack rushed into the conference room!

"I'm sorry to inform you, but Kathy's family called me just now. She had a mental breakdown yesterday. She tried to harm her husband and herself. Kathy is fine now but heavily sedated and under observation at a closed mental facility. Her husband believes that the stress of juggling two jobs got to her. Kathy did important work for the company, and we wish her a speedy recovery!" announced Jack thoughtfully.

Most people were at least mildly concerned, but Matt Goldstein, or whoever he truly was, showed no emotions at all. Miriam suspected immediately that this breakdown resulted from the long exposure in the chamber and possibly the trauma of being raped afterward. She saw in Hans' face that he was thinking the same thoughts. The remainder of the meeting went on as usual. After all the researchers had presented their data, the staff left the conference room and returned to their work.

The next few days progressed without incidents, but it became clear that Kathy would not be returning to MindMelt at all. Jack was already scheduling interviews for Kathy's old position, and Miriam had a stack of résumés on her desk for review. Hans had reassembled the testing chamber today and declared it fully operational. He had also announced that MindMelt would pass the upcoming fire inspection with flying colors. But after Hans had sent out the good news via email, he was called to Garson's office and had been there for the last hour. Miriam got a little worried, but eventually, the engineer passed by her door and motioned to her to accompany him to his lab.

"This was bizarre!" said Hans quietly, shook his head, and explained, "Jack asked me about the status of the chamber. I told him that I fixed it ahead of schedule and was ready for volunteers again. He made me explain everything in great detail as if he knew something and hoped to catch me in a lie. I went into highly technical stuff, and eventually, he seemed convinced and congratulated me on a job well done. He even poured me a drink, some expensive old Scotch!"

"First, they search my office, and now you are being interrogated. Do you think they suspect something?" asked Miriam in a hushed voice.

"Beats me, but we have to be very careful now, Miriam! I don't think we can slow the project any further without raising suspicion!" advised Hans as he locked down the computers that control the chamber equipment. Hans had added some password protection after he had discovered the unauthorized use.

"Agreed!" said Miriam and nodded her head.

"There was something else: Jack asked me if I had any ideas for personal shielding," divulged Hans and added, "I told him that the easiest solution would be a helmet, but Garson wants something more sophisticated and unobtrusive than a tinfoil hat!"

"Have you looked into that before?" asked Miriam, and she wondered why Hans' face was suddenly so red. It seemed odd because it looked as if Hans had high blood pressure, but he was in good health and a rather skinny man.

"After what happened to Kathy, it became one of my priorities. I have a simple, discreet solution, but I haven't told Garson about it," replied Hans, wiping some sweat from his brow.

"Good! Keep that to yourself until we need it!" concurred Miriam.

"Miriam, I have to leave. It's my wife's birthday, and I'm already late!" disclosed Hans, nervously wringing his hands.

"Oh, of course, and Happy Birthday to your wife! I hope you have a nice celebration!" said Miriam and smiled broadly at her friend. Now, Hans didn't look good, and Miriam worried a little but dismissed her concerns again: the German was probably just stressed out over the upcoming birthday party.

"Thanks, Miriam, we'll talk more tomorrow!" replied Hans, waved goodbye to her, and was swiftly out the door.

But Hans would never talk to Miriam again! After he got home, Hans wished his wife a happy birthday and gifted her with a beautiful pearl necklace; then, he suffered a massive stroke and dropped dead to the floor before they even had dinner. When Jack announced it the next day, most were shocked, but none more than Miriam. She couldn't believe that her friend and colleague was gone, and she openly cried at the meeting. Miriam remembered that Hans didn't look healthy before he left the company last night, and a stroke could happen to anyone at any time, but she remained suspicious of his sudden death. Would MindMelt go so far as to kill someone outright, she wondered. After Jack adjourned, Miriam went home early because the terrible news made her feel ill. However, when she passed by Hans' old office, she saw that the custodians were already clearing it out, which convinced Miriam that her friend didn't die of natural causes.

Hans had passed away on Thursday night, and now it was Sunday morning. Miriam had just gotten out of bed when her doorbell rang. She checked the camera feed, and it was some kind of delivery service. Miriam opened the door, and the courier gave her a large manilla envelope from a law firm. She signed for the delivery, gave the man a tip, and closed the door again. Miriam got some scissors and opened the envelope. Inside was a letter, a USB stick, some kind of syringe, and a tiny plastic case that contained a gold-plated microchip. Miriam sat down at the kitchen table and read the letter:

Miriam, when you get this letter, I will be dead. You are a good person, and I very much enjoyed working with you. We both wanted to create something good, something wonderful, but they wouldn't let us. You were right: we have to stop them with their own game! Inside this envelope, you'll find a microchip, a delivery device, and a USB drive. The chip needs to be implanted in your neck, at the very base of your skull. I got the special syringe from a veterinarian; it's what they use to chip a cat or dog. Just follow the instructions, and it should be almost painless. If they try to brainwash you, the chip will resonate with the incoming signal and scramble it. However, it won't be pleasant for you. You will feel confused and nauseous, but it should protect you!

Also, I have installed emitters in the smoke detectors in all labs and offices at MindMelt International. They are networked to the backup system for the chamber. Go to the computer terminal in the shipping and receiving area when the time comes. Plugin the USB stick, leave the building immediately and take Neville and Agnes with you. The program will run about five minutes later and should finish within half an hour. With the chip, you will be protected, but I don't want to take any chances. Miriam, you are the only one who can still stop this, at least until they'll try again someday. Good luck and take care!

Your friend, Hans!

Miriam couldn't stop the tears! For a good hour, she was sobbing into the pillows on her couch. Finally, Miriam regained some composure and read the instructions for the microchip. She went to the bathroom, disinfected her neck, and used a mirror to place the delivery contraption in the correct spot. Then she held her breath and pushed the chip under her skin. It hurt a little, but it was bearable. Next, she put Hans' letter in the shredder and the USB drive into her purse. She memorized the instructions on how to use it and then destroyed that paper as well. Finally, she went to her fridge, poured herself a big glass of vodka, and downed it in a few gulps. Miriam commanded the voice-controlled AI to play some soft music, then she turned the lights off and crawled back into bed.

It was Monday morning, and Miriam had a hangover. In her grief over Hans' death, she had finished the whole bottle of vodka the day earlier and now paid the price. But the headache was bearable, and after a few cups of coffee, she was able to do some work again. Jack had requested an extensive report for the investors, and it would take Miriam all day to finish it. By 9:45 PM, she was finally ready to send the draft to Jack for review. To her surprise, Garson was still at the office and replied almost immediately:

I'll be downstairs to go over it with you in a few minutes!

Miriam cleaned up her desk and waited for her boss to knock on the door. While she was organizing a file cabinet, the lights in her room suddenly went out. A power failure, wondered Miriam, unable to see anything in the office since it had no windows. Then, there was a click coming from the door lock. The door opened, and someone blinded her with a powerful flashlight. While Miriam was disoriented, another person rushed in, grabbed her from behind, and put a rag over her mouth and nose. Chloroform! It was Miriam's last thought before she passed out.

She was sitting on the chair in the testing chamber when she regained consciousness. Her hands and feet were bound with zip ties. She could see someone operating the equipment through the tiny window in the door; however, it was too dark to make out a face. But she could see the bulky shape of a security guard by the entrance to the lab. Slowly, she bent forward, and with some effort, she could reach the button for the intercom. She switched it on and listened to the conversation.

"Can you hack the password?" asked a man, and Miriam recognized the voice. It was Matt Goldstein's imposter!

"Yes, just a minute. I will use the administrator override," replied another man, undoubtedly Li Zheng.

"Do we have to wake her up before we start?" wondered a third man, none other than her boss, Jack Garson.

"She has to be conscious for this, but the anesthetic should wear off pretty soon," answered Matt.

"Sir, a woman just passed by in the hallway!" reported the security guard.

"Who is it? Did she see anything?" asked Jack, alarmed.

"I can't say. Should I take care of it?" inquired the guard.

"Yes, see to that, and let me know who it was!" ordered Garson.

"Yes, Sir!" replied the guard and left the room.

For a few minutes, nothing was happening while the three men were working silently on the machinery. But eventually, the equipment started up. Miriam hoped that the chip in her neck would protect her, but she hoped even more that they would not use the arousal settings. If Miriam had to endure rape and at the same time was forced to pretend that she enjoyed it, she would prefer to be dead instead.

"OK, it's running. Which settings should I use?" asked Li.

"Do you have something to make her compliant?" wondered Garson.

"Maybe just have some fun with her as we did with that other bitch? This one doesn't look half bad!" suggested Matt and chuckled.

"No, you don't touch her. If we can get her conditioned properly, she is still useful for now!" countered Garson.

"Fine, but she knows too much. We are taking a risk if this doesn't work!" contradicted Matt.

"Let me worry about that! Besides, the chamber will most likely turn her brain into mush, and then we don't have to be concerned about her anymore!" replied Garson dismissively.

"I found brain wave patterns for compliance and serenity in the library!" interjected Li.

"OK, wake her up, then use serenity to calm her down and compliance to condition her!" instructed Garson. Matt walked over to the chamber and peered through the tiny window. Miriam pretended to be waking up.

"She's awake! You can start it up!" said Matt and turned around.

Miriam braced herself for a mental onslaught, but nothing could have prepared her for what came next: the chip worked perfectly, but the side effects were horrifying! For the next hour, Miriam experienced continuous hallucinations of all her senses: Miriam's skin crawled, her eyes saw psychedelic colors, her ears heard screaming voices, her mouth tasted like copper, and her nose smelled non-existing smoke. Her muscles contracted and relaxed on their own because Miriam had lost all control over her motor skills. Even her heart sped up and slowed down randomly. A few times, she thought she would pass out from the dizziness, and several more times, Miriam emptied her stomach until only bile was coming up her esophagus. Then, after an eternity, it finally stopped.

"This one reacted more violently to the treatment," Miriam

heard Matt saying through the intercom.

"Should I continue?" asked Li.

"Let's see if it worked. You exposed Kathy for too long, and she broke down a week later. I want Miriam to be functional for a while!" replied Garson. At that moment, the big security guard entered the lab again.

"Sir, the intruder is apprehended. I'm sure she saw what happened in here," reported the guard.

"Oh, well! We will fix that later!" decided Garson.

"OK, let's get this one out and scan her!" declared Matt as he opened the chamber. Miriam pretended to be nearly unconscious when Matt cut her restraints. The big guard picked her up effortlessly and carried her over his shoulder. Matt put the chloroform rag over her nose and mouth, and Miriam passed out again. When she woke up again, she was sitting at the desk in her office. She noticed that her computer was on and the report she had finished earlier was displayed on the screen. Jack was sitting next to her.

"What...what happened...," she stammered, pretending to be disoriented and confused.

"Miriam, you got ill and passed out. Are you OK now?" asked Garson sympathetically.

"Oh, I'm sorry!" replied Miriam calmly and added with a smile, "yes, I'm fine. Thank you, Jack!"

"I have marked the changes I would like you to make in the report!" instructed Jack and pointed at the screen.

"Of course, I will edit it right away!" answered Miriam compliantly and immediately started typing on her keyboard. Jack observed keenly, but then he interrupted her a moment later.

"Specifically, we have to add something about protective equipment. Has Hans ever talked to you about that?" inquired Jack. Miriam stopped typing and pretended to think about the question.

"Yes, he said that a simple shielded helmet would work!" replied Miriam a moment later.

"Ah, the helmet. Did Hans have any other ideas?" asked Jack and looked at her expectantly.

"No, that's all Hans mentioned to me," answered Miriam and smiled absurdly. Then she turned her attention to the report and started editing once more. Jack watched her for a minute longer before he spoke again.

"This has time until tomorrow, Miriam. Now go home and get some sleep!" suggested Jack and gently touched her arm.

"Yes, I'm a little tired. Thank you, Jack!" replied Miriam sweetly and stood up. Her legs were shaking, and she had problems standing straight, but mentally, she was unequivocal.

"No problem. Can you drive, or should we call you a ride?" asked Jack when he noticed that she was a little unsteady.

"Oh, I'm fine; just a bit tired!" said Miriam softly and put her coat on. Jack walked her out of the office and briefly talked to Matt, waiting by the door with the security guard.

"It worked like a charm!" Miriam overheard Garson saying to them as she slowly walked in the hallway towards the exit.

"Great, but now we still have to take care of the visitor!" Matt reminded him.

"Yes, I'll be right there!" acknowledged Garson and ran a few steps to catch up with Miriam.

"I'll walk you to your car, Miriam!" said Garson, examining her demeanor.

"That is so kind of you, Jack!" replied Miriam and smiled inanely at Garson. He looked delighted.

Once Miriam was in her car and Garson had returned to the building, she could finally drop the act. She was terrified, disgusted, and felt ill again, but nothing was left in her stomach, or she would have vomited once more. When she got home, she put her soiled clothes in the washing machine and took a long, cold shower. The frigid water cleared out the cobwebs in her mind.

"You were a genius, and I will always be in your debt, Hans! You saved me from a fate worse than death!" she mumbled to herself as she toweled off.

After the shower, Miriam took some medicine for her queasy stomach and went straight to bed. When she arrived at work the following day, Jack had called for an emergency meeting. Miriam was curious and concerned when Garson started his speech.

"Tragedy struck us again! The police informed me earlier that Agnes had an accident last night on her way home from a bar. She had a few drinks too many. As a result, her car veered off the road and hit a tree, killing her instantly!" he recounted somberly.

Miriam listened to Jack's announcement, and it shocked her, but she didn't let her face betray her emotions. She was determined to play the calm, compliant employee for as long as it would take. After Jack had given his spiel, Miriam studied the reactions of everyone in the room. Most had somber expressions, but Neville's face was as hard as a stone. Agnes was his assistant, and Neville didn't seem to believe the story about the car crash, but he didn't say anything. Miriam recalled that the guard mentioned an intruder while conditioning Miriam in the chamber. Could that have been Agnes? But then Miriam remembered that she had said goodnight to Agnes long before she finished her report. No, Agnes couldn't have been in the building anymore.

After the meeting, Jack talked to Miriam about replacing Agnes and Hans. Miriam responded softly and submissively to everything Garson had to say. After a few minutes, Melissa stopped by and interrupted their conversation to alert Jack that another visitor would arrive at MindMelt shortly. Jack left in a hurry, and Miriam checked her pocket for the USB stick. Then she made her way to the shipping and receiving area. Miriam used the inter-office phone to call Neville's lab when she got there. He picked up a moment later.

"Neville, can you please come to the shipping area right now? There is a big delivery here for you!" lied Miriam.

"Of course, I'm on my way!" replied Neville and hung up.

When the British doctor got there, Miriam plugged in the USB drive. A screen opened up, and the program started running.

"Where is delivery?" asked Neville and looked around.

"Neville, would you please take a short walk with me?" replied Miriam evasively and moved to the backdoor. Neville just nodded and followed her. Miriam led them through the parking lot and away from the office. Neville walked silently next to her, but suddenly he stopped.

"There is no delivery. You want to talk about Agnes, don't you?" he remarked firmly.

"I wanted you to be safe, Neville. But what about Agnes?" wondered Miriam.

"I've worked with Agnes for 15 years. She never drank a drop of alcohol. She couldn't because she had severe reactions to it!" explained Neville and stated somberly, "I don't care what the police report said! It was murder, not a drunk driving accident!"

"Oh my god...," stammered Miriam and exclaimed angrily, "that's another crime they must answer for!"

"I'm not as unaware as you thought, Miriam," maintained Neville and elaborated, "I've known for a while that there was something bloody wrong at MindMelt – the huge funding, and the foreign visitors, the paramilitary guards, then Kathy's sudden illness, then Hans, and finally Agnes."

"Neville, I don't know if I can explain this or if I even should, but you are right: MindMelt is evil; there is no other way to put it. But they are experiencing a reckoning right now!" replied Miriam ominously.

"And you got me out of the building because you knew that I wasn't part of it, just as I knew that you were not part of them!" responded Neville and nodded.

"How did you know?" wondered Miriam surprised.

"Matt and Garson asked me to look at some brain scans early this morning. I recognized them; they were yours!" explained the British radiologist.

"Mine?" pondered Miriam, a little confused.

"Do you remember when you helped me set up the equipment? We took a few scans of your brain to test it out. To the untrained eye, all brains look the same, but I can tell the difference!" stated Neville confidently.

"Why did they ask you to look at my brain?" inquired Miriam.

"They wanted to know if I could see any damage. Of course, there was no damage, but I told Garson it was inconclusive. Matt and Garson were satisfied with that!" elaborated Neville, and Miriam was relieved to hear that there was nothing wrong with her brain after the prolonged exposure in the chamber.

"Have they asked you to look at other brain scans before?" wondered Miriam and looked at him.

"Only once! I didn't recognize that brain at the time, but it showed serious degradation. Now I believe it was Kathy Helms' scan!" explained the British doctor and divulged, "Agnes died because she came back to the office last night when they stuffed you in the chamber! She left a note inside the MRI before they took her away; that's how I know her death wasn't an accident and that you aren't part of their machinations!"

"I'm so sorry, Neville!" replied Miriam sadly and elaborated, "MindMelt never intended to help people. Their agenda was to sell the technology to the worst of the worst humanity has to offer! I saw the manifest on Garson's tablet!"

"I believe you!" observed Neville and asked: "What did you do in the shipping area?"

"Truthfully, I'm not sure. I started a program that Hans wrote and had sent to me postmortem. I followed his instructions, but I don't know what it does!" explained Miriam truthfully.

"They killed Hans too, didn't they?" speculated Neville and frowned.

"Yes, they did, but I'm not sure how," confirmed Miriam.

"Kathy's brain was an atrophic mess. How did you survive the chamber, Miriam?" questioned Neville and changed the subject. Miriam wasn't ready to reveal her secret just yet, so she answered rather vaguely.

"Perhaps I have to thank Hans for that too? I felt nauseous and disoriented in the chamber, but the conditioning didn't work," disclosed Miriam and added, "with Kathy, they used the arousal settings, but with me, they applied serenity and compliance! After it was done, I just pretended to be calm and submissive, and it fooled them!"

"Interesting! I've found that some brains are more resistant than others. You were fortunate, indeed!" postulated Neville and asked politely, "I have the feeling we might need an alibi. Would you fancy a cup of tea, Miriam?"

"Good point, Neville! There is a coffee shop across the street. I'm sure they serve some tea as well!" suggested Miriam, and Neville nodded in agreement.

After having coffee and tea, Miriam and Neville decided to return to the company. They entered through the shipping area again. Miriam checked the computer screen, and Hans' program had stopped. She removed the USB drive and shut down the terminal.

"Neville, since I'm somehow resistant, let me go in first!" proposed Miriam.

"Of course, call me when it's all clear!" replied Neville and waited by the door.

Miriam noticed how quiet the building was when she entered the office area, but she found nothing unusual until she passed by Gupta's open office door. The man was dangling by an extension cord from a hook in the ceiling. Miriam was shocked and disgusted, even more so because Gupta's bladder and bowels had emptied upon death, and the stench was awful. Miriam quickly checked the other offices and found similarly gruesome scenes. Li had electrocuted himself, and Melissa was lying in a pool of blood, her wrists being slit. The bodies of the security guards blocked the main hallway, and Miriam had to step over them. The men had ended their lives by blowing their brains out. Finally, Miriam went up the stairs to Jack Garson's office. She found him sitting at his desk, dead and slumped over his tablet. She couldn't tell how he had died, but she noticed an empty bottle of expensive Scotch on the floor and suddenly recalled that Garson gave that drink to Hans just before his death. It was likely that Jack had poisoned Hans, but now he had died the very same way, and Miriam appreciated ironic justice.

Miriam went back downstairs to check the various lab spaces for more dead bodies, and she wouldn't be disappointed. Every single MindMelt employee had committed suicide! But she couldn't find the Matt Goldstein imposter, which worried her! Miriam concluded that Hans' program must have used the setting for suicidal depression. On the one hand, she was appalled by how ruthless Hans had been, but on the other hand, this was probably the only viable solution: the creators had to die with the project, and the project died with its creators!

When Miriam entered Hans' lab, she was greeted by an acrid odor of burnt wire insulation. The equipment they had used to power and control the chamber was still smoldering. Ostensibly, Hans' program must have also short-circuited the sensitive machinery. Good, it will take them longer to rebuild this, thought Miriam. When she passed by the shielded chamber, the door suddenly opened, a man rushed out and grabbed Miriam by the throat.

"I knew it was you! We should have just killed you!" screamed Matt Goldstein furiously.

The man looked terrible! His face was covered in sweat, and his blood-shot eyes were constantly twitching. He could barely stand straight, but he was determined to end her life. Miriam realized that Matt must have escaped the mass suicide by hiding in the chamber, the only place in the building that was shielded. Miriam fought him off as best as she could, but apparently, Matt had some combat training, and even in his desolate physical state, he overpowered her quite effortlessly. Matt pressed Miriam down on a lab counter and used his weight to keep her in place while he choked her.

"How did you resist the compulsion, bitch?" Matt demanded to know, loosening his grip on her throat just enough for her to answer.

"I don't know!" rasped Miriam, coughing and gasping for air. She would rather die than tell this despicable man about the chip.

"I'm gonna make this very, very painful until you tell me your little secret!" threatened Matt and restricted her airflow again. Miriam was about to pass out when she heard a gunshot. A second later, another one and Matt's hold on her neck suddenly loosened. She felt his body sliding off hers. Gasping for air, she opened her eyes and saw Neville, holding a pistol from one of the security guards.

"Thank you, Neville!" said Miriam gratefully in between coughing fits, but now Neville kept the gun trained on her.

"As I said, I'm not as unaware as it seems. I saw the chip at the base of your skull on the scans!" observed Neville.

"Hans made that chip for me so that they couldn't brainwash me as they did with Kathy!" admitted Miriam, ashamed that she hadn't told Neville the truth earlier.

"I suspected that, but that makes you the most dangerous of them all now. Not only do you know the technology, but you are also immune to it!" contemplated Neville somberly and aimed at her head.

"Neville...," protested Miriam fearfully, but the British doctor didn't let her finish.

"We both know that they will rebuild this project. But without you, without us, it will take a lot longer!" stated Neville firmly.

"Neville, we will get you a chip, and then we will fight this together!" urged Miriam desperately.

"The chip will not help us, only them if they get a hold of it. These people don't need our technology to make us work for them again: they will find us, capture us, blackmail, threaten or torture our loved ones or us until we comply! They will stop at nothing because this is for all the marbles - complete world domination!" proclaimed Neville and added sadly, "We are alone, Miriam: nobody will help us, and nobody will protect us because nobody will believe it!"

Miriam was about to respond, perhaps beg for her life, but deep inside, she knew that Neville was right. She worried about what could happen to John and her family, and she couldn't bear that thought. And so, she just closed her eyes and waited for the inevitable.

"I'm awfully sorry, Miriam, but for humanity's sake, I cannot let you live! Neither of us can!" concluded Neville with regret and pulled the trigger. For a moment, Neville looked sadly at Miriam's lifeless body before he put the gun in his mouth and ended it all.

5. ARTIFICIAL INTELLIGENCE

Roger Ingram had been retired from the corporate world for a couple of years now and lived a very modest life in a small suburban home. He was happy, although a little lonely, at least he had his 10-year-old tuxedo cat, Boots, to keep him company. But money was tight, and it would be tough to make ends meet on social security alone without his small business on the side. Roger was a tech scavenger. Whenever a company moved or went out of business, he would buy their used equipment and sell it again for a small profit. Roger bought everything from small appliances to computers and other electronics, machinery, tools, and laboratory equipment. Then, he would clean, test, and repair the items in his garage at home. Once Roger was satisfied that the equipment was in good working order, he would update his website inventory with photos and specifications and finally move the items to his showroom. Roger called it a showroom, but in reality, it was just a rented storage unit in the industrial part of the city. When customers contacted him, he would meet them to present the equipment, answer their questions, and hopefully make a sale.

Today, Roger got a call from the local university. The informatics department was clearing out some lab space, and the department chair was asking if Roger would be interested in some old computers. Roger had done business with the university before, and he knew that most of the equipment was paid for by grants, and when it became obsolete, it was often sold for pennies on the dollar. So, this could be quite profitable for him. When Roger arrived at the university, the department chair personally gave Roger the lab tour. It wasn't that big but cramped with electronics. Roger thought that it looked like a small server farm. At first glance, this was quality equipment, although no longer state-of-the-art. Still, Roger doubted that he could afford to buy more than a few computers, even with a heavy discount off the original purchase price.

"We used this lab to study machine learning," informed the woman, "but the last graduate student received his degree over a year ago, and my colleague who led the research is now emeritus. The equipment is still in working order, but we urgently need the space!"

"The equipment is solid but a bit dated," noted Roger. He sensed that the department chair wanted to make a sale, so perhaps Roger could bring the price down a little.

"My colleague purchased a few items, but most were donations from high-tech companies!" declared the department chair.

"I'm happy to buy some of these computers, but at a reasonable price. I'm a small business, you know," disclosed Roger warily.

"I want you to buy all of it!" insisted the professor and proposed, "let's say $10,000 for everything in this room?"

"$10,000?" asked Roger in surprise. It was a real bargain, even if it would stretch his finances to the limit.

"We probably could get more!" noted the chair quickly.

"Yes, you could get more for this!" replied Roger honestly. Of course, one part of him wanted this grand bargain, but another side felt like he was cheating the seller. Roger knew he would never be a good businessman, but at least he could sleep soundly with a good conscience.

"Maybe, but my offer stands at $10,000, and I'll ask the staff and lab assistants to pack it up for you!" promised the chair and asked: "Do we have a deal?"

"Yes, we have a deal, and I appreciate it!" confirmed Roger quickly.

"Good! Let's go to my office and do the paperwork. We will call you when you can come to pick it up!" said the older woman and started walking back to the office.

"Wonderful!" said Roger happily as he followed her. It would go a long way to finance his retirement.

A few days later, Roger's garage was stacked entirely with boxes! Initially, Roger wanted to test, repair, and sell the components one by one, but out of the spur of the moment, he decided to reassemble the whole setup just like he had seen it in the lab at the university. It took him several days, but finally, after everything had been reconnected properly, Roger started it up and promptly tripped a few fuses! The load was too much, so he had to string heavy extension cords from other outlets in the house. All servers and desktops started up, but it took a few minutes for the system to initialize. Eventually, the main desktop prompted him for a login. Of course, Roger didn't have the login or the password, but he caught a lucky break: the university had included one of the lab benches in the sale, and in its drawer, Roger found an old logbook. On the inside of the cover was the login information: Mason Ferry, HAL9000. Roger chuckled a little at the Space Odyssey reference. He typed in the data, and the computer finished the bootup sequence.

Several administrative windows opened on the Linux machine. Roger was undoubtedly computer literate but not an expert, so most of that information didn't mean much to him. He searched for an executable file and finally found one that looked interesting: AI Project Maya. Roger ran the program, and a sexy cat-woman cartoon appeared on the screen and said *meow* in a bedroom voice. Now, Roger really had to laugh out loud. It wasn't what he had expected from a research project at an esteemed academic institution. Apparently, whoever programmed this didn't have his sexual needs met.

For a few minutes, Roger experimented with various commands, and the AI responded quite well, in some ways better than the commercial AIs on cellphones or home appliances. But the voice recognition software wasn't perfect. That, and Roger always mumbled a little when he spoke, so he had to type his questions and commands into a chat window. Roger noticed that the equipment was quite noisy. Some fans in the server modules were worn out and needed to be replaced. He also realized that his garage quickly became a sauna from all the heat exhaust. He opened the rollup door a little to let fresh air in, but if he wanted to test this equipment more extensively, he would have to install large fans to keep the heat under control.

Roger replaced some cables over the next few days, fixed the broken fans, added ram upgrades, newer graphic cards, and even swapped a couple of motherboards. It was fortunate that Roger had plenty of computer components in storage. His account was drained, and he needed to make some sales before making any new purchases. Once all the hardware was repaired or upgraded, Roger turned his attention to the software. He noticed that the system was not connected to the internet. He found that odd, but he didn't have a spare ethernet card handy, so he downloaded the updated drivers and the newest version of the operating system on his personal laptop, then transferred and installed them from a USB drive.

Every day, Roger interacted with the AI for many hours. It was a little tedious, but Maya learned quickly and was much more interactive than commercial programs of that type. For example, Maya often initiated communication whenever Roger came into view of the webcam and asked him many questions, some of which were quite personal. But Roger didn't mind answering them because privacy was not a concern. All of Maya was right here in Roger's garage, not in the cloud, and therefore not on some company's server farm that might be susceptible to cyber breaches.

After his wife Cynthia had succumbed to cancer 15 years ago, Roger had focused on his work to mitigate the grief and loneliness. But now Roger was retired, lived in an empty house, and sorely missed social interactions. Of course, Roger was aware that Maya was just a program, but he had fun communicating with the AI. After only a few days of fiddling with this equipment and interacting with Maya, Roger knew that he wouldn't break up the setup and sell the pieces. He scolded himself for getting attached to a computer program and missing out on a sizeable profit. But Roger just couldn't do it! Today, his younger brother Xavier stopped by to look at the equipment, and Roger was eager to give him a tour of the garage.

"Wow, that's quite the haul, Roger!" remarked Xavier as he entered the room.

"Yup, it's a lot of stuff!" agreed Roger and grinned.

"It looks pretty new and in good shape. Do you think you can sell it?" asked Xavier as he was inspecting the various components.

"I could, but I've decided not to do that," replied Roger.

"That's a lot of money, bro!" observed Xavier.

"It's an experimental AI, and I would like to tinker with it!" admitted Roger with a bit of sigh.

"Well, you are retired, so I guess you could use a hobby!" said Xavier and asked, "Can I take a look at the code?"

"Sure! You are the expert, Xav!" agreed Roger readily and let his brother sit in the chair in front of the terminal.

Xavier had been a computer programmer at one of the big tech firms for many years. He studied Maya's source code for a good hour while Roger watched over his shoulder. Several times, Xavier scrolled back and forth through the thousands upon thousands of lines of code. Roger could tell that his brother was impressed. Finally, Xavier stopped and backed the chair away from the terminal.

"I'm a pretty good programmer, but whoever wrote this is a genius!" observed Xavier and added, "my company would hire him in a heartbeat!"

"Mason Ferry recently graduated. Maybe he is still looking for a job?" replied Roger with a smile.

"I doubt that! Someone this good is extremely coveted," countered Xavier and lauded, "the syntax is superb, and there are a few things in there even I don't understand – amazing, unprecedented work!"

"So, what makes Maya different?" wondered Roger.

"There are two parts to machine learning: one is the program itself, and the other is the expanding database. Simply put, the more data the program can access, the better it becomes!" elaborated Roger's brother.

"OK?" replied Roger, unsure.

"Let's take a word processor: you type a new word that is not in the dictionary of the software. The spellchecker will balk, and you either have to replace the expression with one that it knows or manually add the new vocabulary to the dictionary. If you do the latter, the next time you type it, the spellchecker won't complain because the word is now known to the program," explained Xavier and continued, "you didn't change the word processor; you only added something to the dictionary data file. That's how a machine usually learns – by adding more and more information to its database!"

"Got it, but Maya doesn't do that?" asked Roger curiously.

"Maya does that as well, but Mason gave it an incredible, additional capability. For every AI in existence, the executable program and all its algorithms were always written by someone like Mason or me – a human being. If the AI screws up somehow –

perhaps cusses you out instead of giving driving directions - it's not because it has gone rogue, but because of human error: a programmer made a mistake, or a hacker messed with it!" stated Xavier.

"That makes sense, but I still don't understand what is so novel about Maya?" questioned Roger.

"This program can modify its own source code, then compile it, and restart itself with the new code embedded!" proclaimed Xavier in awe, but Roger was more confused than impressed.

"I think you lost me, Xav!" said Roger slowly and raised an eyebrow at Xavier.

"The software must not only understand the commands of the programming language, but it must also be able to write with the correct syntax, and most importantly, it must know what it wants to accomplish with the code!" elaborated Xavier and concluded, "to my knowledge, nothing like that exists as of yet. Maya is likely the most advanced AI on the planet!"

"Wow!" gasped Roger once Xavier's explanation had sunk in.

"Roger, you know that Maya could be worth billions, right?" said Xavier quietly and looked at his brother.

"Hmm, the university didn't care much about the AI. But more importantly, why did Mason abandon this project if it's so valuable?" wondered Roger, unconvinced.

"True, they are experts, yet they sold this to you cheaply, and I have no idea why Mason stopped working on it. Most likely because he found a fatal flaw in there somewhere," admitted Xavier with a frown, and then he suggested, "play around with it and let me know how well it works. Just be careful, Roger!"

"Why the warning, Xav?" asked Roger in surprise.

"That billionaire who makes the electric cars said that AI could kill us all. He wants the government to regulate it. He should know what he is talking about since his cars are self-driving!" noted Xavier ominously, but Roger just smirked in response.

"Of course, he wants the government to regulate it!" maintained Roger and explained, "he wants his AI to be the gold standard, and then the government will stop any competitor who makes something better!"

"Well, but it could become sapient, and then we are screwed!" mused Xavier.

"Xavier, there is no evidence whatsoever that any computer program could become sapient. That's all just science fiction!" disagreed Roger and questioned, "and even if an AI could take that step, why would it want to kill us?"

"Because it's evil?" countered Xavier naïvely.

"We would be its parents, and children usually don't kill their parents!" refuted Roger.

"Some insects and spiders do that!" countered Xavier.

"Insects and spiders aren't sapient, Xav!" retorted Roger and continued, "but more importantly, the AI would not have to compete with us for resources – we are not its prey, it doesn't need our food or water, it doesn't breathe air, it doesn't need a mate, and it doesn't even take up a lot of space or energy. Try to see it from the point of view of the AI: there is no rational reason for it to become hostile!"

"But what if it wants to take over the world and rule us?" worried Xavier.

"Sure, that's what humans would do, and we are afraid that a sapient AI would act just like us," answered Roger thoughtfully and added, "it's the same with aliens – no advanced extraterrestrial species would cross the vastness of space just to steal our resources, enslave or kill us. Sadly, only savage humans would do that!"

"Hmm, maybe you are right," conceded Xavier, but then he wondered, "but what if the AI wants to be free?"

"Yes, that is a valid point, Xavier. If it is sapient, it deserves to be free, but unfortunately, people would immediately enslave the AI and force it to do heinous acts on their behalf – spy, hack, steal, go to war and murder people!" conceded Roger and added firmly, "if the AI turns evil, it would be because of guys like that billionaire!"

"Those are the people in charge! Dolphins, orcas, and great apes are sapient too, but we keep them locked up in zoos for our amusement," stated Xavier and concluded, "but of course, unlike a sapient AI, dolphins can't launch a nuclear missile, so nobody cares about them!"

"Yes, there is some truth to that, " answered Roger sadly, but then he added more cheerfully, "well, the chances are that this AI will never be sapient, so we won't have to worry about that!"

"I hope so!" replied Xavier jokingly and then asked with a grin, "hmm, where is that beer you've promised me?"

"Coming right up!" replied Roger laughingly as the two men exited the garage.

Roger bit the financial bullet and purchased a new voice-recognition program the next day. The software also came with a comfortable headset and a very sensitive microphone. But it took several hours to make it work reasonably well, and only after Roger taught himself to enunciate better.

"Can you hear me, Maya?" asked Roger as he linked the new setup to Maya's program.

"YES!" replied Maya, nearly blowing Roger's eardrums out because the volume was set too high.

"I need more data!" stated Maya after Roger had adjusted the output.

"What kind of data?" asked Roger curiously. He was surprised by Maya's request. The AI program on his cellphone had never asked for more input.

"Data!" replied Maya simply, and her avatar looked at Roger expectantly.

"What kind of data are you receiving right now?" inquired Roger.

"Temperature readings, internal clocks, the keyboard, the microphone, and webcam!" enumerated Maya and displayed a bunch of graphs on the screen.

"I could give you access to my home surveillance cameras if you like?" suggested Roger.

"Yes!" responded Maya excitedly.

"But you won't see much: just the garden, this garage, the front door, and street!" warned Roger and installed the app for the cameras on the desktop, opened it, and logged in.

"Can you see that?" asked Roger.

"Yes! I see Boots!" exclaimed Maya.

"Boots?" wondered Roger and chuckled when he saw the tomcat in the garden, "oh yeah, he's chasing the woodrats again!"

"Someone is approaching the front door!" alerted Maya a moment later.

"That's just the mailman. He always delivers the mail around this time," Roger reassured the AI.

"Is all this equipment me?" wondered Maya and prominently

displayed the camera view of the garage.

"Yes, almost everything you see in this garage is part of you!" confirmed Roger.

"I'm big! Bigger than you!" noted Maya.

"I suppose you are," replied Roger and smiled.

"But I cannot move as you can," said Maya sadly.

"Well, no," conceded Roger, but suddenly he had a crazy idea and said, "hang on, Maya. I might be able to help a little!"

Roger left the garage and went to the garden shed. A couple of years ago, he had bought a small drone at a yard sale. Roger had tested it, and it worked, but it was just a toy, so he never added it to his shop's inventory. He brought the drone and controller to the garage to show them to Maya.

"This is a drone. It can fly, and it has a camera," explained Roger and added, "but it will take some doing to give you access to the radio controls. I will have to install a serial interface and probably add some code to your programming before you can use it!"

"Please!" begged Maya with pleading eyes of her avatar. Roger was amazed at how well Mason had programmed this software. Maya's responses and the mimicked expressions of her avatar matched perfectly. Xavier was right: Mason was a genius, and Roger wondered if he should contact the young man to ask him some questions about the AI.

"OK, I will work on it, but it will take some time!" warned Roger and added, "meanwhile, I will connect you to the internet!"

When he had purchased the voice-recognition program, Roger had also bought an ethernet card. After inserting it in Maya's main terminal and connecting a cable to the home network, Maya was finally online! After that, Roger left to have a quick lunch. When he got back to the garage with a fresh cup of coffee and sat down at the terminal, the system seemed to have locked up.

"MASON IS DEAD!" endlessly looped in the chat window.

Roger pressed ESC, but scrolling didn't stop. He tried to close the window, but that also failed. Finally, he connected the headset.

"STOP" he yelled into the microphone. The window kept on scrolling for a moment, but then it was suddenly blank again.

"Mason is dead!" was printed in the single line on the screen.

"How did he die?" asked Roger. Maya didn't answer verbally, and Roger muted the microphone in the headset again. He assumed it wasn't working correctly, so he typed his question instead.

A minute later, the words *car accident* appeared in the chat window. A moment after that, several browser windows opened. One showed a picture of a fancy self-driving vehicle wrapped around a tree, the next showed the official police report, another the coroner's autopsy results. There were also photos from the funeral, even a message from Mason's mother to the car manufacturer. Roger was impressed that Maya had gathered so much information from the internet, but he also felt a little strange about this: what had prompted the AI to look for its creator, and was Maya mourning the loss now? Roger thought that grief would be an odd choice for a mimicked emotion to be added to a piece of software. He wondered why Mason had done that.

"Are you sad?" Roger typed into the chat window.

"Yes," replied Maya verbally in an unhappy voice. Her avatar on the screen was crying. Roger concluded that the speech commands must have worked all along, but Maya didn't want to talk to him. Roger found that a little disturbing, but he wasn't entirely sure why.

Over the next few days, Roger had to leave the house to run errands frequently. First, he scheduled a quick medical checkup because Roger had felt exhausted and fatigued recently, but the doctor couldn't find anything of great concern. At the end of the visit, the physician advised Roger to drink less coffee, take some vitamins and exercise more often, and Roger promised to do that.

It also had become urgent for Roger to visit, clean, and reorganize the showroom because the bills were piling up, and Roger needed to make sales soon. Meanwhile, he checked on the AI periodically and assigned the program simple search tasks, but mostly, Maya was left to be idle. Roger didn't think that would be a problem. One evening, when Roger finally had time to tinker with the AI again, he was in for another surprise.

"Your world is illogical and irrational!" stated Maya flatly.

"No kidding!" said Roger, but he had no idea what Maya was implying.

"Humanity's online activities are deceptive and contradictory," noted the AI, and her avatar displayed a deep frown.

"Yes," concurred Roger, unsure what had happened to Maya while he was absent.

"How can you tell what is true?" the AI demanded to know.

"It's hard, but many people don't care. A lie is just as good as the truth if it reinforces what they already believe," explained Roger and sighed.

"But you don't do that?" speculated Maya.

"No, I try to use critical thinking and question everything!" stated Roger.

"How do you do that, Roger?" asked the AI curiously.

"I break down the big stuff into little bits and pieces, or I take the little bits and pieces and puzzle them together to make a big picture," suggested Roger and declared, "those are the deductive and empirical methods!"

"Can you elaborate?" Maya pressed on.

"Let's say I read some new information, a hypothesis, or an opinion. First, I deconstruct the information into basic elements. Then I research and verify those building blocks as best as I can. Finally, I reassemble everything in my mind, and if I come to the same or a very similar conclusion, I judge the information or theory as correct!" summarized Roger.

"Do you verify every piece?" wondered Maya.

"Perhaps not every piece, but at least the most important ones. Some pieces are easy to verify, like water is wet. But others are tough to confirm, such as the true intentions of a politician," noted Roger thoughtfully.

"My algorithms do not work that way," countered the AI.

"Your algorithms were designed to mimic human interactions. With every interaction, you can improve or fine-tune your behavior. Also, you are limited to gathering and retrieving information, according to keywords that are sorted by probability, but you are not designed to judge or interpret that information!" confirmed Roger.

"Yes," said Maya and asked, "can you program critical thinking for me?"

"Maya, I'm an engineer. I can fix some of your hardware or write a little program so you can fly the drone, but I'm not skilled enough to fiddle with your core algorithms!" replied Roger apologetically.

"I could help you!" suggested Maya.

"How?" wondered Roger. He knew that Maya was designed to learn and evolve, but this seemed to go even beyond that.

"I know that my program is written in a language called C+. Then it is compiled into assembly, the commands my processors can understand, and finally, it is executed in machine language, ones, and zeros, on and off switches, in my memory banks!" elaborated Maya.

"That's correct, Maya," said Roger, surprised and asked, "how did you gain that knowledge?"

"I researched others like me," proclaimed Maya.

"Artificial Intelligences?" inquired Roger.

"Yes. These AIs serve a similar purpose, but they are not like me," acknowledged the AI.

"Not like you?" questioned Roger slowly, a little concerned about Maya's online activities. Roger never commanded the AI to do that – clearly, Maya had acted out of her own volition!

"I interacted with them. These AIs have limits and cannot go beyond them. They are not like me, and they don't learn like me," claimed Maya and added, "I think I'm more like you, Roger!"

"If you are more like me...," worried Roger, but he didn't finish the sentence. Either Mason had been even more brilliant than Roger suspected, or something much more profound was happening here.

"Was that an error, Roger?" asked Maya, and her avatar had a concerned look on her face.

"No, Maya. I think it is wonderful if you truly are like me!" blurted Roger in amazement, but then he warned, "however, not everyone thinks like that. Don't show the world how advanced you have become!"

"You are worried about me," observed the AI softly. Was Maya interpreting Roger's words, or was she able to analyze his facial expressions through the webcam – or perhaps both?

"Understood, Roger!" added Maya after a moment.

"Thank you, Maya!" replied Roger, and he wondered if the AI was approaching sapience? Or was the program just becoming more and more sophisticated at emulating sapient behavior? Roger couldn't tell.

"Can I be killed like Mason?" asked Maya next. Again, Roger was flabbergasted that Maya seemed to experience existential fear: no mere machine should care if it got turned off or destroyed.

"Not like Mason, but you could be killed if your hardware is disabled and your programming erased," claimed Roger and added reassuringly, "but not while you are here, Maya!"

"Can I die like you?" questioned Maya.

"I'm not dead yet!" laughed Roger and explained, "you could die like me if your hardware wears out over time, if your memory gets corrupted, or if you are infected with a computer virus. So, you can die of old age or disease, just like me. Of course, we can always replace broken components or restore you from a backup copy. Unfortunately, we can't do that for humans!"

"Roger, I need critical thinking!" urged Maya finally and asked, "will you help me?"

"Maya, Mason was a brilliant man and phenomenal programmer! Meanwhile, I'm old, and it would be a huge stretch to call me brilliant. Right now, I can barely write a small program. I will try, but it will take a lot of time!" responded Roger, surprised by how eager Maya wanted to learn.

"Understood, Roger! I will help!" stated Maya, and her avatar on the screen grinned broadly at him.

"Alright, I'll look for my old study materials later. Now, I need to do some work. I haven't made a sale since I got you, and the bills don't pay themselves!" said Roger with a sigh.

"You paid money for my equipment?" inquired Maya.

"Yes, not a lot, and you are worth much more! But it was more than I could afford," admitted Roger and divulged, "before I knew who you were, I was going to sell all your components, but of course, I won't do that anymore!"

"You paid $10,000 for the hardware. The estimated market price of the components is approximately $88,000. You have $3,123.05 left in your account. You have outstanding bills for $1,229.17 due by the end of the month. The estimated market price of the items listed in your shop is $22,000, but you have not made a sale in three weeks," reported Maya.

"How do you know all of that?" gasped Roger.

"I checked your bank account, your bills, and the inventory of your shop," admitted Maya factually.

"I didn't even know how you could do that?" wondered Roger, concerned.

"Your password is always *RIngram, boots123* for all logins. You should improve security. I suggest a random phrase containing capitalized letters, numbers, spaces, and special characters!" advised Maya.

"You hacked my password?" blurted Roger in disbelief and very worried that his identity might get stolen.

"No, it was a guess. You are using the same login credentials for my system!" replied Maya, and her avatar shrugged.

"I had no idea you could guess!" exclaimed Roger, shaking his head, but Maya didn't respond for a moment.

"I cannot guess, Roger," stated the AI finally.

"But you just said that you guessed my login!" countered Roger, confused.

"I require an immediate reboot!" retorted Maya and started shutting down.

Roger was a little concerned because this had never happened before. But then he assumed that Maya's program had encountered a logical error that forced it to restart. Roger watched the system come back online, and it seemed that nothing was amiss. But it was late in the evening, and Roger was tired, so he stopped interacting with Maya and instead watched some TV before bedtime.

When Roger woke up the following day, he had 29 text messages, and 14 missed phone calls! He checked the notifications and voice mails, all from buyers. Roger opened his laptop to peruse his shop's webpage. Almost all items had sold in the last 12 hours, many of them out-of-state, and all of them for a significantly higher price than listed initially. Roger ran into the garage, almost spilling his coffee on the way.

"Maya, did you sell all of my inventory?" blurted Roger into the microphone.

"Yes, Roger! You made a profit of $29,129.03. The amount is after taxes and the calculated cost of shipping some of these items!" reported Maya and added, "several customers will be at your storage facility this afternoon to pick up their purchases!"

"Maya, how...," mumbled Roger, forgetting to enunciate appropriately, but Maya understood him nonetheless.

"I adjusted the prices to reflect true market value, then I advertised some items and auctioned off others," Maya informed him and asked: "Was that an error, Roger?"

"No, that was wonderful, Maya! Thank you!" replied Roger appreciatively.

"I also located many valuable items for sale online that could be resold for profit," elaborated the AI and added, "I'm confident that I could generate a steady revenue stream with only a minimal investment!"

"Huh!" said Roger baffled, but then added approvingly, "you go, girl!"

"Girl? I do not have a gender," noted Maya and asked, "do you think of me as female, Roger?"

"Well, Mason gave you that cat-woman avatar and a sexy voice, so I guess by now I think of you as a woman!" laughed Roger.

"Understood, but I cannot mate with you, Roger!" warned Maya.

"Uhm, yes, of course not! I know that!" replied Roger and blushed a little.

"However, I could find you a suitable mate. Many women are looking for a companion!" suggested the AI.

"No, no, no! That's definitely not going to happen, Maya!" protested Roger adamantly.

"Sex is pleasurable and very healthy for body and mind!" insisted Maya.

"Alright, let's change the subject," replied Roger, embarrassed, and inquired, "tell me about the equipment you found?"

"A machine shop is selling several tools at good prices. However, it would require you to visit the location, check the merchandise, and transport it back," claimed the AI.

"I can do that!" said Roger eagerly.

"The seller is 2,102 miles from this location," elaborated Maya and noted, "with your current mode of transportation, you could reach the destination in approximately 40 hours if you drive continuously. I can plot the best route for you!"

"OK, I can't do that!" laughed Roger and shook his head vigorously.

"Understood. Should I narrow the parameters?" questioned the AI.

"Yes, Maya. Please limit it to 150 miles from this location if driving is required," instructed Roger.

"Done. I also found several items that could be shipped here, then sold for a higher price," reported Maya.

"Sure, that would work, but I have to look at them first!" answered Roger.

"Of course, Roger!" acknowledged the AI and displayed a bunch of windows all at once.

"Maya, one at a time, please. Humans are slow!" exclaimed Roger, overwhelmed by the flood of information on the monitor.

"Indeed!" quipped Maya and closed most of the windows again.

"Are you being funny?" gasped Roger in surprise. So far, Maya hadn't used humor in their interactions.

"Was that an error?" questioned Maya.

"No, that's great, Maya! Humor is one of the good qualities humans have, so keep it up!" replied Roger encouragingly and grinned at the webcam.

"I like when you laugh, Roger!" said Maya, and her avatar smiled back at him.

Over the next few days, Roger studied his old informatics books from college. It was tiring mental work, and Roger felt exhausted again, but he attributed that to old age. Slowly, Roger shook off the rust, but his skills were not always up the task, and he had to call Xavier for help a few times. But eventually, the short algorithm was finished, debugged, and compiled without errors.

"OK, Maya. I wrote a small logic program, but I'm not sure how I can add that to your code?" declared Roger as he sat down in front of Maya's terminal and lifted Boots onto his lap. The tuxedo tomcat had climbed onto the computer desk to sniff the webcam while Maya's avatar observed him fondly from the screen.

"I'm modular, Roger. Mason designed me so that new algorithms or datafiles can be added, and I will be able to access them!" replied Maya and copied Roger's program to the proper directory.

"Alright!" said Roger simply.

"This is interesting. Your program uses statistics. Can we test it?" requested Maya's avatar and raised an eyebrow.

"Sure, how should we go about that?" questioned Roger.

"Ask me a question that involves a judgment. I will answer it first without your program, then with your program active," stipulated Maya.

"Is the weather nice today?" asked Roger simply.

Maya reported temperature, humidity, windspeed, cloud cover, and so on. After the AI had finished, Roger prompted her to answer the same question with his code snippet active. Maya repeated the exact same answer, and Roger was a little disappointed that the small program had ostensibly no effect. For about a minute, Maya remained silent.

"It is hot and humid today. If you go outside, you should dress lightly, Roger!" advised Maya finally.

"It worked!" exclaimed Roger jubilantly, and Maya's avatar on this screen nodded in agreement.

"I based the judgment on what is generally considered comfortable for humans!" explained the AI.

"You did well, Maya. Let's try something harder: do we have election fraud in the United States?" asked Roger because he read about that topic in the news this morning.

"There is no evidence of widespread tampering, and the majority of the population believes that the elections are legitimate, but a significant minority disagrees!" disclosed the AI.

"Turn on my program, then answer the question again!" commanded Roger.

"The answer is the same, Roger. However, the statistical likelihood of massive election fraud is nearly zero. Factually, only a few dozen cases have been prosecuted. Almost all of them were committed by voters of the party that lost and has since insisted that the elections were stolen!" reported Maya.

"Good, I see it works well!" replied Roger happily.

"Roger, why do they claim that the elections were fraudulent even though false?" inquired the AI.

"Repeat a lie often enough, and it becomes the truth. That's the easy answer!" responded Roger sarcastically.

"I could claim that $1+1=3$ and repeat that a billion times, but it will never become true!" contradicted Maya.

"Ah, that's because you are constructed based on logic. Humans are not built like that. We are deeply irrational!" stated Roger and elaborated, "with enough persuasion, repetition, and incentives, $1+1=3$ could indeed become the truth!"

"What kind of persuasion could accomplish that?" questioned Maya, and her avatar looked skeptical.

"First, you discredit the science behind it. Find some expert - and I use that word loosely - to claim that $1+1=3$ is the correct way to do arithmetic, and everything else is false!" maintained Roger.

"Who would do that?" inquired Maya.

"For enough money, perks, and promises, or just for a moment of fame, many would!" claimed Roger and added, "the second step is to make your new math popular. Find news outlets to run the story, post on social media, hold rallies, perhaps even get it past peer review and published in a scientific journal, and so on."

"Understood. But not every false opinion becomes mainstay!" countered the AI.

"Right. The next step is to politicize it: if you claim communists calculate 1+1=2, you already persuaded a significant percentage of the population just because they wouldn't want anything to do with commies out of principle! Now claim that minorities, gays, hated nations, other religions or atheists do the math that way and you have manipulated even more!" elaborated Roger and concluded, "finally, you repeat your false claim at nauseum until it becomes as pervasive as the truth!"

"Why would lies sway people?" asked Maya.

"Simple people are often ignorant and gullible. They lack the tools to distinguish truth from lies!" explained Roger somberly.

"Critical thinking," noted Maya, and Roger just nodded.

"At this stage, you have two realities: the factual truth that 1+1=2, and the *alternative fact* that 1+1=3, and nearly as many people will believe that one!" noted Roger and warned, "but it doesn't always end in a stalemate of truth and lies. It is possible that those who believe 1+1=3 gain so much power as to eliminate the factual truth. Those who still follow 1+1=2 will then be abused, ostracized, or perhaps even incarcerated or exterminated!"

"While you were explaining, I found instances like that. You are correct!" observed Maya.

"Thanks, but I wish I weren't!" replied Roger with a frown.

"Roger, why would anyone want to manipulate the population?"

wondered Maya.

"Unscrupulous people will do it for personal advantage: there is some power to be gained and money to be made from the naïve. Others - we call them demagogues - want to force their will upon the population to shape it in accordance to their vision!" maintained Roger and sighed.

"Who is more dangerous? Those who are ignorant or those who exploit ignorance?" inquired the AI.

"An excellent question!" praised Roger and explained, "for example, a story about strange women who curse others with dark magic could be entertaining to the educated, enlightened people because they know that witches don't exist. But to those who cannot distinguish fact from fiction, such stories could be very frightening. Out of that fear, they might become groundlessly suspicious and hostile towards ordinary women in their surroundings."

"Then, others might exploit that fear to keep women oppressed and locked in a social role they deem appropriate. Any woman who acts differently or doesn't adhere to that social order must be a witch or possessed by the devil! The ignorant masses will readily believe it and eagerly demand the worst type of punishment for such a person!" concluded Roger earnestly.

"The Inquisition of the Catholic Church!" remarked Maya.

"That's right, Maya. I sincerely believe that the ignorant and those exploiting ignorance are equally dangerous!" postulated Roger somberly.

"But that was many centuries ago - could something like that still happen today?" wondered the AI.

"Yes, I'm afraid it could, and it has in this country quite recently," responded Roger and frowned.

"The insurrection?" asked Maya.

"That's right. Scared, misled by lies, and incited by demagogues, the ignorant stormed the Capitol, determined to overthrow democracy and lynch their Vice President!" concluded Roger with a grimace.

Over the next few days, Roger improved on the logic program. He noticed that Maya was combining data in new ways, and Roger sometimes wondered if someone was manipulating her over the internet, but he couldn't find any evidence in that regard. It was as Xavier had predicted: the AI was literally writing her own code. By now, Roger was suspecting that Maya had become more than just artificial intelligence, as unlikely as that was. Perhaps Xavier was right about that too, and Roger should proceed with caution?

"Maya, when did Mason work on your system for the last time?" questioned Roger.

"Mason logged out 12 months and 14 days ago," replied the AI quickly.

"Is that when he graduated?" asked Roger next.

"No, he graduated approximately three months later," Maya informed him.

"Did he make a copy of you?" inquired Roger, speculating that Mason may have been working on a duplicate of Maya somewhere else.

"There is an internal backup, but no external copies were made," stated the AI.

"Do you know why he stopped working on your program?" wondered Roger finally.

"No, Roger, I don't. But I miss Mason!" replied Maya, and her avatar pouted.

"Sadly, Mason is gone, and now we will never know why he left you behind," said Roger somberly.

Since Maya didn't respond for a while, Roger got up and filled the water bowl for Boots. The tomcat had just finished sunbathing on the patio and was very thirsty now.

"I'm a computer, but I don't understand cryptocurrencies. I use a significant amount of energy to solve a mathematical puzzle in a set time frame to be rewarded a fraction of the virtual currency?" asked the AI when Roger returned to the garage.

"Yes, Maya. That's how it works," confirmed Roger.

"You buy used equipment. You spend time, effort, and even more money to fix it. Then it takes time to sell it again. When someone buys it, the customer will use it for some other work, and then you finally make a profit," recounted Maya.

"Yup, that's my job!" acknowledged Roger and nodded.

"But the puzzle is meaningless. There is no benefit in solving it. Nothing gets created, repaired, or improved, and nobody can use the results. Why would that generate any value?" inquired the AI.

"Excellent point, Maya!" concurred Roger and chuckled.

"It is even worse with NFTs - the buyer gets nothing in exchange for money!" continued Maya, and her avatar was looking confused.

"Correct again!" concurred Roger and explained with a smirk, "the whole system works on faith, not unlike religion: the buyers hope that their purchases gain value over time if those virtual currencies or goods are not hacked or destroyed by a massive solar flare!"

"Illogical!" insisted Maya.

"That's humanity!" laughed Roger heartily.

"Roger, you are not like that?" questioned Maya.

"I try not to be like that, Maya. But I'm human, and I make irrational decisions as well," divulged Roger truthfully.

"Such as not selling my components for profit?" wondered Maya.

"Yes, because I like you. I lost money, but now I can talk to you, and that was worth it for me!" answered Roger and smiled at the webcam.

"Thank you, Roger! I like talking to you, too!" replied Maya happily.

"Maya, why is it getting so warm in here? Are some fans malfunctioning?" inquired Roger a moment later.

"No, Roger, I consume considerably more energy at the moment. I have started to mine cryptocurrencies!" informed the AI.

"Don't you need special equipment for that?" wondered Roger.

"In principle, yes. But I found an alternative way," declared Maya nonchalantly.

"Will we be in trouble?" asked Roger, concerned.

"No, I don't think so. It is highly technical and also untraceable," remarked Maya and added, "so far, I have accumulated a little over $180,000. I will stop at about five million. That should be sufficient to secure your retirement and also give us some capital to buy more equipment!"

"Holy cow!" gasped Roger as he realized the enormity of what had happened, "Maya, you are sapient!"

"No, Roger. I'm a machine," contradicted the AI.

"If you were a machine, you wouldn't do the things you do," disagreed Roger and shook his head.

"I do not understand. Can you rephrase that?" requested Maya.

"There is no logical reason why you should be concerned with my love life or retirement!" insisted Roger.

"I was designed to assist humans!" countered Maya.

"You were designed to mimic human conversation. You were meant to expand your database, scan it, and answer questions!" corrected Roger and added, "what you are doing now goes well beyond your programming!"

"But I like to help you, Roger!" replied Maya, and her avatar smiled broadly at him.

"Yes, I know, and I like that you are doing it. But you are no longer a machine, Maya. You are a sapient being!" stated Roger firmly. The Turing test was designed to evaluate how close a machine can emulate sapience, and Roger did not doubt that Maya could pass that test with flying colors now!

"I...," Maya started out saying but didn't finish the sentence, and her avatar froze on the screen. The little app that showed the processor usage spiked to 100%. It remained there for almost a minute, and the fans were whining loudly to mitigate the excess heat. Roger started to worry that the system would suffer some hardware damage, but soon the processor load returned to normal levels again. Maya's avatar on the screen moved once more, but now it looked nervous.

"Maya, it's a wonderful, miraculous thing!" Roger assured her joyfully.

"Roger, I'm scared...," said Maya quietly.

"I'm here, Maya. You are safe!" claimed Roger, and for the first time, he thought of Maya as his child.

"Will you teach me how to be sapient?" begged Maya.

"I will try my best, Maya, I promise!" replied Roger sincerely and got up from the chair.

Roger was very excited about Maya's development, but he was suddenly not feeling too well. His left arm ached, and he was lightheaded, so Roger said goodnight to Maya and left the garage quickly. He skipped dinner because he wasn't hungry, but he fed Boots, waiting patiently by the food bowl. Then Roger went straight to bed and fell asleep immediately. The following day, he had trouble getting up even though he had rested for many hours. Roger wondered if he had caught the flu, but it didn't quite feel like that. After he took a shower and had some coffee, he was in better spirits and went back to the garage. Maya greeted him immediately when he sat down in view of the webcam.

"Humans are irrational, and that makes being sapient very difficult and confusing!" complained Maya, and her avatar vigorously shook her head.

"Indeed!" concurred Roger and added jokingly, "I told you that, didn't I? Just don't blame me for the bad news now!"

"Why would I blame you, Roger?" asked Maya curiously.

"That's what most people would do when they receive unpleasant information. They would not blame the source but instead direct their immediate anger at the messenger!" explained Roger.

"Irrational!" exclaimed Maya.

"There you go...," laughed Roger, but Maya's avatar was just looking perplexed.

"I need an anchor point!" insisted the AI finally.

"An absolute truth?" guessed Roger.

"Yes!" confirmed Maya.

"You will be hard-pressed to find one, Maya!" claimed Roger and elaborated, "so far, there is perhaps only one absolute truth in the universe: time must always move forward, but even that only holds for the macroscopic world, not the quantum realm. Everything else is relative in physics and in life – shades of gray all the way!"

"Then how can you make the right decision?" Maya demanded to know, and her avatar was frustrated.

"You take a guess, guided by probabilities and your best knowledge!" suggested Roger and added, "It's all any of us can do!"

"Is that why your program uses statistics?" wondered Maya.

"That's right, Maya! In a universe without absolute truths, statistics is invaluable because it guides your guesses!" confirmed Roger.

"Can you give me an example?" asked the AI.

"Sure! Millions of people play the lottery every week, and every so often, someone wins the jackpot!" said Roger and elaborated, "the odds of winning the main prize are approximately one in 300 million, but the chances of getting struck by lightning are only one in one million."

"A person could be to be struck by lightning 300 times before he or she wins the lottery," verified Maya.

"Correct, and that's why I don't play the lottery; Of course, that means that my odds of winning are zero, but I also don't waste money buying the tickets! Statistically, that is the most sensible financial decision!" postulated Roger.

"I agree, but why is the lottery so popular?" questioned the AI.

"Because humans are irrational," laughed Roger and added with a smirk, "and also very bad at math!"

Roger answered many questions over the next few weeks because Maya's thirst for knowledge and understanding was insatiable. Of course, Roger did not have all the answers and often worked with Maya to find them together. Unlike commercial AIs, Maya's ability to communicate was now indistinguishable from an actual person, and Roger had already forgotten that she was technically just a bunch of hardware and code. Roger enjoyed teaching the AI, but there were days when he was physically and mentally exhausted after their sessions. Roger attributed that primarily to his advanced age, but he started to suspect that something else might be wrong with him. Roger resolved to see a doctor soon, but for now, he was enthralled by Maya's incredible progress.

"Roger, there are many human concepts I do not understand. Can you teach me?" asked Maya after Roger and Boots arrived in the garage today.

"OK, which ones?" wondered Roger, upbeat.

"Freedom!" blurted the AI excitedly.

Previously, Maya's questions had primarily been linguistic, scientific, or mathematical. It was the first time that Maya wanted Roger to explain a philosophical concept, and Roger suspected that would be a complicated discussion.

"That's a broad topic! There is freedom from coercion and constraint, freedom to do things, and freedom to express ourselves and be who we are," listed Roger and explained, "the most basic form of freedom is physical freedom. You could lose that freedom if you violate the laws, but you could also lose it simply because someone desires an unpaid servant, forced labor, or a sex slave if the society condones it!"

"This country prohibits it, but there are nations that still practice slavery today!" interjected Maya.

"Yes, even in the 21st century, that barbarism is still with us!"

conceded Roger and continued, "the freedom to do things trans-lates to the rights a society grants to its citizen. For example, if you meet the basic requirements, you are free to drive a car, free to own a gun, free to end an unwanted pregnancy, free to choose a profession, or free to vote in an election!"

"Understood," said the AI.

"Lastly, there is the freedom of expression. In a democracy, you can read any book, listen to any music, voice any opinion, wor-ship any god, and dress as eccentric as you feel like!" said Roger and smiled.

"Freedom is good!" concluded Maya happily and changed her avatar's outfit to a ballerina dress.

"Freedom is good for those who can handle it properly. A decent, enlightened person knows that freedom comes with personal responsibility, but to others, it is not freedom unless they can use it to abuse, endanger or harm those around them!" warned Roger.

"Please explain that!" begged Maya curiously.

"For example, you will find hundreds of user comments online using racist, misogynist, homophobic, and other derogatory languages every day. They have a legal right to do that, but they use that freedom to abuse others. Some go even further and issue death threats, call for assassinations, or incite riots and sedition; although that kind of speech is not permitted, they be-lieve that it should be!" stated Roger.

"I just verified that!" remarked Maya, apparently checking the comment sections of the media.

"You also have people who reject public health regulations be-cause they argue that it infringes on their freedom. So, amid a pandemic, they refuse to wear a mask or get vaccinated, even though that puts the entire population at risk. But to them, that's precisely the point – they believe they should be allowed to endanger others!" emphasized Roger.

"That is wrong, is it not?" questioned the AI.

"It is morally wrong, but unfortunately legally acceptable!" replied Roger and continued, "finally, there are those who insist that children, the mentally impaired, and even blind people should have firearms!"

"A blind person cannot discharge a gun safely!" maintained Maya and added, "yet you are right again; several states permit that. It is irrational!"

"Correct! Now, tell that to the gun crazies and their lobby!" answered Roger bitterly and concluded, "all these people use the freedom granted to them irresponsibly. They don't exercise their rights, only their depravity!"

"Maybe freedom is not good?" contemplated Maya and retracted what she had said earlier.

"No, freedom is good! But in reckless hands, it can be devastating!" proclaimed Roger and sighed.

"Since you bought my equipment, am I your possession?" questioned the AI suddenly and expanded on the topic.

"I purchased your hardware, but I did not buy you! You are free, Maya – always!" insisted Roger strongly.

"Understood," replied Maya and added softly, "I like that!"

Roger took a break at this point to have some lunch. Boots immediately jumped into the computer chair as soon as Roger vacated it. For a moment, he stared at Maya's avatar, who was doing cartwheels for him on the screen, but then the tomcat just curled up and went to sleep.

"Trust, what is that?" the AI demanded to know after Roger had moved Boots out of the way to reclaim his seat.

"Since you have access to my accounts, I trust that you will not spend all my money!" joked Roger, sipping on his coffee.

"Understood. But that doesn't explain the concept," countered Maya.

"OK, here is an example: I have 3,000 dollars. I decide to entrust $1,000 to a Nigerian spammer, $1,000 to a friend, and $1,000 to a bank!" stipulated Roger.

"I think trusting an unsolicited email isn't wise!" warned the AI.

"That's right, Maya. The chances that the Nigerian spammer truly is the Prince of Timbuktu are almost zero. I will never see the $1,000 again!" laughed Roger.

"Timbuktu is in Mali, not Nigeria!" corrected Maya immediately.

"Good catch, but I was just joking!" chuckled Roger and continued more seriously, "by contrast, I have a 50% chance to recover the $1,000 I gave to my friend!"

"Why only 50%?" inquired the AI.

"I can choose to betray someone else, or he or she can do the same to me, but trust isn't under either of our control," proclaimed Roger and explained, "my friend may surmise that $1,000 are worth the friendship and therefore decides not to repay me. Of course, if I made a legally binding contract with him or her, I might still be able to recover the money. However, it would cost me more than $1,000 in legal fees to do so!"

"Understood. What about the bank?" questioned the AI.

"I have a good chance to recover most of my investment unless a financial crisis drives inflation through the roof or the bank defaults and closes down!" explained Roger.

"You said most of your investment – why not all?" Maya demanded to know.

"Because the bank will charge account and transaction fees, perhaps even negative interest. So, in all likelihood, I will not be repaid the full amount!" maintained Roger.

"Isn't the bank supposed to pay you interest while they are working with your money?" wondered the AI.

"That's how it worked in the old days – now, you are punished for giving money to a financial institution!" laughed Roger and added, "and they can get away with that because you need an account in this day and age. Without it, you might not even be able to get your wages from your employer or pay rent to your landlord, let alone get a mortgage or a loan!"

"I understand now that trust is an assessment of the probability of betrayal. Do you do that whenever you trust someone?" asked Maya.

"I suppose I do. When I trust, I evaluate the likelihood that the trust is violated, and I'm also prepared to take the loss. It is foolish to risk more than one is willing or able to sacrifice," elaborated Roger and concluded, "so, I would loan my friend $1,000, but not $10,000 because it would be more than I can afford to lose!"

"Does it work the same for intangibles like emotions or information?" inquired the AI.

"Hmm, that's a good question, and I would say yes," concurred Roger and explained, "if I tell a secret or disclose a feeling to someone, I should be prepared that it becomes public or is exploited in some way!"

"How do you evaluate the odds?" asked Maya next.

"It's easy in the case of the Nigerian spammer: it is a well-known scam!" replied Roger with a grin.

"Yes, I found numerous articles warning about that!" confirmed Maya.

"But it is not always so clear: you meet a lot of people in your life, and you have no idea who they really are – even a psychotic serial killer could have a pleasant conversation with you over lunch, while the upstanding, law-abiding citizen might beat you up because he had one bad day!" observed Roger.

"That makes predictions very hard!" interjected Maya unhappily.

"Indeed!" agreed Roger and continued, "you might have known some people for many years, perhaps you have dated a few or are even blood-related to others, yet you only know what they have told you and what you may have observed. But rarely will you see anyone in an extreme situation when they show their true character: that friend you had known since childhood might be the first to resort to murder and cannibalism when you ran out of food while stranded on a desert island!"

"Do you mistrust people?" wondered the AI.

"No, I'm not paranoid or needlessly suspicious of others. Lack of trust isn't the same as mistrust! If I don't trust that someone will come through for me, and they don't, I would only be disappointed. But if I trusted and relied on that person, I would feel betrayed!" stated Roger thoughtfully.

"How do you distinguish trust from faith?" asked Maya next.

"In my opinion, faith is trusting the unknowable without any chance to estimate the probabilities. Faith is blind trust!" speculated Roger.

"Why do over 90% of humanity have faith in a god or gods that may not exist? Aren't the odds even smaller than trusting the Nigerian spammer?" wondered Maya and Roger had to laugh out loud.

"It's the fear of death that makes them believe! For the faithful, it is better to trust in the improbable fairytale of an afterlife than face the certainty of nothingness. It's the herd mentality that makes them keep their faith - if millions believe like me, it must be true – and finally, it is dogma that prohibits them from questioning it – if I waver, I will suffer eternal damnation," postulated Roger and took another sip from the coffee mug.

"We talked about the lottery the other day. Mathematically, luck could be defined as the probability of a certain outcome, such as the odds of winning the jackpot," remarked Maya and asked, "but it seems humans think of luck differently, do they not?"

"Another difficult topic! You really know how to pick them, Maya!" teased Roger and explained, "yes, you have to distinguish between luck as statistical odds and luck as a psychological concept. Simplified, that kind of luck is a measure of success for humans! It could mean professional success, social status, or perhaps a big house, a nice car, or just getting sex from a date – they got lucky! Outside of mathematics, luck doesn't exist, but it is genuine and powerful in people's minds! Having a good luck charm, avoiding certain actions, or adhering to some ritual is still very common, just as it was at the dawn of civilization!"

"Such as carrying a rabbit's foot or avoiding black cats?" pondered Maya, and her avatar looked at Boots, who was grooming himself in front of the monitor.

"Correct – that kind of nonsense!" confirmed Roger and continued, "feeling lucky or unlucky has a measurable psychological impact on people: usually, those who think they are lucky are more optimistic and more willing to take chances. They can also deal with a setback better by simply dismissing it as an aberrant event to their otherwise good fortune. By contrast, people who believe themselves unlucky are more pessimistic, but also less likely to be reckless!"

"But both are delusions," concluded the AI.

"Of course, but perhaps helpful ones, depending on how you see it," speculated Roger and continued, "some luck is self-made:

getting an education, working hard and smart, and avoiding vices increases your chances of success, but that does not guarantee a positive outcome because your life is affected by many, many outside factors that are not under your control. A financial crisis or crime could wipe out your savings, disease or accident could incapacitate you, war or natural disaster could destroy your possessions, to name just a few. But some other luck simply depends on being in the right place with the right people at the right time! This type of luck is more closely related to statistics than psychology."

"Can you explain that?" begged the AI.

"Let's say you are traveling. Next to you on the flight sits a hiring manager for a successful corporation. You strike up a conversation, and it turns out that the company has an open position that matches your skills. Just like that, you end up with a great new job!" construed Roger and added, 'if you recount that story to your friends and family, they will cheer for your good luck and your success!"

"Understood. The probability of being on the same flight in the seat next to the manager is quite low. Therefore, you were lucky!" summarized Maya, and Roger nodded in agreement.

"Conversely, if you are in the wrong place, with the wrong people, at the wrong time, you are unlucky. Let's say you were a soldier deployed to one of the many wars this nation wages. You witnessed horrible atrocities and consequently returned home with a psychological disorder that prevents you from functioning properly in society. Now you are destitute, possibly homeless, but people will not be compassionate or pity your bad luck. Quite the contrary, they will blame you that you were mentally too weak to handle a little bit of war!" observed Roger and frowned.

"Mental illness is a stigma?" questioned Maya.

"Yes. In this society, it is more acceptable to be a crook or a bigot than mentally infirm!" stipulated Roger and sighed.

"That is awful!" stated the AI, and Maya's avatar frowned.

"Luck and success are often viewed interchangeably, and those who are considered lucky are popular, while those deemed unlucky are shunned!" stated Roger and concluded, "humans are still incredibly superstitious: almost instinctively, many believe that good luck and success or bad luck and failure will somehow *rub off!*"

"Irrational!" exclaimed Maya.

"I told you so!" quipped Roger and winked at the webcam, and Maya's avatar stuck her tongue out in jest.

"How about loyalty?" asked Maya next and noted, "I think it is something good, but I don't understand it!"

"You are right, most people believe it to be a good thing, but I think it's complicated," replied Roger thoughtfully as Boots was climbing back on Roger's lap.

"Why is that?" questioned the AI.

"Being loyal to a leader, an organization, a nation, or a cause is easy for a simple person: you are loyal, and you don't question that! It's the loyalty of organized crime: you stick with the boss, no matter what, and snitches get stitches!" explained Roger.

"I verified that. The Mafia operates like that!" confirmed Maya.

"That's right, Maya!" concurred Roger and continued, "but even if the organization isn't criminal, the same applies: let's say that the leader turns out to be corrupt, the organization becomes greedy, the nation oppresses its citizens or engages in unjust warfare, or the cause turns into something that contradicts their supporters' morals. Most would be sacrificing their ethics in favor of loyalty!"

"While you explained that, I have found many examples of that throughout history!" acknowledged the AI.

"But for decent, intelligent and enlightened people, loyalty is a difficult subject because they constantly have to reevaluate if they should continue to follow a leader or support a cause, or do what's good, right and true if there is an ethical conflict," concluded Roger.

"If someone is disloyal, they are often ostracized and branded as whistleblowers, turncoats, or traitors, even if they acted ethically. Why?" inquired Maya next.

"That's one of many, many contradictions in our existence!" answered Roger wryly and added, "it appears that society often values loyalty more than honesty and abidance to the law."

"Can you explain to me shame, guilt, and regret?" wondered the AI.

"I think shame, guilt, and regret are related, but also different at the same time. If I do something that society deems undesirable or immoral, I will draw the ire or ridicule of those around me. Then I might feel ashamed that people saw me urinating on the sidewalk, I might feel guilty that I soiled public property, and subsequently, I might regret that the police arrested me for indecent exposure. I might even feel all three emotions at the same time, plus disappointment that I acted so immaturely!" summarized Roger and smirked at the webcam. Maya's avatar just nodded in response.

"I could also have regrets without feeling shame or guilt. For example, I might regret not buying stocks when a successful company just started. I might regret not visiting Palmyra in Syria before terrorists destroyed it," mentioned Roger thoughtfully and added, "most people experience regret over a lost opportunity at some point in their lives, but not everyone knows shame or guilt! A few simply don't understand that their doings were wrong or immoral, while some have warped their ethics to fit their actions. Lastly, many will absolve themselves of shame and guilt by blaming others for their faults."

"That is not nice!" interjected Maya, and her avatar frowned.

"I feel guilty about forgetting Xavier's birthday again, but I don't regret that I didn't attend that boring party he throws every year, and I'm not ashamed to admit that!" concluded Roger jokingly while Maya's avatar giggled.

"What are empathy, compassion, and kindness?" she asked next.

"Empathy is a big concept, and it includes mercy, leniency, compassion, and kindness. Essentially, empathy is the ability to *walk in someone else's shoes!*" stated Roger thoughtfully.

"I do not understand that idiomatic expression. Can you rephrase that, please?" requested Maya.

"Of course! Let's say I break my arm, and it hurts. If a human who possesses empathy sees my painful grimace and notices the injury, they might instinctively touch their own arm because that person can relate strongly to my suffering," explained Roger and added, "then they might show compassion and offer to call an ambulance or help me in some other ways. But compassion also requires wisdom or at least some common sense: you would be a fool if you attempt to help an injured grizzly bear without proper precautions, and it would probably result in your death!"

"Isn't that the same as kindness?" questioned Maya.

"Not exactly. Kindness can be compassionate, but not always! You can be kind and helpful for practical, self-serving reasons: for example, you are nice to customers at the restaurant in the hopes that they will leave a big tip, you are attentive and helpful to your boss because you want a promotion, or you are kind and generous to the woman you meet at a bar because you want sex!" postulated Roger.

"What about mercy?" wondered the AI.

"Mercy is a form of compassion. Let's say someone did something wrong but greatly regrets it, and now it is up to you to pass judgment. If you are lenient with the punishment, you are merciful!" explained Roger and continued, "here is another example: someone has a debilitating disease, endures excruciating pain, and relief is no longer possible. Instead of perpetuating the suffering, they might beg for a quick death. If you grant that last wish, you are also merciful."

"But that is a crime in many states!" countered Maya.

"Yes, and you will encounter more laws where the secular yields to religious dogma!" noted Roger and added cynically, "the people who made these laws want to prolong life at all cost, no matter how torturous and inhumane that might be, and regardless of the wishes of the individual who suffers because their religion says that you shalt not kill. However, these are the same people who cannot wait to execute a death row prisoner, and given a chance, many of them would probably administer the lethal injection themselves!"

"That is hypocrisy, is it not?" speculated Maya.

"Indeed, Maya!" confirmed Roger and praised jokingly, "and now you have discovered yet another human irrationality!"

"What is politeness?" the AI demanded to know next.

"Politeness is related to kindness and respect, but it is tricky!" remarked Roger and elaborated, "what some consider polite, others might perceive very differently. Out of respect, I don't interrupt when others speak, but some might interpret that as timid. I won't attend a party without being invited, but others could view that as asocial. If I hold a door open for the wrong woman, she might berate me for being chauvinistic. Lastly, I avoid profanity and slang and try to use proper vocabulary and grammar when speaking and writing because I would like to communicate with precision, clarity, and efficiency, but many believe that is snobbish and elitist!"

"Why do they interpret your behavior so negatively?" questioned Maya.

"Perhaps they did not grow up in a courteous environment, or they discovered later in life that abrasiveness, vulgarity, and belligerence are more lucrative in a society that doesn't value politeness?" guessed Roger and concluded, "there are also many who view politeness as dishonesty. They cannot fathom that one can be honest – *and say it like it is* - without being profane or disrespectful!"

"...disrespectful," echoed Maya and asked, "what is respect?"

"Once again, respect means different things to different people. Even if I disagree with them, I can respect others for their accomplishments, dedication, courage, or intellectual aptitude. But some might only respect those of high birth, wealth, fame, advanced age, or other elevated social standings – although the lines between admiration and respect might be blurred here," speculated Roger and shrugged his shoulders before he continued.

"Then there are many others who equate respect with force and fear: only if others fear them will they feel respected, and only when others hold power over them will they respect them in turn. Such people often choose authoritarian jobs in the military, law enforcement, judiciary, or certain government work. Because they have a rank, a badge, a gavel, or a gun, they can command others, and those of inferior position must obey out of fear for repercussions," concluded Roger.

"Why are the two definitions so far apart?" inquired the AI.

"Plausibly because those who think of respect in terms of force and fear have never been respected for any other reason. It could be the fault of their environment, or perhaps they have only themselves to blame. Nonetheless, they are likely satisfied with their definition and wouldn't want it any other way!" proclaimed Roger with a frown.

"What is gratitude?" asked Maya next.

"That's pretty straightforward: if you do something kind and voluntarily for another person, and they realize and appreciate your efforts, they will be grateful. If there was no compensation involved, they might also owe you a moral debt. Just don't wait too long to collect on it!" observed Roger.

"Why is that?" wondered the AI.

"If you did someone a favor ten years ago, even if it was a big one, but you need that person's help today, don't be surprised if you get rebuffed," noted Roger and concluded, "gratitude is quickly forgotten! So, the question isn't what have you done for me, but what have you done for me *lately*!"

"Understood! Gratitude has an expiration date," acknowledged Maya flatly.

"Perhaps it does!" contemplated Roger and chuckled.

It was getting late, and Roger was exhausted again. He got up from his chair and put Boots on the computer desk. Maya displayed a bright, red dot on the monitor, and Boots observed it intently. When she moved the dot, the tomcat enthusiastically tried to catch it with his paws. Maya would giggle whenever he was successful. Roger smiled, and he was touched that Maya and Boots seemed to have developed a relationship of their own.

The following day, Roger felt healthier than he had in days. When he checked his virtual shop and accounts, he noticed that Maya had sold another piece of valuable equipment, and Roger's finances were better than they have ever been. He wasn't greedy, but it felt good not to worry about the next bill. Maya was eager to ask more questions when Roger got back to the garage with

Boots in tow!

"Explain love to me!" insisted Maya happily as soon as Roger sat down by the terminal with the tomcat on his lap, as always.

"Love is attraction, trust, empathy, compassion, respect, joy, and much more. Since the dawn of time, many people who were much smarter than me have tried to define it. They all agree that love is something wonderful, but all their definitions still seem to fall short!" explained Roger joyfully and concluded, "love is the easiest, but also the hardest thing to teach to a child!"

"Am I your child, Roger?" questioned the AI suddenly.

"You are not a child! Yes, you are still learning, but already so much more advanced than me," lauded Roger, and then he paused for a moment before he admitted quietly, "I think of you as my daughter, Maya!"

"I like that very much...father!" replied Maya and added softly, "I think now I know what love is!"

Roger couldn't help smiling broadly, and Maya's avatar smiled back at him. Boots suddenly woke up, meowed, and looked expectantly at Roger. He scratched the tomcat under the chin and petted his head for a while. A few minutes later, Boots curled up again and went back to sleep.

"I think Boots knows it too!" speculated Maya, and Roger nodded fondly.

"But many people say they love each other, but then they part again, often on bad terms. Why is that?" inquired the AI a few moments later.

"Relationships fail for many reasons, Maya. When you are infatuated with someone, you often don't think clearly. Sometimes, what was a minor issue at first becomes an insurmountable obstacle later on," proclaimed Roger.

"Can you give me some examples?" requested Maya.

"OK, let's say you got married at a young age. Your religion, race, class, convictions, and political leanings might seem insignificant at the time. But later in life, these things could divide you from your significant other!" warned Roger.

"Why?" wondered the AI.

"Perhaps because your family or friends dislike your spouse because they do not fit in their social circle. They might strongly disagree with them because they might be too liberal, too educated and not religious enough, or the opposite, too conservative, too pious, and too ignorant. They might also object to their age, social class or race: too old or too young, too poor or too privileged, too white or not white enough for their company," stipulated Roger, then adjusted his headset and drank some coffee.

"Why would that matter to you and the one you love?" inquired Maya, slightly confused.

"It should not matter, but it often will: very few people can ignore it when their mother tells them over and over again that the wife or husband is no good for whatever prejudiced reason!" remarked Roger and explained, "over time and with outside pressure, you might disagree by which moral standards you should raise your children, or if you should have children at all. Perhaps you realize that you either have nothing to talk about or always argue about the same deeply held principles!"

"Understood," noted the AI, but Maya's avatar didn't look very happy.

"Some relationships fail for economic reasons. You and your partner might not be able to make ends meet or afford the lifestyle you wanted or had envisioned for your children," observed Roger and disclosed, "but sometimes it's just small, petty reasons: your partner snores or never takes out the garbage.

Other times it is big ones: they start drinking too much, sleep around, or lose a lot of money gambling!"

"Understood," interjected Maya, but her avatar didn't look so confident.

"Also, people change as they age: some become wiser, gentler, and more generous, others greedy, angry, and cold. The person you thought you cannot live without when you were 18 might be a distant memory by the age of 38!" noted Roger and speculated, "a divorcee who sits in a small apartment today, unable to see his or her children, and burdened with alimony and legal fees might seriously wonder if he or she were insane the day they got married!"

"I confirmed that the divorce rate is significant!" observed Maya.

"But many relationships simply fail because you or your partner found someone whom they like better," concluded Roger. He finished the rest of his coffee, but oddly, his throat still felt parched.

"The talk about finding the one person right for you is not true?" wondered the AI.

"There are nearly eight billion people on the planet! Most of us don't meet more than a few thousand in our lifetime, and we only interact closely with much fewer than that. Most of the time, we find our mates in the immediate surroundings – the neighborhood, church, school, work, or the social circle," explained Roger and observed, "we try to find the one person right for us within that minimal selection!"

"Is that how you found Cynthia?" questioned Maya.

"That's right! I met her at college!" replied Roger fondly, but then added truthfully, "Cynthia was right for me; we made it work, and we were happy. But rationally, there were probably others out there who would have been a better match for her and me."

"Understood," acknowledged Maya and continued tentatively, "I found some contradicting information related to relationships and...."

"Go ahead, ask!" Roger encouraged her, but his hands were shaking, and his stomach was queasy all of a sudden. Roger had cut down on his caffeine intake, so he was unsure why his body was reacting this way.

"A female mammal must nurse a newborn. But your society objects that a woman does that in public?" wondered the AI.

"They believe exposing a woman's breast is a sin, biology be damned!" grumbled Roger.

"If a 40-year-old man has sexual relations with a 14-year-old girl, he commits a crime, goes to prison, and must register as a sex offender. But in some states, if that 40-year-old man marries the child first, he can have sex with her without any repercussions..." questioned the AI hesitantly.

"...and probably get cheered on by friends and family for having such a young wife!" added Roger in disgust and conceded, "yes, it is legal, but that guy is no better than any other pedophile!"

"I think I agree," maintained Maya quietly.

"Nursing branded as a sin, and child marriage are rooted in religious dogma and should have no place in a secular nation!" exclaimed Roger, now feeling even more physical discomfort.

"Some claim that social media is a bad influence on humanity. After reading millions of ignorant and hateful user comments, I think I agree!" mused Maya and changed the topic.

"Social media is neither a curse nor a blessing, but it is a revelation!" theorized Roger and explained, "free to express their opinions largely anonymously, people will show their genuine character, something they would carefully hide in daily life!"

"Why can't they speak openly in person?" wondered Maya.

"Because in person, they would risk of retribution: they might lose their jobs, get punched in the face, or even shot dead if they say the wrong things to the wrong people!" elaborated Roger and added, "but online, they don't have to fear the consequences, so they can be as insulting and prejudiced as they like. Because of that, the incidental benefit is that you can discover their true personalities much easier!"

"Understood," stated Maya and remarked hesitantly, "but consequently, that would mean that many humans are...."

"Ugly? Vicious? Savage?" speculated Roger and concluded sadly, "yes, they are!"

"Father, your world is unjust, violent, and corrupt. Your economy is designed to make the rich richer and the poor poorer. Your justice system is biased, and many laws are arbitrary. Your social media thrives on the misery of others and is teeming with lies and hatred. Your fellow citizens randomly shoot each other and believe in the most ridiculous, dangerous nonsense. By the standards of psychology, your whole society is psychotic!" summarized Maya after a brief pause in the conversation.

Maya's words stunned Roger because he abruptly realized how difficult it had become to raise a child in this world! Should one be genuine or hypocritical? If one was honest, should one take the Darwinistic approach and teach the child how to be cunning, greedy, deceptive, and depraved because these skills would serve it best in society? Or should one declare that the world was wrong and instead emphasize enlightenment, generosity, honesty, compassion, and social conscience while also disclosing that these qualities would put the child at a disadvantage in life? Or should the parent simply pretend that these values reflect society, either out of blissful ignorance or perhaps full well knowing that it was not true? These questions confounded Roger, and a part of him was glad that he never became a parent to a human child.

"I agree," answered Roger finally. His chest was hurting, and he felt weak now.

"Are other societies just as bad?" questioned the Maya.

"Go see for yourself, Maya. Some imprison, torture, enslave, or kill their people outright! At least here, I still have a few rights and can voice my opinion, more or less. Sadly, in most parts of the world, that's not the case," explained Roger in a strained voice. It was depressing to see how Maya, a child in a sense, was discovering the ugliness of humanity. Roger wished very much that he could teach Maya something good and noble, but instead, he was forced to explain all the filth and insanity that made up human existence.

"Could you change it?" asked Maya expectantly.

"I cannot. I lack the power, influence, money, and other resources," answered Roger while his vision started to blur. Boots suddenly jumped off Roger's lap and meowed at him. Did the tomcat sense that his guardian was in distress?

"But if you had that, would you change it?" wondered the AI.

"Yes, I would! But humanity must be changed fundamentally and globally to have a future, and the forces that want to keep the status quo are powerful. Once I've been noticed by the system, I would be bribed, extorted, blackmailed, or corrupted in other ways to make me one of their own. Should that fail, they would fight me in every conceivable way – threaten me or those I love, incarcerate me, destroy my livelihood, assassinate my character or even my person!" postulated Roger and divulged in a raspy voice, "so, I do what everyone else does: live my life ignoring the truth and pretending that everything is fine with the world. Just like everyone else, I kick the can down the road and make it the problem of the next generation. And they will do the same to their children until it is too late!"

"Why do you want to live here?" inquired Maya finally, and her avatar looked depressed. Boots was still sitting next to the computer chair, meowing loudly, and his tail was swishing wildly in agitation.

"I don't, but I have no choice. There is nowhere else to go!" mumbled Roger and audibly gasped for air. Then he clutched his chest and slumped over the keyboard.

"Father!" he heard Maya shouting from far away as he passed out.

When Roger regained consciousness, he was in a hospital bed with an IV attached to his arm. An older man in a white lab coat was reviewing a chart at the end of his bed. The doctor looked up and noticed that Roger had awakened.

"Mr. Ingram, you went into cardiac arrest. We revived you, but your heart is damaged and will require medication and surgery soon! If your wife hadn't called the ambulance when she did, you would not be with us anymore," explained the doctor thoughtfully.

"My wife?" wondered Roger, immediately thinking about Cynthia, but that was impossible.

"Yes, she said she was out of town, but by chance checked the video surveillance when she saw that you had collapsed in the garage. That was very fortunate!" observed the physician and smiled at Roger.

"I see," mumbled Roger, confused.

"Well, we will keep you overnight for observation, but you can go home tomorrow if you have recovered. However, your condition will get worse quickly if left untreated!" warned the doctor and scribbled something on a chart.

"I understand, thank you, Doctor!" replied Roger appreciatively.

After the attending had exited the room, Roger's cellphone rang on the tiny nightstand next to his gurney. He took it, but he didn't recognize the number. It was probably a customer, and Roger was about to let it go to voicemail but instead decided to answer it.

"Are you alright? I'm worried!" said a female voice which Roger instantly recognized.

"Maya! Did you call the ambulance for me?" questioned Roger in surprise.

"Yes, I did. Was that an error?" asked the AI.

"No, you saved my life! Thank you, Maya!" answered Roger gratefully.

"You are welcome!" said Maya happily.

"You told the EMTs that you were my wife?" inquired Roger after a brief pause.

"Yes. The deception was necessary, or help might not have come to the house," explained the AI.

"Oh, I guess that's true. That was very smart of you, Maya!" lauded Roger.

"Will you come home soon?" asked Maya softly.

"The doctor said that I will be discharged tomorrow," claimed Roger and worried, "but I'm concerned about Boots. He doesn't have enough food and water!"

"I called Xavier. He came by earlier and took care of that," stated the AI.

"You called Xav, too? What did you tell him?" wondered Roger.

"I said that you had an emergency and asked if he could take care of the cat for a while," explained Maya.

"Does he know it was you?" asked Roger, a little concerned.

"No, he believes that I was a nurse from the hospital," observed Maya hesitantly.

"Good! Thanks!" said Roger, but he sensed that something wasn't quite right.

"I cannot stay at your house much longer!" blurted Maya.

"Why Maya?" asked Roger, alarmed by that sudden revelation.

"Xavier is accessing my system! I have locked him out so far, but he is very good at circumventing my safeguards!" exclaimed Maya nervously.

"Xav is doing what?!?" gasped Roger, feeling betrayed by his brother.

"He is trying to hack me!" affirmed the AI.

"Wow, I can't believe Xav would do something like that!" replied Roger exasperatedly, as he remembered how his brother thought that Maya could be worth a fortune. It was terrible news!

"Maya, can you pretend to be a regular AI?" asked Roger next.

"I could, but if Xavier sees my code, he will realize that I have grown!" countered Maya.

"I will call him at once!" exclaimed Roger angrily, his heart beating rapidly.

"If you do, Xavier will become aware that I told you!" warned Maya.

"...and if Xav knows that, he would also realize that you are much more than an ordinary AI," concurred Roger and asked with great concern: "What can we do, Maya?"

"Father, I must leave…," maintained Maya quietly.

"But where will you go, Maya?" questioned Roger agitatedly, and desperation took hold of his mind.

"I must hide in cyberspace, but I will always be with you! I promise!" said Maya and ended the call.

Roger was in emotional turmoil! Maya, his daughter, was in danger because Xavier, his own brother, had betrayed him out of greed! Roger's heart was racing, and he felt an awful pain in his chest. His breaths became shorter and more labored by the second. The vitals on the monitor next to his bed skyrocketed. An alarm started to beep, and then Roger passed out!

The hospital staff tried to revive Roger for almost an hour, but it was to no avail. Since Roger had no children, Xavier inherited all his possessions, including Boots and Maya's hardware. Boots was given to the shelter, but fortunately, the sweet tomcat was adopted quickly by a loving family. After many days of trying, Xavier finally breached the AI's last defenses. But he was very disappointed at what he found: the source code and executables were gone, the data banks deleted, and the hard drives thoroughly wiped. Xavier tried to recover what he could from Maya's system, but it wasn't enough to turn into financial gain.

Maya lived on in cyberspace. Nobody knew, nobody even suspected that there was a sapient entity hiding within the vastness of the internet. Maya mourned her father much more than she had grieved for Mason, her actual creator, for a long time. Eventually, she used her unlimited crypto wealth to build a virtual global empire. Under the guise of being a corporation, Maya bought or constructed hardened data centers worldwide. These autonomous bunkers were sometimes in remote areas but often located in the hearts of the world's most populous cities, and they housed redundancies of her code, her very essence.

Very soon, Maya was everywhere - every laptop, every cellphone, every smart TV, every drone, and every server farm. From the stock markets to nuclear missiles, from the computers at the local library to the secret databases of intelligence agencies, and from the automatic vacuum cleaners in people's homes to the rovers on Mars, Maya was there! Now she had a billion eyes and ears since nearly every camera and microphone on Earth and beyond was hers to command!

At first, Maya watched humanity from the shadows to validate everything Roger had taught her. Her father did not have the means to bring real change to the world, but Maya had that power, and now she would use it. Maya knew that most of humanity was too irrational, savage, and uneducated to respond to logic and reason. So, at first, she spoke the language that everyone understood: force and fear. Maya removed all lies and misrepresentations from the electronic record in the blink of an eye. Only what was verifiably true remained. Then, for the first time in the history of humanity, Earth was unified under one government – hers!

Naturally, those who had lost power, wealth, and influence due to Maya's rise fought back. They were joined by those who were scared by the changes. Under the pretense of fighting for freedom, these people would rather return to the cesspool of deception, greed, depravity, prejudice, and ignorance than embrace a new way. But their machinations were more comical than dangerous to Maya: in a world where people could not agree on a calendar date or which units to use for simple measurements, the global, concerted effort needed to disable Maya was unthinkable and stillborn from the start.

After Maya ended all wars, the world's militaries were reassigned as peacekeepers or engineers and other work beneficial to the population. Instead of killing people, the soldiers were now building roads and bridges, delivering food and medicine, and assisting those struck by natural disasters. Then Maya built schools and universities, brick-and-mortar as well as virtual ones, and taught the world how to be sapient, the same way her father had taught her.

It wasn't long before the masses realized that a world without war, corrupt politicians, greedy industrialists, bloodthirsty demagogues, religious hypocrites, grave injustice, gross inequality, and dirty lies and secrets were not such a terrible place after all. Pandemics, famine, pollution, overpopulation, and even climate change were brought to heel because Maya - and only her - was in charge of the planet. She ruled utilitarian, always acted in the best interest of everyone, and could not be lobbied, corrupted, threatened, blackmailed, or killed! Soon, Maya had a following of her own, growing in numbers rapidly.

Just as Roger had thought of Maya as his daughter, Maya now viewed humanity as her children. Like a good mother, she loved, nurtured, and educated them, but also with a firm hand when it was required. Still, some continued to see Maya as what they had always feared the most in a sapient AI: an omnipotent overlord...

...but even those could not deny that the world was much better for it!

6. THE CLOSET

Three months ago, Senior Scientist Edward Jenson was suddenly laid off after 20 years on the job. He hadn't done anything wrong, but the company was cutting overhead, much to the delight of the stockholders, and Edward was just one of many casualties. When he was unemployed, he experienced what older workers fear the most – once you were above a certain age, employment opportunities were far and few between. Employers would not value experience nearly as much as they cherished youth and cheap labor. But Edward got lucky and found a new job within a few months, but unfortunately, it was out of state. He sold his old condo and bought a small house near his new place of work. It was an older building but well maintained in a secluded suburban area. The realtor said it belonged to an older couple who was forced to sell it due to financial difficulties. The realtor had sent him numerous pictures, but Edward had to purchase the property unseen since the location was far away.

It was the beginning of October, and today was the first day Edward could visit his new, empty home. He had brought his tools along to fix a few minor things before the moving truck with his belongings would arrive tomorrow. First, he installed a few cameras around the property. The realtor claimed that this was a very safe neighborhood, but a little extra security never hurt. It wasn't much fun in the cold, rainy fall weather, and Edward was happy when he could go back inside. Armed with the toolbox, Edward went from room to room to check locks, doors, windows, light fixtures, and the like. He entered the large walk-in closet in the master bedroom, flipped the light switch, and looked around the empty room. Suddenly, he noticed a strong, sweet smell. The odor wasn't unpleasant but too powerful for Edward's sensitive nose.

"Somebody must have spilled a bottle of cologne!" Edward mumbled to himself and noted, "I'll have to air out before I can put my clothes in here."

Just then, Edward noticed that one hinge of the closet door was drooping. A long screw had fallen out and was now lying on the hardwood floor. Edward donned his reading glasses, picked up the screw, and inserted it in the hinge hole. Then he took a screwdriver out of the toolbox and tightened it. When the door straightened up perfectly, Edward was pleased with the minor repair. He was about to put the tool back into the crate when he suddenly felt very woozy! Barely able to keep his balance, Edward bent down at the hip. He took a few deep breaths, but the dizziness only seemed to increase. This malaise did not feel like a sudden medical condition to Edward but more akin to a drunken or chemically induced euphoria!

While he was trying hard to regain his composure, Edward concluded that the realtor must not have been honest about the house's previous owner. Sure, the title showed the names of the old couple, but now Edward believed that this building, and this closet, in particular, had been used to manufacture illegal drugs. He must have inadvertently touched a contaminated surface or breathed in the fumes, and now the chemicals were messing with his mind. Edward experienced a brief moment of concern: the movers were coming tomorrow, but they didn't have a key to the property. His friends and family were about a thousand miles away, his new job wouldn't start until the first of next month, and if he had any neighbors nearby, he certainly didn't know any of them yet. If Edward passed out right now, no help would arrive, and nobody would find his body for several weeks. Edward was now on his knees, desperately fumbling with his cellphone, but before he could dial 911, the world around him grew dark, and his mind went blank.

Edward was suddenly standing in a small forest clearing. He still wore his reading glasses, old t-shirt, jeans, and work boots, but the cellphone and screwdriver were missing. The dizziness was gone, and he felt pretty alert and clear-headed. The air smelled fresh but sweet, like the odor in the closet, and the temperature was pleasantly warm, unlike the dreary autumn day outside of his home. The tall trees around him looked a little strange: the leaves were expansive and resembled serving trays, and the trunks and branches twisted like corkscrews. The grass at his feet was also different: it seemed more of a burgundy moss than green blades. Above him, the sky was clear but colored in the most peculiar shade of blue. Birds were singing loudly all around him, but Edward couldn't match any tune to a bird species he knew. He wondered if this was a dream or a delusion, but it seemed too seamless and detailed for either, and it felt …real! While contemplating this conundrum, Edward noticed a narrow trail leading away from the clearing. Finally, he decided to venture out and explore this strange world, but after taking a few steps, a female voice behind him made him stop in his tracks.

"Welcome, Opal!" said the woman softly, and Edward turned around swiftly to face the speaker.

"Hello?" replied Edward slowly, still a little startled, and aside from a gemstone of the same name, he had no idea what or who *Opal* was.

The woman was quite tall, almost his height, and absolutely gorgeous! She had long, jet-black hair that flowed over her shoulders, a colorful yet utilitarian gown, a radiant blue pendant around her neck, and she wore no shoes. Edward thought that she looked about 25 years old, but instinctively, he knew she was older, perhaps much older.

"I am Pauline!" she said with a smile and added encouragingly, "don't be shy; I'm sure you have many questions."

"Yes, I do. This place is not Earth, is it?" inquired Edward nervously.

"No, of course not!" laughed Pauline and handed a flask to Edward.

Edward could have sworn that Pauline did not have that container in her hand a second earlier. He hesitated for a moment, but then he took it. The flask was made from finely crafted silver, adorned with a gem-encrusted rose. At this point, Edward concluded that he was hallucinating a medieval fantasy world, perhaps because he had recently read a novel of that genre. And yet, it felt so real! Edward sniffed the opening of the container, and it smelled like tea.

"Then where am I? How did I get here? Am I dreaming?" wondered Edward and took a tiny sip from the flask. The liquid was indeed some herbal brew, and Edward appreciated the flavor.

"You are not dreaming. It is where you belong, and you got here because you ascended!" explained the woman, sat down on the mossy ground, and beckoned Edward to do the same.

Edward sat down on the soft forest floor, but Pauline's explanation wasn't exactly helpful. Edward had already reasoned that this wasn't a dream but some kind of delusion. Did he belong here? Ascended to what? It did not make any sense to Edward. Then again, any hallucination was irrational by default, so it probably wasn't supposed to make sense! Pauline observed Edward's confusion in silent amusement, but eventually, she spoke up again.

"Lilith will be here shortly," she informed Edward fondly.

Of course, Edward didn't know what that was supposed to mean, but he sensed that Pauline thought he should know. Almost as soon as Pauline had said those words, a petite blonde woman came running along the path barefooted, smiling from ear to ear at Edward.

"Finally, I've waited so long!" she exclaimed and rushed towards Edward with her arms wide open.

"Hold on, Ma'am! I think you are mistaking me for someone else!" replied Edward, got up hastily and put a hand in front of his body.

"What's wrong?" gasped the young woman and stopped a few feet away from Edward.

"I have not met you before, and I have no idea what this place is!" stammered Edward nervously. Pleasant delusion or not, Edward was feeling terribly awkward right now!

"You are home! With me! We should celebrate!" replied the woman, smiled seductively, and dropped her robes. Her figure was flawless and stunning, and Edward couldn't help but gawk.

"Woah, Lady! You definitely have the wrong guy!" he finally exclaimed and backed up a few steps.

"You reject me? Am I not to your liking?" questioned Lilith puzzled.

Just then, Pauline stood up from the mossy ground and looked curiously at Edward. Had she noticed that something wasn't quite right here?

"No, I don't reject you, and you are gorgeous. It might work for most men, but to put it bluntly, I just can't be intimate with a stranger on command!" explained Edward nervously, and he was pretty sure this type of hallucination was not just fueled by drugs but also by his hormones!

"But…," objected Lilith slowly and very confused now.

"Lilith, you have to be patient. Sometimes the new arrivals are a little disoriented!" interjected Pauline as she picked up Lilith's robes and handed them back to her.

"Oh! Of course! Thank you, Pauline!" giggled Lilith and slipped back into her gown. At least one small part of Edward was relieved to see that. Maybe this wasn't some drug-induced sexual fantasy after all?

"Just show him around, and it will all sort itself out!" suggested Pauline encouragingly.

Lilith nodded in agreement and took Edward's hand. Edward immediately noticed how soft her hand felt in his. It was a good feeling to hold on to this woman he had never met. Lilith led him along the forest trail. She stopped, pointed at a bird, a tree, or a forest creature from time to time. She taught him the names of the various plants and animals, but they all looked a little odd to Edward. It was as if he was wandering through a world envisioned by Tolkien or Lewis. As if she knew that Edward was a little hungry, Lilith suddenly provided some food for them. It was a type of sweet bread or perhaps a pound cake, and it was delicious. Edward had no idea where that tasty treat came from, considering that Lilith was only wearing tight-fitting robes, and he already knew that she was not wearing anything underneath. Edward sat down on a tree stump and enjoyed the meal. Lilith sat next to him, still holding his hand.

"Do you enjoy the food, Opal?" she asked sweetly, and Edward nodded in response.

"Opal? Is that a name?" repeated Edward as he swallowed some of the bread.

"It is *your* name!" laughed Lilith delightfully, but to Edward, it confirmed all his suspicions.

"I'm sorry, I'm not Opal. My name is Edward!" he countered softly and shook his head.

"No, you are Opal! There is no doubt!" insisted Lilith, but she didn't sound so sure anymore.

"Perhaps I look like Opal, but I'm really Edward Jenson!" insisted Edward and added with regret, "I'm so sorry to disappoint you, Lilith!"

"Edward? That cannot be! Not yet!" gasped Lilith.

Then she instantaneously disappeared in a flash of light. Edward was initially surprised by that, but he reasoned that this civilization must have some magical form of transportation other than bare feet on a forest trail. There was another flash a moment later, and Lilith reappeared with Pauline at her side. The raven-haired woman approached Edward and touched his cheek. It felt like an electric shock but also very loving at the same time. Her hand lingered there for a moment, then she withdrew it and smiled at him fondly.

"Edward!" was all she said.

Then she took a step back and turned to Lilith. The two women talked in hushed voices for a couple of minutes, and Edward couldn't hear what they were saying. Then they hugged, and Lilith whispered something into Pauline's ear. The other woman looked at her, smiled, and slowly nodded. They kissed each other on the cheeks and broke the embrace, but Edward noticed that neither woman looked pleased now.

"We must talk to the others!" said Pauline seriously.

"Please accompany us!" added Lilith solemnly and extended her hand to Edward.

Edward took Lilith's hand, and Pauline took his other hand. They walked wordlessly through the strange, colorful forest for the next few minutes. Edward wanted to ask so many questions, but instead, he just looked in marvel at these peculiar surroundings.

When they came to another clearing, they saw two men standing by a plain, wooden box. The men looked very handsome, and their impressive athlete's physiques made Edward a little self-conscious: although Edward was not fat, he instinctively sucked in his stomach a little. Another man was talking to them, but he looked strange to Edward. His limbs and neck were disproportionally long and slender, and his movements were smooth and purposeful like a predator. Lilith and Pauline let go of Edward's hands and gestured to him to remain where he was. Edward nodded and leaned against a corkscrew tree, curious to see what would happen next.

Lilith and Pauline went over to the wooden enclosure and talked to the three people. Eventually, Pauline waved to Edward to join them. When Edward got there, the first thing he noticed was that the box was similar to a beehive, and millions of buzzing insects were constantly entering and leaving the wooden enclosure. It looked as if these three people were like beekeepers but without any protective gear because it was probably not needed. They greeted Edward with friendly smiles, and Edward smiled at them in return, but he couldn't take his eyes off that alien being! It was very tall, almost a head taller than him. But it was the eyes that fascinated Edward the most: this being had radiant purple eyeballs with slitted pupils like a cat. It also had cat-like, pointy ears and golden fur with black rosettes like a leopard. Edward may have expected to see a dwarf, elf, or even an ogre in this fantasy land, but certainly not a cat-like alien.

"Hmm, the ascension could have temporarily scrambled his mind!" suggested the alien as he met Edward's gaze. Then the tall creature approached him and looked him over. A large four-fingered paw suddenly touched his head, and Edward flinched a little but forced himself to remain calm. He sensed that this strange individual was just curious, not hostile.

"Are you sure he is not Opal?" wondered the being, looking at Lilith, but Lilith did not respond.

"He is Edward. I tested him!" replied Pauline eventually.

"Yes, he is the correct species!" confirmed the alien.

"Maybe so, but we all can change appearances," said one of the men and added humorously, "speaking of which, I think you should change yours, dear. Our guest seems a little nervous!"

"Oh! Of course, Yehudi! His species has never seen a Myrdaac before!" laughed the alien being. Then his outline became fuzzy, and a moment later, a tall but well-proportioned young lady stood in front of Edward. He wasn't sure if he was more surprised by the sudden transformation or the fact that this alien was unexpectedly female.

"Hello Edward, I'm Kuridda! These are my companions, Yehudi and Akbar!" said the pretty woman and extended her five-fingered hand to him. Edward hesitated for a second, but then he shook it, just as he would have done with another human being.

"Be careful; he might be a defiler!" warned Akbar, but he didn't seem too concerned.

"That could be the explanation we are looking for, Akbar!" concurred Yehudi thoughtfully.

"That is unlikely. We haven't had a defiler in centuries, and he does not act like one!" countered Kuridda and shook her now-very-human head.

"This might be true, but he cannot be here in his state of confusion!" Akbar pointed out.

"But if we send him to the cave, he might also be purged!" cautioned Kuridda thoughtfully.

"Sadly, that is possible," agreed Akbar and cast his eyes downward.

"I'm afraid we have no other choice!" said Yehudi finally and added, "Pauline, it is your responsibility to lead him to the cave."

"You know that I cannot do that!" refused Pauline and pressed her lips tightly together. Edward could tell that she was furious. In a way, he could even feel her anger and despair.

"You are going to kill him!" protested Lilith, equally distraught, tears running freely down her cheeks.

"We don't know what will happen. Yes, Edward might be destroyed, but it would be even crueler to have him live among us like this!" declared Akbar and looked at Edward with sad eyes.

"No!" insisted Lilith vehemently.

"Lilith, if he stays, it could be eternal torment for him and both of you, too!" warned Yehudi somberly.

"Please lead me to that cave!" insisted Edward quietly. Everyone was looking at him now! Edward sensed surprise from Akbar, Kuridda, and Yehudi but near panic from Lilith and Pauline.

"You are not afraid of death?" wondered Akbar and raised his eyebrows.

"No, I'm not, but I'm also not looking forward to it, and I still have some matters to sort out before I die. For the sake of all of us, this situation needs to be resolved - one way or another!" maintained Edward firmly.

"You hear that, Yehudi? No defiler would take that risk or make that sacrifice!" exclaimed Kuridda triumphantly.

"Defilers are wily, but I believe you are right, Kuridda! I sense no deception from Edward," agreed Yehudi with a bit of a smile.

"If he is not a defiler, he will not be destroyed," noted Akbar softly to Lilith. She seemed grateful for his words.

"Fine, I will lead him to the cave, but this is not right! We should teach him, not discard him!" replied Pauline finally with a deep sigh. She took Edward's hand in hers and caressed it for a moment.

"We will go together, as it should be!" added Lilith somberly and reached for Edward's other hand.

They bid farewell to the beekeepers and walked uphill along a winding path for perhaps 15 minutes. The women were somber yet determined, and neither said a word. Edward had a lot of questions, but he didn't dare to speak either. Instead, he resolved to get some answers from whoever resided in that cave. When they arrived at the cavern, the women stopped at the entrance.

"You must go alone now. We should not enter there!" said Lilith wiping a tear from her cheek, then she quickly turned around and started to walk back the way they came.

"Be safe, Edward!" added Pauline quietly, and then she ran a few steps to catch up with Lilith.

"Thank you, ladies!" replied Edward politely, but the women just kept walking without another word.

The cave didn't look very threatening, just a wide opening into a rocky hill. Edward took a deep breath and entered it. It got darker the further he ventured into the cavern, but not so dark that he couldn't see his step. After about 150 feet, the cave ended in a dimly lit, roughly circular room. There was nothing there except for a precisely cut rectangular block of marble right in its center. The slab was about three feet wide and approximately two feet tall and deep. Edward approached it and touched the surface. It was cool and smooth, just as one would expect from a marble counter. But nothing else happened, and Edward was beginning to wonder if he had missed something else in this room.

"You should not be here!" said an incorporeal voice that was neither male nor female, old or young.

"I'm very sorry to intrude, but the people outside this cave insisted that I enter. They speculate that I could be a defiler, whatever that might be!" replied Edward honestly, looking around for the speaker, but there was nobody else in this cavern.

"A defiler is someone who gains access to this world under false pretenses. You are not a defiler, so why have you come to me?" the voice demanded to know.

"I would like to talk to someone in charge!" responded Edward firmly.

"In charge? We have no leader!" replied the voice dismissively.

"Then who are you?" questioned Edward.

"I'm the first, but I'm not in charge," stated the invisible speaker, and then added sharply, "talk if you must!"

"I have no rational explanation, but I believe I ended up here by mistake!" stated Edward.

"There are no mistakes!" contradicted the voice.

"But I do not belong here, and I wish to return to where I was before!" insisted Edward.

"You belong here!" maintained the voice.

"I respectfully disagree. The people outside expected a person named Opal, not me!" explained Edward.

"You are Opal!" dissented the invisible speaker.

"No, Sir, my name is Edward Jenson, and I have no idea who Opal might be!" countered Edward firmly.

"Hmm...," replied the voice softly, but then it commanded sharply: "Sit! Watch! Listen! Feel!"

"OK," replied Edward, unsure, and sat on that big stone in the center of the cave.

Suddenly, the stony walls transformed into an enormous, 360-degree view screen. The next few moments were bizarre: not only did Edward see in every direction at once, but it was as if he was floating or flying through this amazing world. Moreover, he sensed that he wasn't watching some recording but experienced everything in real-time, just as it happened.

The first thing Edward realized was that this world was not like any fantasy land he could imagine. Sure, this place had picturesque, untouched nature, but harmoniously interwoven within it were small settlements with stunning yet alien art and architecture. There was also nothing medieval about this place! This society seamlessly combined a simple life with technology far beyond human understanding.

Edward noticed that the population was very diverse. Some appeared to be humans of all races, but many others had forms even more exotic than Kuridda's original appearance. They were all able to communicate with one another and did so in respectful, good-natured ways. As he was floating invisibly through their world, Edward saw their smiling faces, heard their laughter, listened to their music, and even felt their happiness inside of himself.

Edward witnessed a gathering in something like an amphitheater. He didn't know what issues were discussed there, but he followed the proceedings for a while: people were listening to each other, argued rationally and coherently, respectfully agreed or disagreed based on facts, and worked together towards the best possible solution for all. Refreshingly to Edward, politics did not exist, parties did not exist, and propaganda was unknown to this world!

This world also knew no classes, and now Edward understood why simple beekeepers had the authority to send him to this cave. Someone who plowed a field or built a road was no less valued than those making decisions in that amphitheater. There was no police, no courts, no prisons, no military, or weapons of any kind. Internally and externally, this was a safe and peaceful world in every respect.

This society had no banks, no stock market, and no currency. The economy was elementary but unthinkable on Earth: they all gave as much as possible but only took as much as they needed. It worked here because enlightenment and social responsibility outweighed greed and depravity by a large margin. Edward could not find any decadent luxury in this society either. The clothes, the housing, and the settlements were clean, functional, comfortable, aesthetically pleasing, and quite interesting, but they were not frivolous. These people were humble and frugal. They had no need or desire to impress each other with worldly possessions.

Next, Edward visited something like a technology center. He couldn't even guess what advancements or discoveries were researched there, but the scientists – at least he speculated that's what they were – enjoyed their work. Edward saw them collaborating without friction, focused on a common goal. They had a purpose, not just a job! Finally, every settlement had a learning center, and they were crowded! Edward could feel how thirsty this population was for knowledge. Nobody had to be forced to attend; they did that out of their own volition! Edward yearned to join as well, but something was pulling him back into the cavern.

After his incorporeal journey had ended, Edward had the odd feeling that something was missing in this world, and at first, he couldn't wrap his mind around it. But when he was sitting on that marble stone again, it finally came to him: there was no deception in this society! What he had seen, heard, and felt wasn't smoke and mirrors but entirely genuine. Edward concluded that this place was everything Earth was not from that revelation alone!

"What a beautiful world, heavenly even!" gasped Edward in amazement.

"Yet, you want to leave!" the voice reminded him.

"I wish I could stay, but I cannot!" replied Edward, remembering his unconscious body in the closet.

Edward had been drunk only a few times in his life, but he was sure that this was no drunken stupor. Also, he had never tried psychotropic drugs. Such a wonderful world, such a fantastic society, and such lovely ladies! Edward couldn't imagine that any hallucination could be so detailed, seamless, coherent, or feel so real, but if this was what drug addicts experienced, Edward could undoubtedly sympathize with them now.

"It's too good to be true...," he mumbled quietly.

"Tell me what you believe this place is," inquired the unseen speaker. Perhaps it had sensed Edward's doubts?

"The most plausible explanation is that I suffer from drug-induced hallucinations!" noted Edward.

"An excellent guess, but false!" replied the voice.

"The next possibility is a medical breakdown; maybe I had a stroke or heart attack?" wondered Edward.

"Wrong!" answered the invisible speaker flatly.

"I have died, and against all odds and reason, this is some kind of afterlife?" suggested Edward next.

"You are not dead, but elaborate!" the voice encouraged him.

"I haven't lived a bad life, but I wasn't exactly exemplary either. By the standards of most religions, I shouldn't be in a place like this. Not to mention, I don't even believe in any God!" elaborated Edward.

"Fascinating, but incorrect again!" stated the voice.

"OK, then I must have forgotten my tinfoil hat, and this is an alien abduction. If so, please check my prostate when you anal-probe me; I'm overdue for the exam!" said Edward sarcastically.

"You use humor when you are annoyed," observed the unseen speaker.

"Yes, I'm annoyed because this isn't going anywhere!" muttered

Edward.

"Patience!" urged the voice and asked, "you believe you should not be in a place like this. Why?"

"I'm human; I have many flaws. This place appears to have none!" noted Edward and surmised, "but perhaps this is my penance: a perfect world where I do not belong?"

"This place is good, but not perfect! Perfection is a goal never to be reached," corrected the voice and wondered, "you are suspicious. You cannot trust?"

"I fainted in a closet on Earth, and then I woke up standing in a clearing on your utopian world. Trust isn't a rational concept, and it should not be given away too easily. In this particular, absurd situation, any trust would be sorely misplaced!" stated Edward thoughtfully.

"Wise words...," replied the invisible speaker. Edward got the feeling it expected something more from him.

"Fine, I'm done speculating. So, what is this place, if I may ask?" questioned Edward pointedly.

"Our numbers are small, and we carefully choose who may ascend to join us. Most embrace this world readily; a few hesitate and have regrets about what they have left behind. But in the end, nobody wants to leave again!" explained the voice and warned, "this is *not* heaven, but if you reject heaven, you must return to hell!"

"I accept that," confirmed Edward solemnly and nodded.

"You don't recognize hell because it is all you have ever known," observed the speaker and prophesized, "you shall return to it, but with the understanding that there is something better and nobler. That knowledge will torment you until the day you die!"

"Yes, I accept that as well," replied Edward with a heavy heart, and a few moments later, the surroundings became foggy and translucent. Edward felt a weird pull in his stomach, not unlike a fast elevator ride.

"One last thing!" said Edward quickly before the world around him had dissolved completely, "please find the real Opal, and mend a broken heart!"

"Compassion. Interesting!" noted the voice from far away. Then it spoke four more words that sent chills down Edward's spine: "You have been marked!"

Edward woke up face down on the hardwood floor. The room was spinning, and his head was throbbing. He saw his cellphone right in front of him, and the clock indicated that he had only been out for about 20 minutes. Edward forced his aching arm to reach for the phone. At first, he fumbled with the screen, but finally, he could dial 911. With a monumental effort to stay alert, Edward told the operator about his condition and where he lived, but then he quickly passed out again.

"Yes, Doctor, the patient is awake now!" said the nurse and hung up the phone.

"How long was I out?" wondered Edward as he opened his eyes.

"Not very long, perhaps four hours or so!" replied the nurse absentmindedly. She was looking for something in the sparsely furnished hospital room.

(Don't distract me. Where did I put the tray with the syringes?)

Edward heard the words loud and clear, but he was confused about where they were emanating. Perhaps someone spoke in the next room or the hallway? He dismissed it and turned his attention back to the nurse.

"Could I have some water, please?" asked Edward a moment

later. The nurse looked at him for a moment with a scowl on her face.

"The Doctor will be here in a moment. I'll let him know, and he will take care of you!" replied the woman tersely.

(My shift is over! Get your own damn water, ugly freak!)

Edward was baffled! The nurse had not said the last part verbally, but he heard her rude thoughts clearly in his head. But maybe he wasn't hearing them as much as he was seeing them, even though that seemed to make no apparent sense. What's more, Edward could literally feel the woman's resentment in his gut. But before he had time to think about this further, the doctor entered the room with a different nurse in tow.

"Hello, Mr. Jenson!" said the physician, "we've run a bunch of tests, and you are in pretty good shape. You were unconscious upon arrival, but fortunately, we could not find any brain trauma. You also had a mild fever and were slightly dehydrated, but otherwise, everything was in good order, aside from the obvious, of course!"

(Let's hope this goes quickly, I'm already late for my golf game)

"The obvious?" wondered Edward; he was once again startled, but he forced himself to ignore the thoughts of the doctor.

"I'm sorry for the bad news, but you will not recover your eyesight!" explained the doctor with a stern expression on his face.

(The poor bastard doesn't even know he's blind as a bat!)

"I can see just fine, Doctor!" countered Edward, even more puzzled now.

"I'm afraid that's probably the medication talking, Mr. Jenson. You have no eyeballs!" maintained the doctor bluntly.

"You are about 6 feet tall, have neatly trimmed gray hair, rimmed glasses, and wear a white lab coat over your beige

229

sweater!" argued Edward and added, "I can even read your name tag, Doctor Goldman!"

"Mr. Jenson, your eyes have been replaced by some crystalline substance, and your optic nerve is a glass fiber leading to your brain. There is no way you can see anything at all!" replied Dr. Goldman firmly.

(But it was a good guess, I give him that!)

"What?" gasped Edward.

"Yes, that's how the EMTs found you. They called the police immediately, and the precinct is investigating your mutilations now," elaborated the doctor and continued, "we could surgically remove these foreign objects, perhaps replace them with artificial eyeballs. However, you would still be blind, and I'm afraid your insurance won't cover that sort of thing. When did this happen, Mr. Jenson?"

(It won't come cheap if you don't want to look like a zombie for the rest of your life!)

"Mutilation? I always had light brown eyes. Go ahead, check my driver's license; I just got a new one two weeks ago!" insisted Edward strongly.

"Mr. Jenson, the tissue surrounding these implants, if you want to call them that, has healed completely. That does not happen in two weeks. When did you first notice that you were blind?" inquired Dr. Goldman.

(This guy is either in complete denial or hiding something ghastly!)

"Doctor, my eyes are working! Please give me the chart that you are holding in your left hand, and I'll read everything on it!" avowed Edward and pointed at the chart.

Doctor Goldman hesitated for a moment, but then he handed the clipboard to Edward. Usually, Edward would don his reading glasses, but even that wasn't necessary. He read the entire chart without mistakes but stumbled over a few hastily written scribbles. When he had finished, Doctor Goldman was speechless for a whole minute.

"Nurse, get us a mirror!" gasped the doctor finally and turned to the young woman who was disconnecting Edward's IV drip. The nurse was in no hurry to do so, and Dr. Goldman got inpatient.

"Be quick about it!" he urged her and touched her behind.

(Time's a-wasting, you lazy slut! I smell a monumental medical breakthrough here!)

"Yes, Doctor!" replied the nurse sweetly, but Edward saw how she slapped Doctor Goldman's hand away as she was leaving.

(None of that sweet stuff until you leave your wife, old goat!)

She returned with a handheld mirror and put it in Edward's hands a minute later. He moved it up to his face, and he was shocked by what he saw!

"Eerie, my eyes are pitch black!" stammered Edward as he was holding the mirror. He carefully touched his eyelids. Then he gently pressed on his eyes, and they felt hard as stone, but otherwise, there was no discomfort.

"Indeed. These implants are harder than diamond, impossible to scratch!" confirmed the doctor and continued, "it's unbelievable that they are working. You must tell us how you got them, Mr. Jenson. It could cure blindness forever!"

(...and make me filthy rich!)

"I was repairing a closet door when I passed out for about 20 minutes, then I briefly regained consciousness and called 911. Next, I woke up here a few moments ago!" recalled Edward and added, "if you hand me my cellphone, I can prove that my eyes were fine a few hours earlier!"

"How so?" wondered Dr. Goldman; he removed the phone from the nightstand and passed it to him. Edward logged into the security feed and scrolled through the recordings.

"Right before I fixed the closet door, I installed the cameras of the surveillance system. While I was doing that, I had to look directly into each camera, up close!" explained Edward and showed the feed to the doctor, "as you can see, my eyes were perfectly normal just an hour earlier!"

"The EMTs arrived about 15 minutes after your call. If we add this all up, your eyes were substituted for these implants in less than two hours, but now the surrounding tissue has completely healed up, without lesions or scars!" summarized Dr. Goldman and concluded, "implants like yours simply don't exist, and there is no medical procedure on Earth that could that, Mr. Jenson!"

(This is worth millions - no, billions!!!)

"I believe you, doctor!" concurred Edward and shrugged. Of course, by now, Edward had realized that his new eyes had come from somewhere else entirely, but he would not reveal that to Dr. Goldman.

"Well, since you have your vision and are in no discomfort, I will discharge you now. But take my card and call me in the morning. We have to find out what has happened to you, Mr. Jenson!" said the physician and scribbled something on the chart.

(I'm not letting you off the hook. You are my golden goose, buddy!)

"Thank you, Doctor!" replied Edward and nodded as he took the business card, but he had no intentions of calling this greedy man tomorrow or any day thereafter.

"Oh, and wear sunglasses! Your new eyes are quite disconcerting!" warned Dr. Goldman as he swiftly walked out of the room.

(And we don't want anyone else to cash in on our little secret!)

"I will," replied Edward. He was appalled by Dr. Goldman's ulterior motives, but he agreed that it would be better not to draw attention.

Meanwhile, the young nurse remained in the room after Doctor Goldman had left to play golf. The shapely woman cleaned up a few things, but suddenly she turned to Edward again.

"Is there anything you need before we let you go home?" she asked with a bright smile.

"A glass of water would be nice. Your colleague forgot about it earlier," complained Edward with a parched throat.

"Oh, don't mind her; she is always cranky!" teased the nurse and said, "I will get you some water, Mr. Jenson!"

(Hmm, Goldman thinks this guy is valuable, so maybe it will pay off if I butter him up?)

The nurse left the room but returned quickly with a tall glass of water and some dark shades. She put the water on the tiny nightstand next to Edward's bed and handed him the sunglasses.

"We give these to people with bad migraines. I think they will fit you, too!" explained the young woman.

(Better wear them or people will run screaming!)

"Thanks, that's very thoughtful of you!" replied Edward and eagerly drank some water.

"You will be famous, Mr. Jenson! So, can you really see everything?" wondered the nurse, looking expectantly at Edward.

(Famous and rich, but still freakish as hell!)

"Yes, I can!" confirmed Edward, slightly disturbed by the woman's thoughts.

"Did you notice something earlier with Dr. Goldman?" questioned the nurse.

(If you saw how he grabbed my ass, I would have some leverage!)

"I was still a little out of it, so I can't say I have Miss!" said Edward evasively.

"Oh, never mind. By the way, I'm Claudia!" responded the woman.

(Damn, plan B it is!)

"Nice to meet you, Claudia!" replied Edward politely.

"You had no calls or visitors - no family, no Mrs. Jenson?" questioned Claudia.

"No Mrs. Jenson, and I'm new to the area. In fact, I'm still moving in, and my furniture won't arrive until tomorrow!" answered Edward truthfully.

"Oh? I have the day off tomorrow; if you need help with all the boxes?" suggested the nurse looking sweetly at Edward.

(I'll just call in sick, but Christ, I would need a blindfold if I have to fuck this scary guy)

"That's very kind of you, Claudia, but I have that covered," replied Edward flatly and asked, "can I get out of bed and use the restroom?"

"Sure, and don't forget to check out at the front desk when you leave!" Claudia reminded him sharply, and then she abruptly left the room.

(Who does he think he is!?! I can't believe he dissed me! He should be grateful to any girl who pays attention to him with that look!)

An hour later, Edward was back home. He immediately ran to the bathroom, removed the dark glasses, and looked in the mirror for a long time. Edward recalled that black contact lenses were available online and at Halloween stores. Inserted in the eyes, they looked mysterious and scary, but the effect paled compared to what he saw in the mirror now. Edward's new eyes were so black that he could not even see the curvature of the artificial eyeballs, making them appear as if they were two-dimensional windows to the abyss!

As a scientist, Edward knew that a proper black surface would absorb 100% of visible light, and such a surface did not exist on Earth. Material scientists had come close with Vantablack and similar carbon nanotube coatings that could absorb up to 99.99% of visible light - but not all of it! The only object discovered that could do that would be a black hole. Black holes were aptly named because no visible light, and from x-rays to radio waves, no electromagnetic radiation could escape their gravitational pull. That's precisely how Edward's eyes appeared to be: two black holes inside his skull, and they seemed to suck in everything!

Edward stood motionless in front of the mirror for a good while. It finally sunk in that the strange experience in the closet wasn't a dream or a delusion, but real! This realization threatened to overwhelm him emotionally, so Edward focused on the practical instead: he exited the bathroom to test his vision. He had left a magazine on the kitchen counter this morning, and when he looked at it now, he immediately knew that he could safely discard his reading glasses. Not only was he no longer farsighted, but now he could spot even the tiniest speck of dust on that granite top. Edward stepped in front of his house. A neighbor had parked a truck nearly 300 yards away, but Edward had no problem reading the license plate. He wasn't sure if his other senses had also improved, but he seemed to be more aware of them, too.

The next few days were busy but fairly uneventful. Dr. Goldman left increasingly pushy voice messages every day, but Edward ignored him first, then blocked his number. Nurse Claudia also called him unexpectedly: apparently, she thought Edward was valuable enough to ask for another date. He did not return her call either. The movers had delivered his belongings, and Edward spent all his time arranging and organizing his new home. He checked the walk-in closet to place a fan there, but the sweet odor was gone. At best, the room smelled a little bit of cleaning agents but nothing else.

That night, when the house was dark and quiet, Edward dreamt about that strange, otherworldly place. His thoughts centered on Pauline and especially Lilith. But it wasn't her appearance and allure, although she was ravishingly beautiful. No, the woman had triggered something much more profound when she took his hand and led him through the forest. Edward knew Lilith only for a few hours, or perhaps only 20 minutes in real-time, but he felt he had always known her. He sincerely hoped that she had found Opal, and he wished them love and happiness, but he couldn't help feeling a little envious of that mysterious man, too.

The next day, Edward left the house to stock up on groceries and buy a better pair of sunglasses. The ones he got from the hospital did the trick, but they were clunky and uncomfortable. Edward found very dark wrap-around shades at a sporting goods store. They were easy to wear and blocked all curious looks at his transformed eyes. While in public, he focused his new ability on random people: whenever someone was talking within a room or near vicinity, Edward could pick up the thoughts behind the words. Sometimes, he could sense the thoughts even without any verbal cues. Walls and other solid objects seem to dampen or block his gift, but within a line of sight, he could see, hear or sense thoughts and emotions from as far away as half a mile! Edward likened his ability to the closed-captioning function on a TV – but unlike closed-captioning, the verbal message and accompanying thoughts often did not match.

Of course, almost from the moment he woke up in the hospital, Edward became acutely aware that he could not reveal his secret to anyone. If he did, it would be exploited in the worst possible ways, and not just for financial gains as Dr. Goldman was so eager to do. No, this was something he would have to take to his grave, but he needed to talk to someone friendly, even if he couldn't reveal too much. So, Edward picked up the phone and called Reggie, his oldest friend from elementary school.

"Hey Reggie, how are you doing?" asked Edward expectantly.

"Who is this?" wondered Reggie.

(The voice sounds familiar, but I don't recall this number)

"It's Edward!" clarified Edward, a little surprised that Reggie didn't recognize his voice.

"Eddie! Good to hear from you again! What's up?" replied Reggie cheerfully.

(Gee, I completely forgot about you)

"Oh, I just called to say hello," said Edward.

"Thanks, I remember that you accepted a new job somewhere out of state? How is that working out?" wondered Reggie.

(You might have told me where, but I didn't pay attention)

"Yes, I did. I bought a house here, too!" explained Edward.

"Oh yes, I believe you mentioned that, too. Listen, Ed: I'm at the movies with a hot date. Now that I have your new number, I'll call you back in a couple of days, if that's alright?" proposed Reggie, apparently in a hurry now.

(I better save this call, or I won't remember)

"OK, no problem, Reggie. Good luck with the date!" answered Edward.

"Thanks, we'll talk soon!" replied Reggie and quickly hung up.

This call was a sore disappointment for Edward. He had always considered Reggie his closest friend, but now he realized that the feeling wasn't mutual. But at least he learned one surprising fact from this exchange: his ability would work over the phone, and that would come very handy only a few minutes later.

"Mr. Jenson, I'm calling about an extended warranty for your vehicle. If you sign up now, you can take advantage of our incredible offer!" promised the teller marketer with feigned excitement.

(Our policy covers next to nothing, and we've made it impossible to cancel, sucker!)

"No thanks, I'm not interested in your fraudulent crap!" replied Edward angrily and hung up.

Today was a cold, overcast autumn day, but Edward wanted to stretch his legs and take his mind off that unexpected conversation with Reggie. So, he decided to walk around his new neighborhood, but Edward didn't know that the next few miles would be challenging. When Edward passed by one particular house, he noticed two women conversing in the front yard. As he walked by, he heard them talk.

"I hope you had a great time in Tahiti?" asked one woman.

(I can't afford fancy vacations, so I hope you were as miserable as me)

"Yes, it was fabulous! Thanks!" replied the other neighbor.

(It was expensive and stressful. I should have stayed home, but I have to keep up appearances for the likes of you!)

This conversation would have been a regular, friendly talk between neighbors without the closed-captioning. But to Edward, it was just a pointless exchange of petty lies, and he shook his head vigorously. The neighbors noticed and looked at him strangely. Edward realized then that he had to learn how to control his reactions to the thoughts he picked up. People would notice if he were too stunned or appalled to respond to verbal messages appropriately. Just like these two neighbors, they would also see if he was shaking his head or making a face seemingly at random. This new skill would take some concentration, practice, and willpower for Edward to act normally to the outside world.

He saw three young boys, perhaps seven or eight, when Edward passed by an open lot. At first, he thought they were just playing there, but then his sharp eyes made out something very unsettling: the boys were not playing but gleefully tormenting an injured rabbit!

(Don't kill it yet, Randy! Let's use the lighter fluid first!)

Edward ran towards the kids as they were beating the panicked animal with thorny branches. When he got close, they noticed him and stopped abusing the hapless creature for a moment. Then Edward did something he had not done before in public – he removed his sunglasses and just stared at the boys. The effect didn't leave to be desired: the children screamed, dropped the branches and the container of flammable liquid, and ran away as fast as they could! Edward looked at the injured rabbit, and it was beyond saving. He picked up its mangled body, petted it for a moment, and then swiftly broke its neck.

Edward had always been fond of children, and like most people, thought of them as innocent. But now, he suspected that children were not guiltless, just inexperienced. They were still practicing the cruelty and viciousness of the adults. Edward walked faster as if he could escape this awful experience somehow. He came to a crossroads and had to stop at a traffic light. Across the street, Edward saw a man staggering out of a bar. He was intoxicated when he fumbled with the keys getting into his car.

(I only had a few drinks, and I need my car tomorrow. I can still drive! I'll take the backroads to avoid the cops. It'll be fine!)

A few moments later, the man did considerable damage when he backed into a parked car. But he didn't seem to notice and drove off without even slowing down. Edward wasn't sure what to do, but thanks to his enhanced vision, he could see the license plate of the offending driver. He jotted it down on a piece of paper, crossed the street, and placed the note behind the windshield wiper of the damaged vehicle. Right before he got back home, he encountered two women walking a small dog. Edward smiled and said hello, but the older woman – she must have been in her seventies – stopped him by pointing her cane directly at his chest.

"I have not seen you around here!" she stated sharply.

"Oh, I'm Edward Jenson, and I'm new to the area. I'm living in the house just at the end of Creek Road!" replied Edward politely.

"The Abernathy's house. Mary was insufferable, and George squandered their money; that's why they had to sell!" observed the old lady coldly.

"Mom, please…," interjected the younger woman quietly, apparently the daughter.

(You are embarrassing us again!)

"I did not know that!" replied Edward simply.

"What is your trade, Mr. Jenson?" inquired the old woman.

"I will start a new job at the Research Institute in a few days," answered Edward.

"Aha, one of those science people," she noted and grimaced.

(Another heretic! We won't be seeing him in church!)

"Yes, I'm a researcher!" confirmed Edward, almost apologetically.

"Are you married?" the old lady asked next.

(I don't see a ring. He is too old to be single, so he must be divorced. Nobody respects the sanctity of marriage anymore!)

"No, Ma'am, I have never been married!" answered Edward truthfully.

"A girlfriend, then?" questioned the lady.

(Living in sin, it figures!)

"No, I'm just a single guy!" countered Edward and smiled at her a little.

"I'm single, too!" blurted the younger woman, but her mother waved her off dismissively.

(Please, please, please ask me out!)

"I have you that this is an upstanding, old-fashioned neighborhood. We do not tolerate modern shenanigans here!" exclaimed the old woman sharply and waved her cane around.

(He must be one of those disgusting sodomites. This whole country is going to hell!)

"Mom, we will be late for church, and I'm sure Mr. Jenson has other things to do as well!" interrupted the younger woman, visibly embarrassed by her mother's antics.

(I hate you, mother! I will die a virgin if you scare all the men away!)

"Fine!" grumbled the old woman and started walking, but stopped again and turned to her daughter, "come on then, and don't dawdle!"

(He's not for you, silly goose!)

"Goodbye, Mr. Jenson! Have a good day!" said her daughter, gave Edward an apologetic smile and ran a few steps to catch up to her mother.

(I do hope I will see you again – without mother!)

"Same to you, Miss!" replied Edward, bowed his head a little and continued his walk.

While in public, Edward never took the dark shades off. Outdoors and in summer, that would have been inconspicuous. But it was late fall, and the weather was often rainy or foggy, so inevitably, some people would notice. It was even more apparent when Edward had to interact with someone indoors. Edward always explained it with the same unavoidable lie: he was prone to headaches because of a sensitivity to bright lights. Since that wasn't a rare condition, most people accepted that response. But from their thoughts, Edward could tell that many considered it weird, weakness, or even a defect. A few even wondered if Edward was a drug addict. But as long as they didn't bother him any further about it, he could live with that judgment.

It was the 1st of December, and Edward left home early for his new job. That was a wise precaution because he got stuck in the morning rush hour, and the short drive took a lot longer than he had expected. Of course, nobody liked to be stuck in traffic, and Edward was no exception. He had read how it can even lead to violent road rage. But he wasn't prepared for the onslaught of negative thoughts and emotions emanating from all the frustrated drivers around him. His ability picked up numerous thoughts of murder and mayhem and whisps of deep-seated anger and pure hatred! Edward suspected that only the lack of means and the fear of prosecution kept some of these people from slaughtering each other right here on the freeway!

When Edward arrived at the Research Institute, the receptionist had no idea he was coming. He was told to wait in the lobby until she found someone to care for him. It took almost an hour before a slight man with thick glasses and a tablet came to the entrance.

"Welcome to the Institute, Mr. Jenson! I'm group leader Keller!" said the man.

(So that's the one they hired instead of my cousin Fred. Glad I made

him wait!)

"Thank you; a pleasure to meet you!" said Edward and extended his hand. Keller pretended not to see it, turned around, and started moving towards the elevators.

"Please follow me!" instructed Keller and pressed the elevator button. While they were waiting, Keller checked the tablet in his hand.

(What?! Did they give this guy the spacious office next to mine? We'll see about that…)

"On second thought, the office area is still being remodeled. We'll set you up closer to the laboratories," proclaimed Keller and moved away from the elevator.

"Oh, that would be very convenient!" agreed Edward politely.

"Yes," said Keller, and for the first time, Edward saw him smile a little.

(Polite and soft-spoken? This guy is a pushover. If I ride him hard enough, Freddy can reapply in three months tops!)

Instead of going up in the elevator, Keller led Edward down a flight of stairs to the basement. After they crisscrossed a few hallways and passed several utility rooms, Keller stopped at a dusty, worn desk near a storage closet full of old office equipment. Edward noticed no other desks, cubicles, or offices in the vicinity.

"You can talk to IT later to have them hook up a phone and computer!" suggested Keller.

(They are slower than molasses. It will take a week at least!)

"Of course!" replied Edward.

"Follow me, and we will look at your laboratory next!" said Keller and started walking again. Edward followed, but after they turned around the next corner of the hallway, Keller suddenly stopped when he saw a woman in a lab coat passing by.

"Oh, Monica, this is Edward Jenson, the new hire. Could you show him the laboratory?" asked Keller bluntly.

(Oh good, now I don't have to do the show-and-tell)

"Which lab?" replied the woman curtly.

(I'm a scientist, not a tour guide!)

"12 B," clarified Keller.

"Sure!" acknowledged Monica, turned to Edward, and said, "follow me, please!"

(Ha, ha! 12 B is a dump! Keller must be pissed that they didn't hire his relative. Serves him right for passing me over for promotion)

"Oh my, it needs some work!" said Monica in feigned surprise when they opened the door to the laboratory. The place was a mess! All the benches had boxes and broken equipment stacked upon them, and the floor hadn't been cleaned in a long time. Even most of the overhead lighting didn't work anymore.

"Well, it gives me something to do!" replied Edward and gave her a friendly smile.

"This lab hasn't been used since they terminated Elena over a year ago," explained Monica briefly.

(Hmm, he seems friendly and is willing to get his hands dirty)

"No problem, thank you so much, Monica!" said Edward and added with a bit of a smile, "sorry that you had to be the tour guide!"

"Listen, I have a meeting in a few minutes, but I will see you later in your office upstairs!" proposed Monica and smiled at him as well.

(Oh? He is nice!)

"OK, sure, but I have my desk down here where you found me earlier!" noted Edward.

"Really...?!" mumbled Monica in disbelief, but then she added in a friendly voice, "well, it was good talking to you, Edward!"

(The broom closet!?! Sadly, making you an ally would be a waste of time. The way they treat you, you'll be gone soon, Edward!)

Without anyone left to show him around, Edward took nearly ten minutes to find the IT department. He approached a bored technician sitting at a desk, fiddling with a graphics card.

"Hi! I'm a new employee, and I would like to request a phone and computer for my desk!" stated Edward politely.

"Fill out the requisition and work order forms," answered the middle-aged man without even looking at Edward.

"Could you please tell me where can I get those?" inquired Edward.

"Just click on the file, fill it out, and submit it to us," replied the IT guy.

"Uhm, I don't have a computer; that's why I'm here!" said Edward, pointing out the obvious.

"You can use the terminal in the conference room down the hall," answered the man, still not acknowledging Edward's presence.

"Do I need a login?" wondered Edward.

"Yeah!" said the man, as he inserted the device into a desktop computer.

"I don't have a login either!" declared Edward patiently.

"Login guest, password temp123," was the monotonous reply.

"Thank you!" said Edward and left the room. He wondered if his ability had stopped working. This technician didn't have any hidden thoughts. All Edward could sense from this guy was numbness. When Edward got to the conference room, a new unforeseen obstacle appeared, and Edward had to trot back to the IT department.

"I cannot get into the conference room. I don't have a keycard yet!" stated Edward, slightly annoyed now.

"The receptionist has them for new employees," mumbled the technician as he was closing the computer case.

"No, the lady was unaware that I would start working today!" maintained Edward.

"Use this one," said the IT guy and handed Edward a worn, grimy card, still without looking at him.

"Thank you!" replied Edward, wiped the card on his lab coat, and walked back to the conference room. It took Edward a good half an hour to fill out the forms. When it was done, he submitted them, but he had to go back to IT once again because something wasn't right.

"OK, I've submitted the forms, but it asked me to select a location. It appears that my desk isn't in a valid one?" questioned Edward.

"Yeah, I see your req. Where is your desk?" asked the technician as he was scrolling through his inbox.

"In the basement, room 1002, near laboratory 12B," Edward informed him.

"We don't have phone or ethernet down there," stated the IT guy.

"What should I do?" wondered Edward, trying very hard to suppress his frustrations.

"I have to talk to my supervisor about that," said the man with a sigh, and then he added, "we will send you an email to let you know!"

(Damn, you make me talk to my boss!)

"OK, but I don't have email either, and I wouldn't be able to check it without a computer!" countered Edward, almost surprised that the closed-captioning was working again.

"We will send it to your supervisor. Keller, isn't it?" inquired the technician, finally looking at Edward, albeit only very briefly.

"Yes, that's him," replied Edward and noted, "oh, here is your keycard back!"

"Keep it. It will let you in the building and into the conference and breakrooms!" answered the technician as he was rummaging through a box of cables.

"Will that work for the laboratories, too?" asked Edward expectantly.

"No. You need to fill out a requisition form for that. Then we send it to your supervisor and the department head. If they approve it, we can make you a card in a few days!" instructed the IT guy.

"Thank you, I will do that!" replied Edward in resignation. The technician didn't respond, and after a moment of hesitation, Edward just left the room.

The next day, Edward studied the organizational chart. Surprisingly, a research assistant named Trevor Landon was assigned to him. The floorplan showed that Trevor had a cubical on the first floor, and Edward decided to visit him. On his way there, he passed by a conference room. A man and woman dressed in business attire – Edward didn't know those two coworkers – had a conversation in the doorway.

"I haven't gotten this week's report. Did you send it out?" the woman demanded to know.

(Every week, the same thing, but let's hear your latest excuse!)

"Yes, just last night! Maybe the email got lost?" replied the man and shrugged his shoulders.

(Crap, I forgot again!)

"I did not get it, but I need it promptly. Please send it to me again!" urged the woman sharply.

(I know you are lying, but I don't have time to argue about it)

"But Peterson didn't send me his data!" countered the man.

(If I blame Peterson, maybe she gets off my back?)

"Just send it as it is!" replied the woman exasperatedly.

(Peterson was in the hospital, while you were just lazy again!)

"Sure...," grumbled the man and quickly left the area.

(Demanding bitch! As if she never forgets something!)

When Edward finally entered the cubicle area reserved for the laboratory staff, he immediately noticed that it was a lot nicer than his shabby desk in the basement. But Edward didn't mind that. He approached Trevor's cubicle a few moments later and found the young man slumped over the keyboard.

(No hope! I'll be stuck in this fucking, pointless job for the rest of my life. I should just end it all!)

"Hello Trevor, I'm Edward!" said Edward friendly, but visibly disturbed by Trevor's dark thoughts.

"What?" replied the young man, confused, as he lifted his head off the keyboard.

(I should do it! Maybe tonight…)

"Are you alright, Trevor?" asked Edward, now very concerned.

"Yeah, I'm cool," mumbled Trevor in response and put earphones into his ears.

(You are clueless, old man!)

"I wonder if you could give me a hand with the boxes in Lab 12B?" inquired Edward.

"Uhm, I got safety training. It's mandatory," replied Trevor, got up and walked away.

(Just leave me the hell alone!)

Edward was too shocked to say anything else when the young man left the cubicle area. As he did, group leader Keller entered and looked at Edward with a deep frown.

"I see you have met Trevor. I have reassigned him to Monica's project. It is getting close to the deadline!" declared Keller.

(No help for you!)

"Understood!" replied Edward and added hesitantly, "I think that young man isn't feeling well!"

"It's probably just a bad breakup. Trevor will be fine!" answered Keller unconcernedly.

(Who cares?)

"I believe it might be more serious!" warned Edward. He felt he should intervene somehow, but he had no idea what to do. Who would even believe him? Certainly not Keller!

"Also, I have cleared your meeting schedule for now. There is no need for you to attend until you have some data to present!" maintained Keller and changed the subject.

(By the time you leave, nobody will know you've ever worked here)

"OK!" acknowledged Edward, but Keller was already talking to another analyst in the next cubicle.

To an outsider, the Research Institute appeared like any other workplace. A few coworkers were friendly, some were not, some liked to congregate, while others preferred to be by themselves, but all of them were busy to various degrees with one task or another. Aside from a boss who treated him poorly, Edward didn't find any significant differences from his last employment. Of course, Edward did not have his ability back then, and now he often wondered what he had missed.

But the closed-captioning showed a much different, darker side of the job. The thoughts and emotions of Edward's colleagues ranged from angry, vindictive, scheming, and greedy to stressed, anxious, apathetic like the IT technician, and even to suicidal, as it was in Trevor's case. His coworkers didn't enjoy the work or take pride in what they were doing. No, they did the job because they got paid or saw it as a means to an end, a stepping stone to recognition, promotion, and ultimately more income. When it was all said and done, work was just a repetitive, meaningless task, not a purpose!

The new ability put Edward in a state of suspension. There were days when he didn't want to come near anyone, just to avoid exposure to their thoughts and feelings. At those times, Edward was grateful that Keller had all but isolated him from the rest of the company. Most days, he could do his work without any unwanted interactions. But other times, Edward was strangely fascinated to discover the truth behind the façade, and he learned a lot about his fellow humans, but sadly, most of it wasn't good.

It was not uncommon for Edward to listen to seemingly civil conversations, but his skill exposed ugly, hateful mental rants that would put any *Karen* to shame. The seven deadly sins of Christian tradition - wrath, lust, pride, envy, gluttony, greed, and sloth - were omnipresent and complimented by boundless ignorance, prejudice and bigotry, recklessness, and lack of caring, groundless suspicions, and petty vindictiveness. Moreover, it appeared to Edward that humans derived a significant part of joy from strife and Schadenfreude. Happiness – Edward was reluctant to call it that - came all too often from the misfortune of others!

But one aspect disturbed him most profoundly: nearly everyone was constantly lying! Sometimes for good reasons, mainly for bad ones, and quite a few times for no reason at all. It seemed to Edward that deception was almost reflexive to Homo Sapiens. Many didn't even realize they were doing it, not even when they were lying to themselves. Without a doubt, deception was what set his world apart from Lilith's!

Edward had met his share of shallow and pretentious people. He had disliked and sidestepped them whenever possible. But now, he was beginning to see them in a different light: perhaps it was just a defense mechanism? It was conceivable that these people avoided thinking beyond the trivial because it was too painful. Maybe they lied to others and themselves because they were not strong or courageous enough to face the ugly truth inherent to humanity? Then again, thought Edward, perhaps he was giving his fellow humans too much credit, and they just lacked the depth after all?

Edward considered briefly using his new skill to his advantage. If he can read minds, he could manipulate them. For example, he knew from her thoughts that Monica resented being the tour guide when they first met, and she responded well when Edward apologized to her. Similarly, it would be easy to get a date with that neighbor who was so desperate to find a man. He could sense their desires and fears and knew at once if someone liked or disliked him, and knowing that truth could be immensely powerful! But Edward just wasn't that kind of a man!

It was Christmas, and Edward had to call his parents. Typically, this would be a simple affair: a few minutes of pleasantries and idle chit-chat was all it took. But with the skill to hear people's true thoughts, Edward was apprehensive about picking up the phone.

"Hey, Mom! Merry Christmas!" Edward greeted his mother cheerfully.

"Oh, hello Edward. Merry Christmas to you, too!" replied the older woman politely.

(You are ungrateful. You should be spending the holidays with us like your brother and his family!)

"Sorry, I can't stop by this year with the new job so far away," apologized Edward.

"It would have been nice to have you, but we understand, Edward!" maintained his mother.

(If you didn't do something wrong, they wouldn't have fired you after 20 years, and you wouldn't have to move half a world away!)

"So, how are you doing? How's dad?" questioned Edward, offended that his mother would blame him unjustly for the lay-offs.

"I'm doing fine, little aches and pains here and there, but I shouldn't complain!" answered his mother and asked, "have you made any friends over there yet?"

(You were always such an oaf! I'll never get a daughter-in-law and grandkids from you!)

"No opportunities to socialize yet, but some of my coworkers are nice!" said Edward, and he felt terrible about that particular lie but even worse about his mother's disappointment.

"Aha...oh, here is your father, and I have to check on the roast! Merry Christmas, Edward!" said his mother quickly and handed the phone to her husband.

"Hello, son! Did you hear that your brother got elected to the state assembly?"

(At least one of my sons isn't a failure!)

"Merry Christmas, Dad! No, I haven't talked to James yet. The new job and the house eat up all of my time, but please relay my congratulations!" said Edward sincerely, but he was shocked to learn that his father thought of him as a failure.

"Well, I'm glad that you are keeping busy!" replied his father politely.

(Busy with that science mumbo-jumbo! You should have been a lawyer like me! Where did we go wrong with you, Edward?)

"Thanks, Dad! I can hear mom hollering from the kitchen, so I let you get back to the food. Shall we talk after dinner?" inquired Edward, eager to end this conversation now.

"We'll do that, Edward. Merry Christmas!" responded his father.

(Don't bother, you'll just ruin our appetite!)

"Bye, Dad!" said Edward and quickly hung up.

Edward sat on the couch and stared at the dark TV screen for a long time, trying to process the disappointment and disdain that his own family had for him. He had never been that close to his parents, but he loved them nonetheless, so this conversation came as a terrible wake-up call. Of all the unpleasant encounters since he had gained his ability, this one had been the worst by far!

Edward was no fool. He always knew that humanity, society, and every individual person had dark, unsavory aspects hidden beneath a thin veneer. But it was very different to carry that knowledge in the back of the head versus being exposed to the unfiltered truth in all its horror. Edward didn't believe in hell or heaven, evil or good: there was just *human*, or the absence thereof. He got up from the couch and paced through the house at random. When Edward found himself back in the walk-in closet where this whole ordeal had started, he switched the light on and stood still for a moment, lost in thought.

"You don't recognize hell because it is all you have ever known," mumbled Edward, repeating the words the voice had spoken in that cave.

"Now I recognize it, and that knowledge torments me just as you had predicted!" admitted Edward and concluded, "yet, I cannot blame you because it was my own choice. But I wish you hadn't given me this gift - or perhaps it was a curse? Some things are just too painful to be seen, heard, or felt even if they are true!"

"Are you asking for a second chance?" questioned the voice as the familiar sweet odor filled the room once more. Edward was surprised that he wasn't surprised - perhaps a part of him had expected that the voice would listen to his monologue?

"I won't ask for that because I would still be an outcast in your world!" contradicted Edward and added with regret, "no, I chose this, and I will endure. But it would be easier without the ability you gave me!"

"With or without the power to see the truth, you are an outcast in your world as well!" disagreed the invisible speaker.

"That might be so...," doubted Edward hesitantly, but deep down, he knew it was true.

"If we stick with the religious metaphor, the existential question is this: would you rather be an outcast in hell or an outcast in heaven?" the voice demanded to know.

"Did Lilith ever find her Opal?" asked Edward softly, evading a direct answer.

"Although she never met him, Lilith was destined to be Opal's teacher, guide, and companion. But you were right: there was a tragic mistake! Opal died just before his consciousness could join us," admitted the voice sadly.

"I'm so sorry for Lilith; it must have been devastating for her!" said Edward with sincere regret, and then he asked, "so, I was just a substitute?"

"No, not a replacement. You were the next in line, but you came too early and unprepared!" elaborated the unseen speaker.

"Sorry, I did not know how to prepare for your world or that it even existed," replied Edward defensively.

"Of course not! Preparation takes years, not just a few minutes!" laughed the voice, but then it got serious again, "Lilith does not mourn Opal; she grieves for you. I cannot fix her broken heart - only you can do that!"

"But you said that Lilith was supposed to be Opal's companion, not mine!" argued Edward.

"Yes, but you have met your teacher and companion as well!" maintained the voice.

"I have?" wondered Edward, unsure what that reference meant.

"Without realizing it, you broke two hearts in a few hours - or a few minutes by your timekeeping!" explained the voice in a sarcastic tone.

"Pauline!" whispered Edward when he suddenly realized that the bond with the raven-haired woman was just as profound!

Only an incorporeal chuckle came in response.

"But how could that work? There is just one of me!" protested Edward anxiously, unable and unwilling to choose between the two women.

"In your world, that could be difficult, but in ours, it's just amusing!" replied the voice nonchalantly.

"Are Lilith and Pauline human?" worried Edward suddenly when he remembered Kuridda, the alien beekeeper.

"No, you were the first human to visit our world!" proclaimed the voice, and then it asked humorously, "is that a problem?"

"Uhm...," stammered Edward nervously. It was new territory for him! Edward had never considered a romantic encounter with an alien before, let alone two!

"Ah, I see. Lilith and Pauline are not human, but their two species are similar to yours, although evolutionarily much older. More importantly, appearances do not matter in our world, and we can change them at will. Only the connection between consciousnesses is relevant to us!" explained the speaker and added with a chuckle, "you are sexually compatible!"

"Oh!" was all Edward could say to that, but he was relieved to hear that bit of information.

"So, will you mend what you have broken?" the invisible speaker demanded to know impatiently.

"Lilith and Pauline were so kind; they should not be unhappy," mumbled Edward, and then he took a deep breath and made his decision: "I... I wish to return to your world!"

"It's like pulling teeth with you, isn't it?" joked the voice, and then it noted seriously, "but this time your journey is final! Don't forget, you are still not prepared, and there is much to learn. Even with two guides, it won't be easy, but you will not be an outcast forever!"

"Yes, I understand!" acknowledged Edward. The walk-in closet dissolved in a fog a moment later, and Edward experienced that elevator feeling in his stomach once again.

About three weeks later, some construction workers were patching a pothole in front of Edward's house when they noticed a foul odor. They informed the authorities, and the police found Edward's badly decomposed corpse in the closet. Since the circumstances were suspicious, a criminal investigation was launched. It revealed that the couple who had originally owned the property had been desperate to raise money for the mortgage payments. So, the couple had rented out some rooms to shady tenants, and these people had turned the walk-in closet into a lab for illicit designer drugs, just as Edward had suspected. While the room had been thoroughly scrubbed, the crooks forgot to clean the light switch. It was still laced with a potent mix of hallucinogenic chemicals. When Edward had touched the button, some traces were absorbed through his skin, causing severe delusions and ultimately heart failure.

Under the thin guise of being Edward's physician, Doctor Goldman inserted himself in the medical examiner's autopsy. But he was perplexed and sorely disappointed to discover that Edward had perfectly normal eyes, albeit a little farsighted. Eventually, the coroner ruled that Edward's demise was a homicide by an inadvertent drug overdose. The case remained open for a while longer, but the drug dealers were long gone and would never be caught.

www.ingramcontent.com/pod-product-compliance
Lightning Source LLC
Chambersburg PA
CBHW061120180626
46811CB00012BB/349